EVER EDEN

King of Spades

A Darkrose Novel

ISBN: 978-0-6480524-0-1

This book was professionally typeset on Reedsy.
Find out more at reedsy.com

Thank you

Mum, who taught me to be a legit bada$$ and never saw a reason why I couldn't achieve anything I wanted, Pat H who has believed in and encouraged me from all the way across the world, my Domo, Daz S, The Great and Powerful Chris M, Timon, Alan C and my CAIA family
and
everyone I know I've forgotten who has put up with my Darkrose-related quips over the years.

Your excitement and encouragement sustained a fire. I hope I can burn this mother to the ground. <3

1

NUMBER ONE'S OFFICE WAS COOL when Cleo entered and the hefty bulletproof door locked behind her. The four giant bodyguards were wearing black shirts straining over pecs and biceps, standing with submachine guns hanging from their shoulders, ready to kill any smart-mouth MDS agent who threatened Number One or said something a little too stupid. One pair flanked the doorway and the other split either side of Number One behind the desk.

She sat opposite, glancing over freshly painted powder-blue walls to the window behind Number One, imagining the view down to the cement benched, rose-covered courtyard and the airfield beyond. The office was simple, unlike wherever Number One turned in for the night. Superiors liked the illusion of accessibility, it was why they were sitting in an office on the fourth floor of the Red Tag Building, literally around a corner and a few pot plants from her own dorm room.

The ever-changing décor showed Number One staring from all walls, paused in clichéd photographs and posed with leaders from The Outside; presidents and prime ministers, all in the middle of handshakes that had gone on too long so photos could be taken. Fake smiles morphing to grimaces on everybody's dial.

Other pictures showed squads of Majestic Defence Syndicate Combat Agents on desert sand, filthy and holding bulky firearms. She was among them, features half-hidden under dirt and someone else's blood and surrounded by Red Tag CAs. She'd been a rank lower then, tell-tale blue band around her right bicep. She rummaged memories for something from a few years back but a squeak of leather brought her attention back to the front.

Number One's black leather chair revolved so they could talk face to face over the smooth onyx desk. Something in the air changed and the bodyguards tried not to stroke their weapons, ugly faces near excited at the prospect of a kill if something went wrong. Someone she used to know called them "yetis." She understood why.

"We want you to be part of a...collaborative effort." Number One said.

The flinty, out of place British-accent words tumbled down Cleo's spine as she took in all Number One's long platinum hair hanging around narrow shoulders in the usual light grey suit jacket. The superior's utterly androgynous features were predictably emotionless as the meeting began and the bodyguards melded into the décor.

She could still feel the weight of their pervert stares though. Most MDS agents saw each other as relatively genderless, weren't suckers for half Latin brunettes with big dark hazel eyes, full lips and a shitload of black mascara...but they weren't agents. They were beefed up bodyguards contracted from some place she didn't know, repeatedly scrutinizing her for a hidden motive and getting a good look while they were at it. Cleo felt their eyes rove her five foot five frame from top to bottom and back again. They were itching for an excuse to kill her or restrain her.

"You look tense, Darkrose," Number One said, "It can't be the guards. They've followed procedure, confiscated your weapons upon entry but they'd likely be dead in seconds if you wished, correct?"

Number One leaned forward wearing a curious look, ignoring the uncomfortable glances bouncing around the room between everyone else. Yeah, Number One had just challenged her. It was how Number One rolled; all snide remarks and half jokes an agent couldn't dare take seriously unless they wanted their head blown off.

"I am gifting you this next assignment, I thought you'd jump at another chance to redeem yourself after your...*unscheduled* leave of

2

absence a year or so ago."

"I was under the impression I had." Cleo said, her husky voice careful.

"You took to Fugitive Recovery Operations better than I'd imagined but your disappearance left me to wonder if you had ideas of going as rogue as those you hunt." Number one said, "We did not speak of the reasons you left us but I concluded your failed relationship with a certain other highly-ranked Red Tag had something to do with it, among other things."

"Among other things," Cleo said, "I didn't leave MDS. It was a break, for a month."

"Quite. I took your word, you are still one of my most revered, Darkrose. You met with some unfortunate and wanton civilian resistance on your way back here last night and you did not use your RavenEye. It seems my constant requests for you to refrain from its use on The Outside without permission are getting through."

Cleo nodded. She didn't mention it had been hard as shit not to go for the customized firearm while in an alley being jumped by some random wannabes in the city. She was even feeling the loss of it from her thigh rig as they spoke, uncomfortable without it in reach.

"You used more brute force than I'd have suggested but the heart attack administered by the CRONE, marvellous idea."

"Thank you."

"I was watching your vitals, barely an elevated heart rate. I thought your TC chip may have broken. You need a challenge," Number One declared, "We have intelligence suggesting a bombing is going to take place in a city a few states away."

"What do I have to do?"

Number One's face changed, a small hint of what could have been a smile appeared across colourless lips. Cleo waited for ghostly eyes to move over her, decide if she had any emotion to play on behind the flat expression on her face.

"MDS is being compensated greatly for our involvement. Your

retainer is quite large for not much work, maybe more funds than your TC chip can take."

Number One made a small sound at the end, maybe a laugh. Cleo couldn't resist the glance to her fingertip to picture the chip inside with her identification and earnings stored on it. She used the moment to figure out if she was supposed to laugh too.

"I want you to Delete *Alan James Pierce*, the man responsible for planning this bombing."

Cleo nodded and stood. Same old story.

"*Wait.* He used to be one of ours," Number One said, "For long enough to know things foreign governments would find valuable. He calls himself a *Patriot*. You are familiar with these types from previous lectures on Domestic Terrorism, these people want little or no government and believe agencies such as ours should declassify operations we conduct. This man will be leading a protest rally and a seminar. His group will be responsible for detonating the bomb."

"You wish me to stop him?"

Number One seemed amused by the question.

"No," Number One said, "We have decided the detonation and potential for civilian casualties will work in our favour. Just see to it that this man doesn't leave the scene alive. He's been nicknamed the *'grandfather'* of his activist movement. He will likely be hard to miss and can be identified by a very large tattoo on his right upper arm."

"Depicting?"

"The Spades symbol from a deck of playing cards. He is referred to as *'SpadeMan'* by his peers. You will also find the information in the Personal Operative Device I will issue you after this conversation. One more thing."

Cleo waited for it, a runner on her mark.

"*Civilians.*" Number One said.

"What about them?"

"You will need to secure two. I require these specific civilians *before*

4

the detonation," Number One said, "They are his family and they are in danger. Pick them up and bring them back here."

"Civilians aren't permitted entry at HQ. They're prosecuted, lethal force protocol if they even get close. It'll take hours to get them through security–*all the outposts*–the fingerprinting,"

"Perimeter Patrol are aware Red Tags have only one fingerprint, you know that. The biometric scans at the outposts are not a problem, you usually come through quite quickly."

"Always do."

"Ah, another perk of being well-known here at HQ, no?" Number One blinked a few times, "It's one of the reasons why *you* have to be the one to do this. No one else operates like you. You didn't even flinch when I told you we see opportunities after this bomb injures or kills, you understand the greater good. *Bring me the civilians*, Darkrose."

Number One ended the sentence staring her out and the bodyguards watching closely for a reaction. Okay, fine. She had to bring some civilians back to HQ then let a guy blow up some stuff before she got to kill him. She was already wondering if the city she was going to had good tacos, anything south of HQ was usually pretty good for that kind of thing. Yeah, she guessed not too many people operated like her.

"I will send instructions to your current POD and have a Yellow Tag run down a new one after the civilians arrive, you know how the young agents like to feel involved. The Personal Operating Device will display the next parts of the assignment as you complete the objectives."

Cleo nodded and headed to the door for the bodyguards and her weapons. The meeting had been casual, she hadn't needed to salute at any stage, let alone wear the official MDS Blacks, but the assignment was huge. Civilians didn't just walk into HQ. Ever. Being the agent who wrangled them would look good on her record. For that, she would endure them for as long as she could stand it.

2

THE HALLWAY WAS A DARK CATWALK, two rooms either side and the last one further back on the right. This was what some people called a Fatal Funnel; exposed, potential attacks from numerous angles while silhouetted by her entry point. Lighting was about thirty percent when Cleo breached the front door and clipped it behind her. She blinked the code for Nightvision in the Adonai contact lenses and a green world was born in front of her eyes, showing her everything in the room. She moved soundlessly on the wooden flooring, Beretta M9 out in front, CRONE holstered on her right hip, RavenEye secure in the rig on her left thigh. That, and her knife meant she was as armed as she was going to get.

The front door had been the best option, cover in the front yard, shrubs and plants and pillars around the entrance she could use if she had trouble on the way out. Intelligence via the POD suggested the area was usually quiet and the two occupants of the house were going to be towards the back of the structure where the kitchen and main bedroom were. It looked like they were right, the entry alcove was dark and empty.

She skulked the shadows in the hall, closing in on muffled voices up ahead. Her MDS-issue black boots padded the flat hallway carpet silently as she coasted past framed photographs and side tables with vases and wilting flowers that had been expensive once.

She approached the room on her right first, gradual strafe steps around the open door, clearing a few inches at a time without entering. It showed her a switched off TV and an old-style couch patterned with some flower design, probably cream coloured in the daytime. The glass coffee table in front sported two recently abandoned mugs side by side. Adonai exposed steam coming off them.

Adrenalin secreted with no use. Cleo breathed in nice and slow to counter the flow. No one jumped out of the darkness to ambush her and she slunk back out and into the hall again...but someone was going to die, she could feel it in her guts. Good intuition blessed all the Red Tag Combat Agents.

The lowered voices were coming from the second room up on the left, sounds and hurried whispers she couldn't understand. The door was wide open inwards, giving her a full view of the room as she approached to engage from the dark of the hall. The POD had been clear, *secure the civilians.* Translated, it meant extract their asses and get the hell out. Someone wanted them dead, and for some reason, Number One actually cared.

Her eyes darted over the scene in a second from the doorway; *two females, centre of the room, a woman hunched over a bed frantically grabbing at clothes and passing them to a teenage girl sitting cross-legged on the floor.* The girl snatched them and piled them on top of photos in an open suitcase by a dull lamp before she looked up and screamed, eyes on the gun in Cleo's hands.

Cleo shoved the M9 in the shoulder rig, striding across the room and jerking the girl up by the shoulders, wrenching the spaghetti straps on her top until they threatened to tear in her hands. She didn't know when the girl stopped screaming but she'd shut her big mouth when they were face to face and she could smell lipgloss–*berry, cherry, strawberry*–some shit.

Adonai recognised her face instantly, probably some social media syphon; an online profile sucked dry. The square lining the girl's face blinked bright green twice when the match was made and threw up the name *"Tanya Pierce"* at chin-level in clear font in front of Cleo's eyes.

"Tanya Pierce, I am Agent Darkrose. There are people coming to kill you. Come with me," she said, voice habitually ominous with lack of emotion. She gave the girl a full second for it to sink in then pushed her towards the door and turned around for the older one.

A black double barrel jutted forward and struck her in the chest like a long cattle prod trying to shoo her in the other direction. The woman's breath was shaky behind the long firearm, her hands lumbering and desperate to keep control of it. The thing was probably going to go off by accident and the recoil was going to shit them both up.

Cleo kicked the gun up from the woman's grip. Precision flipped it. It smashed her in the head before plummeting down and landing in Cleo's hands as though it was magnetised. Tanya Pierce screamed again from somewhere near the doorway and then both civilians fell mute, didn't know what to do next, standing in the dark separated and unarmed.

A crash across the hall ruptured the quiet panic. The older woman's eyes got wide and fixed in the direction of the splintering glass. Adonai blinked the frame around her face and flashed the name "Julia Pierce." When her eyes were back on Cleo, they were wild. Someone had kicked in the kitchen window and cocked a gun. Shit just got real but Julia Pierce didn't run for the door.

She swooped down and began scooping up more clothes from the bed, clumsily tossing them into a giant handbag with some notebooks. There was a half-second of disbelief before surging outrage and Cleo grabbed her wrist and twisted it. Julia was off-balance and rocking when they were looking at each other.

"Just go!" Cleo thrust the shotgun back to her, swapping positions with her and pushing Julia and Tanya into the hall then to the right, towards the front door before the intruder could clear the other room and come into the hallway. It was going to be close.

Both civilians snivelled, messily grabbing at each other in the dark and pushing and bouncing against the walls as they ran. They tripped over small items in the shadows and looked back to see if they could be salvaged. Cleo trampled everything and ripped the side tables down to the ground so they were obstacles for anyone who followed. She shoved Julia Pierce in the back, smelling sweat, fear and perfume mixed into a sick blend of something she was forced to breathe in while she brought up the rear.

Heavy steps crushed glass in the other room and someone kicked furniture out of the way and sent it scraping along the ground. Cleo drew the RavenEye and cocked it while she pushed the civilians forward. They snapped their heads back at her, sensing she had gone to her main weapon.

Cleo squeezed between them with the safety off when they reached the front door. The risky move left the civilians unprotected from behind while she opened the door and surveyed the street but she didn't want them walking out into a storm of bullets. The black SUV she'd driven up was waiting out of the streetlights to the right of the yard. She pressed the 'unlock' button on the controller in her pocket.

"Duck and run in a zig-zag," she said, leaning into Julia's shoulder, *"Lock the doors, keep low. The windows are bulletproof."*

Julia and Tanya gave her a look then pulled each other into the yard. Cleo watched them go, her back up on the side of the wall, RavenEye covering them but she didn't follow. She listened to their messy footsteps turn to mild thumps through the grass then she stepped back into the house and shut the door when they reached the vehicle.

She put her back against the door and squatted down waiting for Adonai to adjust again. She could hear two intruders sniffing in the night air and tracking through the house like hunting dogs. Their breathing was uneven and laboured like the break through the window and climb into the kitchen had tired them.

She could feel the weight discrepancy between them through the floorboards before the male duo came into view. They were silhouetted partners walking side-by-side and holding handguns out in front. The one on the right was taller, had a flashlight too and was pointing it at various items around the house. The beam lit up the tacky wallpaper then the floor so they could navigate the upturned tables.

Cleo leaned her head back against the door, high dark plait pressing into her head as she pushed the RavenEye back in her thigh rig slowly until it clicked. Then she slid her hand inside her right sleeve to the knife strapped to her forearm and undid the push-stud to release the weapon, coolness of the handle familiarity as it came away.

A torch beam shot past her face and forced Adonai to compensate. She breathed out and stood. Torchlight spotlighted her the same time she flicked her right wrist and ran at the wall on her right, enough momentum to go upwards.

Her knife plunged towards the silhouettes as she pushed off the wall and somersaulted backwards, above probable trajectory if they opened fire. The following sound confirmed her blade struck the target, burrowed through the sinus cavity of the taller man and he dropped the torch as he went down. She landed the same time he did, only he was on his ass and losing half his brain out of a nostril. She had the CRONE in her hand the moment her boots hit the floor.

The second man fired his weapon, desperate and off-target, and bent to make a grab for the torch. Cleo used the moment to slink by him in the dark so she was behind him then she put a hand on his shoulder as he straightened and fired a blue charge into his back.

The guy was instantly gasping and clutching his chest, back rigid like something had hit him from the front instead. His gun clattered on the ground and he writhed. Cleo slid her arm around his neck and grabbed her other bicep, squeezing while he thrashed, keeping him in the chokehold until he was still and sucking shallow breaths. She saw a small tattoo on the back of his neck through Adonai as he slumped. It was a black spades symbol, the type found on playing cards. Her mouth was on the side in some kind of smile as he hit the floor at her feet.

3

THE RED TAG DFAC WAS EMPTY WHEN THEY ENTERED. Stainless steel tables were bolted to the floor like in a military Chow Hall with matching long metal benches either side, vaguely reflecting long fluorescent lights hanging from the ceiling.

Cleo glanced over the metal counters and drink refrigerators looking for the sucker on duty. She could hear him somewhere out of view, clearing his throat and toiling with dirty dishes from that night's dinner rush. Must have been a big one because it was late and he was still cleaning. She knew he'd be a Yellow Tag with Extraordinary Clearance for the building, mopping up spills and leftovers like it got him extra credit. Maybe it did, she didn't know. Working a Red Tag DFAC undoubtedly looked good on a dossier. She tended to collect confirmed kills instead.

The kid lurking behind the counters was about sixteen when she spotted him, wearing a shiny black apron over his uniform, two thin yellow lines diagonal across the front. Wicked acne on the right side of his face tried stealing her attention while she watched his scrawny pale arms work a mean scrub on the kitchen surfaces, knuckles white around the rag he was using. He seemed surprised when he saw her.

"Sit anywhere you like, darling." Julia said and watched Tanya begin a lap around the room to choose a table.

Cleo hung back. They had come through metal detectors and Mal-Intent Scans when security cleared them but Julia's long purple skirt swished around her ankles, loose enough to conceal weaponry. They were never actually patted down and she was pushing up the sleeves on her too-long grey sweater and following her daughter, exposing chunky fake gold bracelets and acting a little too casual for a civilian whose life was threatened only hours prior. Cleo had heard they usually went crazy after something like that.

They had been granted access to a highly-classified facility but neither Julia or her daughter had asked much or given up any information in the car the whole way to HQ. There was just some whispering to each other about how long they'd been driving, one request for a bathroom break around the three hour mark and some other civilian bullshit Cleo hadn't been able to hear properly from up front.

She couldn't tear her eyes from the pink tank top and faded denim mini skirt Tanya was almost wearing as she circled. Bare legs and strappy sandals on the desert floor seemed fucking stupid but there she was, a "*miss thang*" teen idol strutting around like she was in a music video from The Outside and wearing the same outfit as before despite the drop in temperature and the big leather bag of clothes and junk Julia had lugged through security. It was hanging awkwardly from her shoulder now, far too full to be held comfortably while her slightly overweight legs hurried after her daughter.

Tanya trailed bony fingers over tabletops before she stopped near the giant arched window at the end of the room, planted her ass on a bench and swung pale legs over, waiting for Julia to catch up. The look on her face was 'inconvenienced.' Girl had presence, something entrenched in her snaggled-toothed smile at Julia awkwardly clambering to get her bag under the table and sit beside her. Then they were commenting on how the place was different to what they'd expected outside, glancing at Cleo to prompt her involvement. No dice.

HQ had come up on the ink blue horizon like a vast Emerald City hours before, nothing special really, but one of them had gasped at the sight. It was all fences, moving taillights and spotlights sweeping the grounds like prison security floodlights then a bunch of other buildings past the main entrance; some white, some camo and the rest dark and old. Probably a surprise to someone who'd never been deep in the desert, unaware civilization existed miles in from all the *"Deadly Force Authorized"* signs.

The Yellow Tag was still scrubbing counters when Cleo slid her right index finger over the sensor near the number pad on the counter and avoided eye contact with the greenhorn. $100 on the small orange rubber keys had to be enough to pay for whatever the civilians were going to eat and the Yellow Tag nodded when he recognised the series of beeps approving the transaction.

She took a seat across the table from the civilians and put one boot on the ledge underneath the table, legs wide enough so there was space between them to put a magazine on the bench near her crotch if she needed. The civilians watched, smiling and expectant before they realised she wasn't going to engage.

Julia dropped her wide smile gracefully. She was attractive up close, glittering eyes and a mane of curly chocolate hair she kept putting behind her ears and exposing earlobes punctured with more metal than Cleo was carrying. Tanya was the younger, straight-haired version with slightly less holes in her head.

Cleo released the magazine for the M9 and slid it onto the table to check how many rounds she'd used in the last 48 hours. Tanya was watching but it wasn't exciting and the gun was getting replaced with another side arm any day now. Cleo didn't like the weapon, but they catered for the ambidextrous with a reversible magazine release and PVD allowed them to work well in the desert. Sand got everywhere, jammed and corroded things otherwise. Physical Vapour Deposition was a God-send, but Cleo's heart belonged to the *RavenEye*.

"You like guns?" Cleo asked.

"We hate them." Tanya said. Julia nodded.

"Ever fired one?"

"No."

"Then how do you know you really hate them and not just the people who fire them?"

The question was flat and she didn't expect an answer. The kid could take that and ponder her Liberal shit.

The Yellow Tag didn't flinch at the gun on her side of the table when he made trips to and from the kitchen, retrieving scrambled eggs, bacon, fruit, pancakes and orange juice to lay on the civilians. It was breakfast for the next few hours because it was close to sunrise and he was going all out because she'd paid more than enough and he'd recognised her.

Tanya reached for the eggs the same time Julia used a fork to stab pancakes and the Yellow Tag sauntered over again to place a large beige sloppy milkshake in front of Cleo. Yeah, the contents of her glass looked like shit, figuratively and literally but she didn't acknowledge the look on Tanya's face.

Tanya's hazel eyes moved to Cleo's thigh and the butt of the RavenEye next. She was mid-action, half-standing with pieces of egg falling from the fork on the way to her mouth when she asked, "What kind of gun is that one?"

The RavenEye was sweet and no, whatever watered down, dumbed-down description she told Tanya wouldn't be sufficient, she could see that. There were going to be another hundred questions if the girl didn't get an answer she liked. Cleo settled for a halfway point. Sort of. She didn't think it was breaking the rules, even figured it could entice them to cough up their own info.

"This type is custom designed for Red Tag ranked agents," she said and pressed the stud to draw it a little more than halfway from the thigh rig, "Fifteen rounds in a magazine."

The *RavenEye* was fucking perfect, right down to the finger ridges on the grip, and fired with physics-defying velocity. The ergonomic design minimized recoil but it still hurt like a bitch when it slammed back in her palm. Without the thick and fingerless Firing Glove she wore on her left hand almost permanently, it may have shattered her wrist but all that really mattered was that the rounds splintered as they passed through the air, expanding for maximum damage when the target was hit. It was fast, so hot the exit wounds were often far bigger than the entry.

"The gun says your name," Tanya read the fancy shmancy red scrawl down the side of the barrel, "I can read *Darkrose*, what's the C stand for?"

"It doesn't matter." Cleo said. It didn't.

Tanya opened her mouth to say something else but their attention went to another agent entering the room, weaving the tables like a homing missile. He was positively pubescent, barely filling out the uniform, yellow stripe around his skinny right bicep. *Another rookie.* He was only armed with his M9, probably a second thought because he'd come straight from sleep or a double shift and Number One was using him as a messenger pigeon.

"Agent Darkrose, sir," he said, "Number One asks that the civilians are brought to the office after Call."

Cleo nodded once. The agent saluted, turned on his heel and left the way he'd entered. Cleo watched his back, trying to figure how he'd got clearance without having to make her a sandwich. The whole last twenty-four hours smacked of mystery.

"That guy called you sir," Tanya was making another face when Cleo turned back, "You're a *girl*,"

"It's acknowledgement the other agent is superior," Cleo said.

"So you can be *sir* and be a female?"

Tanya looked like she was having a hard time digesting the fact, dainty brown eyebrows–bent perplexion. It was going to blow her mind when she saw urinals in the female toilets. Female agents could piss standing up, devices built into the uniform to allow for it. They could even have sex without worrying about getting pregnant and go for years without a period. MDS had figured there were certain things that made agents equal and then made it happen. Was it too classified to tell the girl? She didn't know. It was probably none of her damn business though.

"Do you have friends or...a boyfriend?" Tanya probed, "Or a girlfriend, even."

Julia laughed, eyes sliding to Cleo like she was supposed to laugh too but she was also waiting on the answer.

"We only have relationships if we receive permission." Cleo said.

"Do they die? Is that why?" Tanya asked, fork on the table now, eggs abandoned, "Did your boyfriend die?"

Cleo started downing the vitamin shake in big impossible-to-answer-anything-else gulps that threatened to end up in a brutal icecream headache. Julia gave Tanya a look until she picked up her fork and started scraping pieces of egg again. Then there were a few minutes before Julia took up the mantle.

"Back at home, Agent Darkrose, did you have permission to stay in our house and hurt those men? Did you kill them? We got out, you stayed behind even though we were safe. I'm disturbed by that. Are you going to kill Alan too? What kind of agency is this?"

Cleo couldn't help the expression on her face. What kind of agency was this? What the fuck kind of question was *that*? Julia lowered her eyes when she didn't get a reply. Cleo wasn't going to explain the way things worked or how she'd been trained to operate. No, they hadn't given much away about themselves but they didn't need to. It was clear Julia was going to hate her stay at HQ.

4

"AND MAY WE ILLUMINATE THE PATH TO MOVE SWIFTLY, COURA-GEOUSLY AND PRECISELY TOWARD A NEW WORLD ORDER."

Hundreds of voices stopped abruptly. Everyone stared ahead, a few throat clears in the silence either side of Cleo. She was stationary at the centre of a long line of agents in the air-conditioned hall, straight-backed and standing to attention, respect for the oath and elaborate muster.

Agents either side and in front of her wore a thin bright red line around their right biceps, sewn into the black uniform. No fancy badges or medals like other agencies, just a line of colour to show rank. Only hers and a couple of others had double red lines, displaying the elite of the Elite as she stood shoulder to shoulder with her peers on the polished oak floor.

The meeting hall was almost at full capacity. Morning light glare flooded tall narrow windows while all the shuffling echoed. Lines of lower-ranking agents were rapidly breaking in front of her, discomfort allowed to be rectified after re-pledging. The high domed ceiling made for good acoustics, encouraged sound to travel along the walls and carry vibration. A hundred voices reciting the oath could sound like over a thousand but now it just sounded like thousands of people trying to blow the joint and get on with their day.

Cleo backed up against a wall by the big-ass Majestic Defence Syndicate insignia so she didn't have to be a part of the circus. The royal purple hexagram was outlined black, popping like 3D beside her, gold pyramid and watchful eye shining out proud from within the capstone. The X inside the pyramid sat about the clear letters and motto; *Oculus Mundi -the eye of the world.* Yeah, the swanky logo was often on show around the place but it never made it to the armband on the uniform, good thing too because she barely felt worthy to stand beside something with so much history let alone wear it on her body.

The cinema-size screen at the back of the room burst to life, rolling footage of MDS agents in the field as the hall cleared around her. Cleo watched clichéd shots of agents abseiling down rockfaces and running over hot sand in the Mohave then her own face flashed and snazzy graphics moved in and out of each other around the edges.

For some reason it now took a colossal twelve-foot image of her projected on the back wall to teach rookies that of all the career paths or specialties on offer they should become CAs; be *like Cleo Darkrose,* the top-ranked, Double Banded Red Tag Combat Agent, poster child for MDS. If the room had agents from all ranks in attendance, the thing was getting beamed up for all to see.

People told her it was a good picture sometimes, but having pouty lips never saved your ass. It occasionally bought some time on The Outside, that was it. She wondered if the recruiters mentioned that part while they were grooming MDS kids raised on site for various career paths at the age of thirteen, bang in the middle of puberty when they had no idea what the fuck was going on with anything.

She pushed off the wall and felt someone eyeballing her–*nosey-ass Yellow Tags*–staring like she was some celebrity from The Outside, phones in hand, failing to covertly record her mundane strides to get the hell out in full HD until they realised she was looking back at them over her shoulder. *Three males, one female all about fourteen years old and on the verge of wetting their pants with excitement.* They looked up one by one, embarrassed and fumbling to stuff their crease-able phones in pockets. She had nothing for them, no catchphrase or *"stay in school"* motto.

She didn't even have a fake smile for the two civilians loitering in the doorway pretending they hadn't been watching Call, looking like a bad game of *"which one of these things is not like the others?"* in their clothes from The Outside. They stepped back so other agents could pass, looking them up and down as they walked away like they'd never seen anyone in an official uniform before.

Two escort bodyguards were close, minding the civilians while Cleo was in the hall, asses up against the wall opposite the door, big beefy arms crossed in front of their wide chests and tight black shirts. She didn't know who they were because she'd removed the Adonai contacts earlier but they look clichéd as fuck, standing side by side like nightclub bouncers, scanning the crowd for troublemakers.

They weren't there to protect Julia and Tanya, they were making sure they didn't wander off and see too much. They'd probably had to reprimand them a few times already but Julia and Tanya were smiling when Cleo reached them. She looked up over their heads to the bodyguards instead.

"Agent Darkrose," One of the guards pushed off the wall and towered over her, blonde hair combed back and stuck to his head like he was mafia from last century. He pulled out a familiar device, "We need your signature."

The small machine was tight in his hand while he reached into his back pocket and handed her a Mondo-stylus. She didn't have one anymore, now she just mashed the screen on her POD like a savage because she'd lost it in a dead guy and they hadn't graced her with a new one. They were great too, doubled as tiny blowtorches when you needed to melt door hinges. His was sweaty when she took it and leaned in to read the screen on the machine.

She was going to have to sign the civilians over like a consignment note she usually submitted for transporting weapons and other inanimate objects. The machine had vein reader capability for ID checks but he was making her go old school, probably another one of Number One's quirky orders. She skimmed the details on screen before she squiggled her name in the box at the end of the jargon and slid her finger across the print scanner on the side.

The other bodyguard stood up off the wall, attempting and failing at a stealthy glance to his watch. Yeah, they had probably been told to escort her and the civilians to Call, hang around, go get something to eat and clock out. They wanted to wrap it up. The blonde one gave a tight-lipped smile when she handed the Mondo-stylus back and his partner took a step closer to the civilians like he was going to grab them.

Julia and Tanya exchanged a look and intimidation swirled between the five of them as the last of the agents spilled out of the meeting hall and disappeared down the corridor. The bodyguard with the wristwatch rested a thick hand on the butt of the gun at his hip. Cleo watched Tanya's eyes follow the move.

"They have to come to the office, now," he said, "Number One wants to personally debrief them."

Tanya mouthed, *"Number One?"* Neither bodyguard acknowledged it.

"Let's go." Cleo said.

She started walking for the elevator at the end of the hall. She imagined there was a look between the bodyguards before the blonde one took a stride forward, smart enough not to reach out and touch the back of her shoulder to get her attention.

"You're coming up too?"

"I just signed my name, handing them over out of my charge. I want to see they arrive at Number One's office in satisfactory condition."

The bodyguards wanted another look at each other, she could tell, but they fought it and gave her a small, synchronised nod instead. She waited for them to flank Julia and Tanya then the five of them headed for the elevator.

5

SOCIAL MEDIA MADE IT DAMN EASY TO FIND TARGETS, maybe even too easy and she didn't need any upscale tech from the depths of her compound. The average civilian idiot could get an approximate location for practically anyone. There was rarely need for a stakeout or surveillance anymore, the way the first agents did it back in the nineteen fifties and sixties. The slaves all spied on each other and themselves with dashcams and overpriced smartphones that could be hacked by any agency on The Outside. It was rampant with CCTV, GPS and people on the lookout for 'terrorists' and it made it so she could do her job upside down.

Number One chuckled about perpetuating fear so everyone became nosey and distrustful and watched each other, something about a culture shift in the population out there; a *psychological operation* on a generation. That and intrusive mod cons made it so finding Tanya and Julia Pierce hadn't been a challenge at all, unless Cleo counted the lack of aircon in the SUV she'd driven to their place. The nine-hour drive out there hadn't been the longest she'd done but it had been a hot one.

She'd messily swiped her finger across the reader by the door to her dorm and been retina scanned mid-morning after dumping the civilians once Number One's door was in sight. Now her watch said it was early evening and it had recorded a restless sleep but she was gearing up by the round table in the corner opposite the beds.

A series of hooks sprouted from the wall for hanging belts and weapons but she'd always unclipped the thigh rig off the tactical belt,

21

unstrapped it from her leg then thrown it all onto the table with her wrist sheath before she crashed out. It was lying in a mash of objects now like grey and black spaghetti when she grabbed up the RavenEye, shoulder and thigh rigs and throwing knife.

The CRONE was still juicing up in a cradle adjacent, sitting by the sink on the piss-yellow counter under the wall cupboards. Great invention, one even the low-ranking agents carried but it only had enough power to Delete a handful of people before it needed a charge and she'd forgotten to hook it up as soon as she'd got back because she'd had two snivelling civilians to babysit. The charging light was blinking depleted red.

She sat on one of the three military-precision-made beds to strap up the throwing knife on her forearm, black leather buckles pulled tight under her sleeve before she made the ritual pre-deployment grab under the bed for the dog-eared photo.

She was self-conscious even with no one else in the room, holding it too carefully. She looked like shit in this picture too, like the one in Number One's office, dirty and standing on desert sand outside HQ, flanked by two other agents. It was a clichéd black and white reminder of how far she'd come, her ability and strength to push forward and be a shit-hot Red Tag, *get it done,* even when her insides were splintered.

The other female agent in the snapshot was dead, died soon after the photo was taken; some botched hit that turned bad on The Outside and she'd never been told the specific details of. The male was her old partner, his tall frame wasn't to attention and he was just waiting for the pictures to stop so he could go home. He'd been shipped off in a draft to war on The Outside two years ago. She didn't know if he was alive.

She slid the picture back under the bed onto a second-rate ceremonial cushion she'd made with some yellow sheet she'd found neat on the tiles in her shower two ranks ago. She'd been a Green Tag just shy of her eighteenth birthday and didn't have a use for it until the picture took on its new meaning.

A knock at the door cut her thoughts and she went for the button at the side of the doorframe. The hunk of metal hissed upwards into the ceiling and revealed the Yellow Tag who had come up to the DFAC hours ago, looked like the guy was cleared for all sorts of levels in the Red Tag building.

"Agent Darkrose, *sir*. The civilians you accompanied inside are unable to be located, *sir*."

"Say again?"

The guy didn't reply but he didn't have to. She fought not to mirror the expression on his face. Yeah, it was a stupid fucking idea to bring any civilian to HQ in the first place. Cleo wanted to sigh, maybe punch a wall. She held both urges in while in front of the lower-ranking agent.

"It's Number One's request you aid in the search, if you are able, until you are due to deploy into the field."

"Thank you, agent," she mumbled.

She followed him out into the hall, even walked a half-assed lap around Level 4, checking the locked doors to dorms assigned to Red Tags who were rarely home. Number One's office was quiet, on the right side of the U shaped floor, reinforced with a bombproof door. Exotic plants in tall beige ceramic pots oversaw her search from either side of the elevator where the other agent made his getaway and none of it turned up the damn civilians.

There were hours of CCTV footage to be reviewed and miles of desert to comb if they were stupid enough to have snuck out into the grounds...and she wasn't getting stuck on that duty. If the civilians weren't in the DFAC when she checked downstairs, they were on their own.

6

THE ELEVATOR DIDN'T GO THE GROUND FLOOR. It was dead still, defiant and daring Cleo to snap. She was about three seconds off obliging, stabbing the button with her finger but the damn thing was just sitting there, doors open and motionless on Level 3 after carrying her down and stopping for no fucking reason, on a floor she didn't even want to go to.

Her face was instantly up against the black glass rectangle for it to capture a more accurate biometric reading, scanner to recheck the green and brown flecks in her irises nice and slow like no civilians were missing and they both had all the time in the damn world. She didn't know why it hadn't worked properly the first time but the maintenance guy apparently wanted an appendage ripped off.

She pressed the button for Ground Level again and *all* the numbers turned green. Then the elevator was shuddering instantly, shooting upwards, threatening to crap out and drop or get stuck halfway between floors so she'd have to wait for some underling to bail her out. *She couldn't afford to be suspended in a metal box for hours!*

She flung open the metal door under the numbers for the Emergency Stop button but the lights in the roof flickered and the elevator jerked to a stop, forcing her into a stumble backwards trying not to land on her ass. She was watching the number panel flash green while she was up against the back wall, arms out, legs apart for balance, bracing for the drop.

The elevator began a slow ascent instead, coming to a gradual halt like nothing was wrong but Cleo was still breathing through her mouth when the doors parted to darkness. She couldn't see shit past a portion of flat navy blue carpet outside in the light thrown from the elevator. The rest of the room was black when she stepped out.

She shot the elevator a dirty look over her shoulder and turned her attention to locating the stairs down...and she had to do it in the dark because she wasn't completely geared up. The RavenEye was in the thigh rig and she had the throwing knife but no CRONE and, more importantly, no torch.

Across the room, the sky was a long wide snapshot of navy blue and glittering stars through an enormous window, losing her attention to various lights thrown up from the airfield. Dark vertical blinds were an accordion on the left of the sill behind a small round black table and chairs that seemed out of place somehow.

She hadn't been up on Level 7 for years. She vaguely remembered some sort of lobby with a bunch of unused furniture but she didn't recall the window or the piles of boxes and stacked chairs to her right. She bet the exit stairwell she needed was on the left, down a long-ass shadowy hallway where the ambient light wouldn't stretch.

Her eyes adjusted slow without Adonai, still relying on the light coming from the elevator when she walked around the table and chairs and stood in front of the window. The sill met her thighs and the glass jutted a foot into the air outside so she could see down to the Red Tag courtyard. The fountain and stone benches looked like a weird mini Stonehenge in front of the mostly-empty airfield lit with small green orbs running borders and blinking light paths for aircrafts to land. She could see people in high-vis vests and protective earphones pacing around the tarmac and driving small maintenance buggies, unaware they were being watched.

Yeah, the view was nice but she didn't have all night. Julia and Tanya Pierce needed to get found and she was wasting time on the wrong floor thanks to a useless elevator. She clicked her tongue and felt a lick up her spine. There was something on the end of her "tsk," another sound using it for cover so she wouldn't notice it was there. Someone was watching her.

Cleo stared into the glass hoping for a reflection of the room behind. She considered reaching for the RavenEye, even just pressing the retention button on the thigh rig...but drawing a RavenEye at HQ was a punishable offence and if she *was* being watched from the darkness, they would see her go for the weapon and probably shoot her in the back of the head first.

She put her arms together, like she was folding them, and slid the throwing knife from inside her right sleeve. She didn't marvel at the stunning handle with all the carved inscriptions the way she did in downtime. She just gripped it and waited for a cue.

She could *feel* someone else in the room when the elevator doors shut and cut the light. The air turned heavy, floating on the inside of her skull and under her skin. *She could feel life-force.* It wasn't some New Age bullshit concept, it was something all good Red Tags had. You could just sense another person, deeper than sound. And it told you to watch your ass.

They wanted to take her by surprise otherwise they would have said something when she stepped out of the elevator, spotlighted in fluorescence and unable to see a damn thing. Logic tried to remind her that she was at HQ and nothing sinister could happen. Her gut argued anyway.

She watched the people on the tarmac work storeys down and unable to hear if she banged on the window for backup. She could feel her stalker approach already, controlling their steps with perfect balance, totally silent on their creeping journey and coming at her through the darkness with ease despite the obstacles and lack of light. Invisible bugs began crawling under her clothes. She breathed in through her nose and slowly out of her mouth.

Cleo spun and slashed a quick X shape across her stalker's chest, shoulder to hip. She didn't know how deep the blade went when she pulled it back and shot forward again. He blocked her arm and twisted her wrist so it locked up and she had to let go of the knife or get her bones broken. Then he shoved her backwards, propelling her towards the table and chairs, no room to hit the ground and roll to recover.

It cost a valuable second to dodge the furniture but her stalker didn't take the opportunity to strike so she flexed her calf muscles and pushed down–*function without instruction*–springing at him in a somersault. She snatched the RavenEye from her thigh rig, upside down mid-air, landed and rushed him, one arm across his neck driving him backwards and slamming the RavenEye into his body when his back smashed into the wall by the elevator.

Momentum made the RavenEye drill his chest as she cocked it and hissed, *"Now what?"*

The nerve someone would attack her at HQ made her fucking crazy. The fact drawing a RavenEye on-site was forbidden unless on a range, forgotten. Her finger was heavy on the trigger, itching to teach the bastard a lesson. *You don't fuck with a Red Tag.*

He was trained to fight, she could tell by the way he moved and it wasn't second nature, it was first but she would Delete him if she had to. Hand to hand or with the gun. Her stalker's calm taunt flowed down to her ear like a hot wave.

"Shooting me point blank with a RavenEye?" he muttered, *"Talk about overkill."*

Cleo's breath caught in her throat. She knew who it was. Low tones, Canadian accent and perfectly formed words. Yeah, she knew. She pushed off him hard, digging her elbow into his chest like a springboard and hoping it fucking hurt as she walked away, forcing him to unstick himself from the wall and come into the vague light from the window.

She turned to watch him materialize like a ghost. Combat boots first, military-issue not MDS, desert and camo coloured and laced up the ankle. She followed them up to where his pants stuck out over the tops of the boots and they weren't black either, they were some kind of multi cam, digi-cam printed ACU number.

His face was half-hidden under the cap, only his strong jaw and smooth mouth and chin visible until he turned and she saw the tip of his nose, the way it curved up so slightly at the end. She swallowed hard. Double Banded Red Tag, *Agent Trent Starr* was standing there in front of her after nearly two years in the Middle East.

She checked his six foot two or three frame over for injury, eyes darting to his arms and legs then his posture, without realising until she was through, remnants of old habits dying hard, despite a strange breakup and so much time apart.

Shit yeah people were going to be glad he was back. The super-talented MDS Sniper was one of Number One's favourites. Number One had seen hologram replays of his fights and been astounded, or so the story went, then someone at his home base in Canada informed Number One he also possessed the IQ of a genius and he was drafted for CA duty at HQ within hours. It took a few months after his arrival for everyone to fall in love with him. And he fell in love with her.

He was intuitive, skilled, downright sexy to some, she was sure...but not to her, she reminded herself, getting ready for eye contact. No, he was *not* sexy, despite the smile and those eyes; green, almost chatoyant and so...*clear*. She'd noticed those things and made a mess of her life with him once before. She set her expression to *"unamused"* and looked him right in the face.

"You wouldn't have used the RavenEye," he said, half smile.

"If I'd known it was you, I probably would have."

Agent Starr screwed up his face, hand on his chest like something had gone through it. Cleo watched his slim fingers as he dropped his hand and grinned.

She picked up the throwing knife and headed towards the window for the table and chairs she'd almost fallen into. He followed when she took a seat. She saw him hang one knee out from the side of the table when he sat because it was too low for his legs to fit under comfortably.

"I take it the elevator was you," she said.

"Gotta make an entrance somehow."

She slid the RavenEye away and couldn't help the glance around the room through the shadows, trying to sight the ever-present long dark bag containing Agent Starr's beloved rifle. It usually went wherever he did. She suspected it even had a name.

He was watching her from under his military cap, face half-lit by weak lights from outside, running the length of his jaw until he gave the window a glance and the light caught the other side of his neck. She just made out the familiar vertical string of tattooed letters spelling '*faith*.' The scripted font just looked like small dark squares in the lowlight.

"I was with the Military and other forces in the Middle East. As you know, a few of us were drafted," he said.

"A '*few*' of us."

Hundreds of MDS agents went over, were *still* being sent. People on The Outside thought the so called *"War on Terror"* was limited to bullshit hacking and the odd radicalised idiot now. Biased media and smooth-talking politicians made it so the public never knew just how many boots were on the ground in so many countries, how many soldiers were sacrificing their lives.

"I had to go. Mandatory, didn't have a choice," he said, like he wanted to remind her, "Number One didn't want us there under our own banner, so to speak, being a big scary secret agency and all. It's not documented *our* agency was ever there. They distributed us into battalions and units with the others."

Cleo stifled a tsk. No big surprise there, MDS presence was rarely documented. If they died in the field, their names wouldn't grace any memorial plaque of remembrance. They would just be forgotten, carbon on the wind. She'd managed to make some kind of peace with it over the years but getting absolutely no credit for fighting a war on The Outside? That was pretty shitty.

"Other soldiers knew who we were, they wanted to break us the second we stepped off the transports. I thought they just wanted to break us in," a one-shouldered shrug, "But it wasn't like that. They separated us, I ended up in a unit with...*regular* soldiers, no other MDS agents."

"No one that knew what your rank is here," she said.

"No and we're trained differently to the way they are. I passed all the physical fitness stuff easily but the rest was new to me, I had to learn pretty quickly."

"Why are you back here? What happened?"

"I made a mistake, things went wrong," he said.

She studied the shapes and colours on his uniform when he folded his arms on the table. His eyes were lowered under the cap for a second. It looked like some kind of Dishonourable Discharge to her but she didn't voice a guess. Whatever it was, she bet it sucked to be him right then.

"You know, even *Basic* is like riding a bike that's on fire...through Hell. Mandatory to get trained their way. It was fast-tracked for me because I'm MDS but it was still hell. We were issued an M9 as a side arm over there too, standard."

Cleo made a face.

"Yeah, I finally found a group of guys who shared my extreme dislike of having to carry it. Using them when you've had the privilege to fire a RavenEye is..." He shook his head, a small smile.

"You're digressing," she said, "You made a mistake, was there a body count?"

"Yes, there was," he said flatly, "But it could've been worse."

He took the cap off and looked at her, eyes glowing emeralds between rows of black lashes in the light from the window. His almost neck-length black hair was tied back. *They'd let him keep his hair?* Okay.

"My form slipped after that, I wasn't performing the way they needed me to," he said.

"Number One must be-"

"Furious, yeah. They're launching an investigation into my actions. They believe if what I did is leaked to the media on The Outside, it'll promote further decrease in public opinion. They said it'll affect the soldiers stationed overseas as well as political agendas here," he shook his head, "They don't get it, soldiers are already affected. *I'm* affected, can't get it out of my head."

"Which part?"

"All of it...nothing's concrete anymore," he wasn't looking at her then, favouring the table surface, "What goes on there is different than here. We're Red Tags but it's not the same there. What I've seen, what I was made to do..."

"They asked you to use it," Cleo said, and suddenly finding the missing civilians didn't seem so important.

"Yes, they did. I told them no. Number One called me personally, demanded I use *NovaRose*," his voice went into a whisper and back, "I was told it didn't matter there, that it was too far out for anyone to report it."

"Who did you use it on?"'

"I can't talk about it."

"But it's *yours*, you designed it," she said.

"It doesn't matter to them. They want me to sign it over to MDS completely, so that Number One solely controls its use, so that I can't refuse to use it again."

Cleo didn't expect to be talking about such heavy things the first time she met him after so long. She didn't expect to be sitting across from him saying anything really, she didn't even think she'd *see* him again until five minutes ago.

NovaRose was a big deal. Maybe the biggest. The weapon was so devastating only two people in the world could command its use; Agent Starr and Number One and they both had to be in agreement before it could be deployed. Number One's command only overrode the rules if Agent Starr was incapacitated or dead.

NovaRose came in a pale mint-green liquid and evaporated to gas when exposed to the air. Cleo saw the bioweapon in action on test subjects in the early days, pigs and mice meeting a demise worthy of a horror film. It agonizingly stripped flesh and devoured bone from the inside, attacking the nervous system and causing targets to experience panic and confusion. Then they would bleed from orifices and sometimes empty bowels while they died. The effects differed for organisms within radiuses of the initial detonation or spill. All results were unpleasant and most fatal.

She remembered Agent Starr's face changing from excited, proud to delight Number One, to being covered in regret she never saw leave him when he spoke about NovaRose any time since. He refused to provide copies of the data to anyone after the tests, keeping all results and data on an old-fashioned portable hard drive and in two hardcopy folders he locked in a lab at HQ. She watched him swallow hard. The things he'd done overseas were eating him like acid and if he'd used NovaRose, the analogy wasn't far off.

"I've been offered a part in an assignment while they investigate my actions over there..." Agent Starr said slowly.

"*No*," she said. *Fuck no.* "I don't need your help with this one. It's mine."

"Other Red Tags are on standby too. The ones that are back at HQ are waiting on your call, usually it's Blues or Greens for backup, right? Everyone's clambering to be your second for this, Number One hasn't told you?"

"No and they're probably just home to get it done if I don't do it right."

"Whatever this is, it's important. Number One said I'm at your disposal. I've officially been assigned to you, if you want me."

"Why just you and not the others?" She felt her eyes narrow.

He leaned back in his chair and shrugged but they knew the answer. Number One was making sure the assignment was executed without fail...or Number One was playing matchmaker with something that had already run its course and ended in pain and drama like a bad romance novel from a thrift store. Number One was quirky like that sometimes.

"I was told my involvement would *redeem* me a little, as it was put to me." Agent Starr said, saving them both feeling awkward any longer but he was still avoiding eye contact.

"I can do this alone."

"I don't doubt that. At all. I'm asking you a favour, I think I need this."

His eyes were on her now, regular intensity lost behind uncertainty. She couldn't read the look on his face and stared him out, surprised when he stood up like he didn't have the energy for a battle of wills. He walked to the window in silence and looked out over the grounds instead.

Her gaze moved to the back of his head and the broad shoulders under a uniform he was never supposed to wear. He was a big guy with the speed of a man half his size, executing decisions and fight technique before he was consciously aware, an effective MDS agent but he looked tired now, palpable unease coming off him. He was out of options, she could practically hear the cogs in his head spinning, trying to conjure a plan B if he couldn't tag along on her assignment.

Cleo joined him at the window, watching the small figures working on the tarmac again. It was a minute or so before he looked at her and she skimmed his eyes for an agenda he hadn't mentioned. There wasn't one.

"Okay," she said. She pretended she didn't see the quick smile he tried to stifle, "If you accompany me on this assignment you need to understand we're going to do things my way. This is my assignment. Are we clear, agent?"

"*Crystal,*" The last half of the word came through his teeth, trying to control his face, "I have something for you."

Cleo watched him fumble around in one of his billion pockets. When he brought his hand out it was wrapped around a white circular plastic compact, A POD, with the next set of instructions.

33

"But Number One said a Yellow Tag was going to–" She stopped. Number One had intended them to work together from the start. Touché, Number One, touché.

Her right index finger found the small red panel on top and cleared the print check and implant scan the first time. The POD clicked open like a clamshell and the top half came to life, MDS insignia blazing across the small screen in vivid colour. Disclaimers rolled up, warnings against sharing the information, that it was meant for the intended recipient only.

Agent Starr leaned over to read with her. The words on the screen instructed her to take care of some kind of camp on the outskirts of HQ, some group that had snuck in further than any had in years. It sounded like they were being given a warm up, probably because Agent Starr had been away for so long. It was fine by her. She almost smiled as she read the last line; *deadly force authorised.*

7

CLEO AND AGENT STARR LUCKED OUT. Another team brought down an SUV and not some beaten up undercover car. It had front seats, seating for three or four people in the back and then another compartment that acted as a trunk. They didn't have to open the back of the car to get to it either, they could just throw things over from the backseat if they wanted.

The stainless steel canisters of water, the flares and other junk came packed in the back of any cars signed out–*standard*. Cleo knew a few MREs were piled up there and she wouldn't touch them because most of them tasted like shit but MDS vehicles were always stocked for fast deployment, usually enough supplies for 2–4 people, for about a week whether they were going urban or not.

She'd left HQ with Agent Starr past midnight after he changed into his MDS Red Tag uniform. They blew through most of the checkpoints in record time even with every group on patrol wanting to welcome Agent Starr back when they'd recognised him, shaking his hand and reluctantly breaking their serious–to–impress–Darkrose demeanours to greet him outside the car while she sat there like a department store dummy.

Agent Starr's features were weakly lit with pale green glow from the dials and devices on the dash now. He was so quiet in the passenger's seat. When Cleo looked over, half the reason was to make sure he was still there. He was slightly thinner than she remembered but everything else looked the same, muscle tone, prominent cheekbones leading to that faultless profile. He was lucky his shit hadn't got messed up when he was deployed overseas.

She didn't know the etiquette for seeing someone after a military deployment on The Outside or whether she should forget about it and go straight into how they were going to tackle their objectives. Red Tag agents didn't talk about who they'd Deleted on assignment or where they'd been. It was probably the same when someone returned from the Middle East but he was decked out in MDS attire again and sitting right next to her, a lengthy drive ahead and nothing but dark sand to look at.

She probably had to say something. He saved her the anxiety and cleared his throat.

"How are you, Cleo?"

"Well."

"Yeah?"

"Yeah," she answered, "How was the Middle East?"

He breathed out audibly, "It's...different."

"I can imagine."

"No," he said quietly.

Cleo didn't say anything back. *Stupid.* He was right, she *couldn't* imagine, she had no fucking clue. She'd never been to war, not the kind he had. She looked at him then, maybe to say something else, maybe just to watch the look on his face change as he drifted through his thoughts and left her dumbass reply behind.

"I missed HQ," he said, "And the people...and you."

"Have you seen anyone besides Number One since you've been back?"

"No, I wasn't briefed much. I got home this morning, zero four. Went through the medical checks, all fast-tracked. If they did everything they were supposed to, I'd still be there but they didn't make me stay for a psyche screen so, uh, that's a good thing. I can't sleep lately...but that's all right."

She didn't look back at him, you didn't stop a Red Tag when they were reeling off personal information. It was rare as fuck.

36

"I just got the standard—move this, stretch this, turn that way, cough—any sexual activity whilst away? Have you ingested foreign foods or water you believe to be suspicious or detrimental to your previous health status?" He rattled off the questions like a script. She knew the one. "I wasn't told much but Number One said the man we're Deleting is a known figure, works with mafia and known terrorists. He's the 'grandfather' of the *Truth for Life Movement.*"

"Truth for Life Movement," Cleo repeated, "Protest group?"

Agent Starr looked across at her, frowning before he continued.

"Uh, I guess they are," he said, "They demand investigations into government conspiracies, levels of radiation in airport security scanners, staged terrorist attacks, chemicals in water, and medicines to thin out the population. You know, the concept of Eugenics."

There was some kind of excitement in his voice. He'd done more research than her in the short time he'd been aware of the assignment. Yeah, well, good for him, she'd been running around trying to find two snot-nosed civilians she'd chosen not to bother mentioning.

"He's building an army to infiltrate government establishments to expose what he calls the *truth*. They call him the King of Spades or *SpadeMan*," Agent Starr said, "The Spades suit has been known to symbolise death, rumoured to have been used in Vietnam and other military operations as a calling card and an intimidation tactic, painted on the bodies of dead enemies and on parachutes, bombs, things of that nature. It's also obviously the highest card in any number of card games when depicted as an Ace...I'm guessing this man is using it in that context, a powerful, dominating symbol."

"You know a lot about this group. Do you believe their stories?" Cleo frowned, "Their *truths*?"

"I didn't."

"But now?"

"I don't know, it doesn't matter really," he shrugged like he'd changed his mind she was worth the long explanation.

Cleo kept her eyes on the dirt road, taking note of the white markers beginning to appear, wooden stakes in the ground every few metres either side of the path. They belonged to MDS, signalling anyone coming the other way that their ass was on the verge of being arrested or shot at if they proceeded.

The SUV was almost out of HQ grounds, headed to areas where civilians wanting to see "UFOs" tried to camp, still over twenty two miles in from the regular tarred roads. People used to be able to come out legally years ago, before MDS expanded the perimeters and radius of permission for use of deadly force. Back then there were tour groups run by shonky con men taking money from tourists to show them a shitty view of MDS buildings in the distance from over some rocks.

They had stopped that shit when she was a lot younger but she had to hand it to those people, hiking out there was hell. There was no shortage of rocks and heat and thin air. She knew all about it because part of her training had been to get dumped out in the middle of nowhere and hike her way back toward HQ enough to be picked up before her water ran out or she died of exhaustion. She wondered if any of those *Truth for Life* suckers knew what it was like to really tough it out in the desert with all the red dirt and rattlesnakes.

"I fought two men on The Outside in a civilian household," Cleo said. "One of them had a spades tattoo on the back of his neck. I was told SpadeMan–*Alan Pierce*–is tattooed with a large spades symbol on his arm."

"Everyone in the group is tattooed with the symbol or wears a variation of it on their body at all times, from what I read on internet forums earlier," Agent Starr gave her a glance, "Maybe a way of identifying men and women under his command and who isn't...maybe a symbol of their dedication."

"I wasn't briefed much on this man's Deletion. I have the POD, obviously, no personal instruction how to carry it out. I'm only aware of the locations and expected ETAs. I have to take them into account."

"Number One usually gives us the name and only a few facts about the target to ensure we don't develop a personal opinion before the Deletion," he said, "But Number One's given you his family, I was told you'd met with them."

"That is correct. Different procedure was noted. Why are you stating this?"

"Number One trusts you but it's like part of this is to reassess your ability to Delete without conscience, it just seems a little late for that."

"Are you saying I have no conscience?" She looked at him and back to the path.

"Would you be insulted?"

"It is a statement, nothing more," she said, "I understand what you're saying, I've been serving for too long to be...*tested*."

"This man's Deletion is going to affect thousands of people and a handful of key figures around the world."

"That means nothing to me, my loyalty lies with Number One and my orders."

"As does my own but there are many people who would probably kill for this man or die to save his life. It's interesting," he said.

"Where are you taking this interaction?" *Can the BS.* She saw Agent Starr shrug before he continued.

"Number One believes you'll complete the orders despite the family and that you won't be swayed into this man's way of thinking when you meet him."

"That's a given. Are you *swayed*?"

"No. I'd never betray MDS but there are a lot of questions his group asks which I also believe are relevant. I spent a lot of time with different people in the Middle East, soldiers, civvies. I was able to hear many opinions that differed from my own."

Agent Starr shifted in his seat as she drove. When she looked at him again he was looking back at her, figuring out how he was going to say the next part. Yeah, it had been a while but she could still read the expression on his face, the way that small crease appeared over his right eyebrow when he was apprehensive. He didn't like what he was about to say.

"Number One, sent out a message a few hours ago, made sure Alan Pierce was informed you were the one assigned his Deletion."

Cleo turned her head to look at him. What. The. Hell?

"Who knows why," he shrugged, "Provoking a surrender?"

Upping the stakes.

"You know your name travels in many circles, it's possible just mentioning you would have SpadeMan take courses of action he wouldn't usually. Maybe Number One wants him to make a mistake or give himself up, save us the trouble."

"Or the tax dollars," she said.

"Yeah. I heard we got new dessert in the MREs. Some poor civilian bastard probably gave his left nut for my pack of candy."

The desert paths and dunes looked the same and minutes spilled into another hour easily. The next time Cleo looked over, Agent Starr was slumped in his seat, eyes closed, head down. He'd stepped off a transport and straight into hours of tests and a major assignment, he was probably tired as shit. She didn't need him until they passed the camp on the way out so she let him rest until there was random chatter between perimeter patrols crackling over the radio.

The volume was down low, murmurs, but enough to wake him. He sat upright and looked around the car, reaching to the thigh rig on his right leg, making sure he was still armed. She didn't look at him when she turned the volume up.

Half the conversation was already gone. One patrol was telling another about action to the south. Some MDS pilot had flown over on the way back to HQ and sighted unauthorised activity a few more miles out. She syphoned the information from the jargon and got the gist. No one said they were going to check it out and report back.

Yeah, that had to be the group the POD was talking about. She pressed her foot down on the accelerator and the car leapt forward. Her eyes drifted from the path and over the dunes in the distance, searching for the target. The desert had no rules, you didn't have to watch the road, you could take in the view at night. In the daytime the whole place looked like something out of an old Coyote and Roadrunner cartoon some agents snuck into the rec room once. Vastness meant you could do whatever you wanted. Out here she could do whatever the fuck she wanted.

She was permitted use of deadly force at their current distance from HQ, they were still on private property belonging to MDS. If she saw anyone who wasn't supposed to be there, it was trespassing so they could be taken out after a warning and choice at an optional surrender. She wasn't going to lie, she liked it when they didn't choose the latter option.

She cut the lights and eased off the accelerator as an object came up on the horizon, upper left over the sand dunes, flickering orange. *Campfire.* Agent Starr was peering through the windscreen, a dog getting a scent, skin glowing from the console again and looking like he was radioactive. They weren't close enough to tell how many people they were up against and getting nearer meant the view would diminish with the sand dunes rising in front of the site. No way to get good recon.

Cleo steered away from the dirt path toward the three large sand dunes separating them from the site. They stretched long and wide in front of the windscreen, silver moonlight running across the tops as they merged into each other like some giant frozen wave.

The car was slow in quiet darkness, a giant black shark stalking blue velvet ocean sand. The dunes were a rolling sea around them, waves expanding out of nothing to stand higher than they looked from back near the path. The SUV climbed smaller ones effortlessly, no groaning or complaining the tilts were too steep, never threatening to roll them but the big ones weren't going to be the same.

Cleo stopped the engine alongside the trio of dunes, car parallel to the piled sand and hidden from the other side. If she and Agent Starr were going to check out the campfire, they had to go on foot because the SUV was quiet, but it wasn't invisible. Hell, if someone walked up over the dunes from the other side, they were going to be found out. Still, there was that Use of Deadly Force permission...

She opened the driver's door slowly, instinctively trying to tune into sounds carried on the wind. Agent Starr stayed in his seat too, waiting for the desert to give up a secret. There was nothing first...then winds picked up and they could hear voices and laughing, curse words and banter over a spitting fire.

"One of those UFO groups, probably. Really shouldn't've been able to get this far in." Agent Starr said, a lick of suspicion to his words. His hand was near his thigh rig again as he reached for the radio with the other one to call it in and tell HQ they were going to check it out.

Cleo reached into the backseat for the case with Adonai contact lenses. It was the size of a handbag, dark grey plastic clipped together by a suitcase-like latch she flicked open. Only one pair of contacts sat in the compartment, the other slot was empty. Agent Starr was out of luck.

"Gear up, we're on," she said and slid out of the car.

She dropped the Adonai contacts in her eyes on the first attempt and everything changed to various shades of green in the moonlight after she blinked the code for Nightvision and stepped around the side of the car to face the dunes.

Agent Starr was still in his seat and lit by the console, eyes down setting up his rifle. She could tell he had a big piece of it balancing across his lap as he took another one out of the bag he'd put on her vacated seat. She waited for him to look up, telling him wordlessly that she'd probably meet up with him in a moment after some recon. He gave one small nod.

She turned back to the dunes to survey the climb, not much opportunity to build up momentum to run near vertical. The dunes started near her boots, in line with the tyres on the SUV behind and climbed to a few feet taller than where she was standing.

She checked her weapons were secure and would survive the hike then she started toward the sunken gap between two of the dunes, ready for the glute workout of a lifetime. The edges of her mouth twitched on that one, *Personal Trainers on The Outside would be out of a job if their clients had access to a desert.*

The incline was steep enough to make her slide backwards, a literal version of two steps forward, one step back and she dug in and powered through gravity, incline and the mini waterfalls of sand trying to engulf her boots. She didn't look back to check on Agent Starr's progress. He was free to keep building his weapon or stare at her ass and laugh as she struggled. Either or.

She was prone on the sand moments later, cool grains submerging her hands as she lay flat on top of the dune, lucky enough to score a shelf stretching about three feet ahead before the dip down the other side. It was a good rest stop and an even better vantage point for recon.

A bonfire spat wide in a shallow pit on her lower left, giving off heat and highlighting the roadtrain-sized truck parked right under her position but the tents standing in a semi-circle opposite were her focus. They were white or beige, a navy blue one in the centre, tall enough that someone could stand and walk around inside. Almost military looking. Not the regular type most UFO Hunters brought in and Cleo had never known alien chasers to bring a truck, mostly because something like that would never get through security outposts without detection. Yet here they were.

She blinked another code and turned on Adonai's Thermal Imaging to estimate the number of occupants inside the tents. She counted five before her attention moved to the right and she saw another mass of heat approaching in the distance. It was another truck, gradually moving to the area with headlights off. She was probably going to need Agent Starr for this one.

The last time they'd been on assignment together, he'd been armed with a souped up, MDS-modded, sniper rifle. It was a hybrid between something Special Forces would use and some civilian gun-buff would sell a kidney for; an MDS *Tern.* She didn't know too many specs on it though. It weighed about thirty pounds, usually came in two pieces before assembly, had a bipod and a detachable magazine box, 50 caliber, bodyarmour-piercing shit, *enough to penetrate concrete and keep going.* Oh, and that bullet compensating reticle and anti-reflective system. Anything else was beyond her and he'd never bored her with the details but she hoped it had been the weapon he was setting up.

She blinked Adonai off and shuffled backwards to turn and step down the dune, straining muscles to control the descent so she didn't trip and roll. Agent Starr was waiting at the bottom.

"What have we got?"

"A bonfire, a campsite. Five people, no weapons sighted...and a vehicle approaching from the south-east," she said.

"How do you want to proceed?

"I want the moving truck first. It could be carrying weapons or reinforcements to the site," she said, "I don't have much time to get it."

Agent Starr nodded. She was going to need control of it before the people at the camp started noticing it approach or the driver radioed in his co-ordinates.

"I'm going to get a decent range at the campsite. Do your thing, I'll be there." Agent Starr said.

8

THE TRUCK WAS MUDDY GREEN WITH A SEMI-TRAILER CON-TAINER ATTACHED, stretching back about 26 feet. The wide tyres were rolling steadily over the sand with ease and leaving tracks and plumes of dust blowing in their wake like no fucks given. It looked kind of military but it didn't belong to any army Cleo recognised.

She landed a boot on a U-shaped metal rung in the ladder at the back and leapt for a handhold, sand conveyer-belting below. It wasn't her first time hitching a ride on the back of a moving vehicle but it wasn't easy the way they made it look in those Hollywood movies Number One banned from rec rooms. It was an art; timing, endurance and good skill not to trip and be sucked under and crushed.

She couldn't see into the driver's cab from her position but she knew it was wide. Adonai had shown the truck was right-hand drive with one big mass behind the steering wheel earlier, so either someone was sitting on the driver's lap or he was a real big fat guy. It was all Adonai gave her and she was hoping for the latter.

The steel and rubber on the truck was scratched and dented, seemed old, containing a metal Adonai couldn't see through enough to pick up any thermal. She couldn't tell what was inside the container she was scaling, potential anxiety as she stepped up the last few footholds to the roof to get up and over before anyone noticed.

Her palms found enough grip when she hauled herself over the edge, scraping the thigh rig against the container and feeling her pulse strain against its straps. Every bump in the sand below became a boulder threatening to take her balance and cause a spill. Slight change in altitude and the human body got stupid and wanted to bail. But that wasn't an option.

She crawled across the container, vibrations from the engine in her fingertips and knees until she stopped at a sunken plastic trap door in the midst of the steel. A thick padlock hung open through a rusty metal loop, begging her to mess with it. The silver child-size handle under it was blinking in the starlight and slimy when she grasped it.

Her stomach clenched, wanted her to rear up and risk falling off-balance. She brought her hand up to her face and she didn't need Adonai. Ambient light in the desert was always enough to make a relatively accurate identification but it was the texture of the shining wet goop on her fingers that told her it was *blood*. The metallic odour drifted into her nostrils to confirm.

She wiped her hand on her pants and padded around the hatch to yank it open, hands slipping on the bloody handle twice before it came up and exposed black nothing. She couldn't see inside and leaning in for a better look wasn't going to happen, she wasn't going to give anyone an easy shot if they were waiting to blow her face off. She hung back from the edge and blinked the code for thermal again.

Green, red and yellow lit her vision in the black-heat signatures on the floor inside the hatch- strange orbed rainbows shivering with the motion of the truck. *Bodies*. She drew the RavenEye and waited but nothing moved so she dropped down into the hole.

The smell hit first. *Rancid*. Blood, meat and shit. Cleo landed squatting half on a body and holding her breath involuntarily. Another bump in the sand pushed her off-balance onto a second lifeless mound. Her free hand went down to brace and straight into a slick of something wet and sticky, sliding a few inches on the truck floor so she almost landed on her ass.

She stood fast and planted her feet to compensate for the off-balance sway. The RavenEye was still tight in her left hand when she looked down and saw the body that cushioned her fall was male. He was lying on his back, face tilted away from her and staring off into the dark.

She could see the outline of his motionless jaw and the side of his neck. Body heat was gone from his extremities but the colour changed through Adonai when her vision went to his core. He'd only been dead a couple of hours at the most.

The front of his throat was ripped out when she leaned over, a gaping hole and no lower jaw, like a ventriloquist dummy that made it so Adonai didn't even waste time trying to identify him. He'd taken a round to the neck with a large caliber weapon. She saw smaller bullet wounds all through his clothing too. They had bled and started drying, covering him in congealing, gummy blood.

The other guy she'd fallen on was long gone, no need to check for a pulse when she looked over her shoulder. The heat in his body was snuffed out completely. Probably killed long before his body was dumped in the container.

A third body sat half-propped up at the front end of the container and lit with red and yellow heat fields. The moonlight from the hatch hampered Adonai's reach but Cleo was sure the body was male too. She could see rips in his clothes, hacked into shredded pieces, along with the skin under it—*some sort of machete attack*—she couldn't tell for sure yet and her eyes were already focussed on something else on his body, highlighted in Adonai's nightvision.

She got low again, a short distance to the floor if the driver hit a large dune and she fell, making her way towards him, hands out to her sides for balance and stepping carefully after each jerk the truck made. The container was a too-long black tunnel on the inside, heat signatures fading all around her, dead human bodies pitifully bleeding out in the dark. It was a fucking nightmare.

Her chest got tight when she reached the guy with the shredded skin. She was right, even from back where she'd entered. She'd been able to see the thin strip around his right bicep. *He was MDS.*

Adonai was going crazy trying to get the read but she wasn't looking at his face long enough, squatting and reaching to his throat to check for a pulse. There was just whirring and vibration from the tyres rolling below and blood-wet skin registering on her fingertips. He was recently dead, maybe even just the last few minutes.

Nightvision said the stripe around his bicep was probably blue. Things were serious and she didn't want to call HQ. She didn't want them to send her backup now. Her veins were boiling anger in their red networked tide. She was *pissed*.

She blinked Adonai off and breathed out. The flavour of death was blunt on her tongue when she inhaled, surrounded by three dead MDS agents in a truck headed towards HQ. She needed to warn Agent Starr. The people at the campsite weren't just some idiot UFO-hunter group. They had enough skill to kill Blue Tags, one rank down from theirs, a rank away from being the most respected CAs in the MDS.

She shoved the RavenEye back in the thigh rig and dug her pockets. She hoped she still had Agent Starr's number stored from years before and that he had his phone set to silent, she was probably going to blow his cover if he didn't. She almost had the collapsible phone scrunched all the way out of her pocket when she stopped fumbling because she'd heard something from the back of the truck and realised she wasn't alone.

9

THE FEMALE AGENT WAS ALIVE, watching Cleo through half-closed eyes with her head resting back on the wall of the shipping container. Adonai hadn't given up a positive ID and Cleo had the thermal off now so it was just Nightvision. Everything was dark and olive-coloured as she got low and approached.

She was wearing a Green Tag uniform; buttons down the front and a lower neckline than Cleo's, with no collars. It was under a bulky standard-issue MDS jacket, mostly zipped up but torn across the chest. She had avocado eyes through Adonai, probably mid-blue in daylight. One eye was staring upwards blankly, a blowout fracture to the socket that Adonai was refusing to ignore and identify through.

Her blonde hair was matted together with dirt and blood, half tied back. Bruising around her face made her jaw sharp and gaunt as her good eye roved Cleo's face, watching her survey the damage.

"You're MDS," she mumbled, "I can tell...by the way you move."

"What happened here, Agent?"

"Agent *Darkrose*?"

"Yeah."

"God, I'm...sorry, sir," she whispered.

Cleo didn't know what to say. Agents didn't say sorry. She could count how many times she'd said it in her whole life on one hand and still have a couple of fingers left over. The only person who got an apology for shit was Number One, and it was some kind of weakness you only gave into if you were fucked otherwise.

"Why are you apologising to me, agent?" Cleo frowned.

"We sold you out."

"Who did?"

"Me, me and Jimmy Stone, my...partner. He's the one you landed on...I'm Agent Hooper."

Cleo heard the laboured breath after the other agent's words. She wasn't doing well, wincing and holding her stomach, a dark stream trickling down her pale neck into her uniform. An overflowing internal bleed? Fuck.

"We did an induction with Yellow Tags out here days ago...Jimmy got phonecalls after it, unknown number. Civilian line," she took a small pained breath out, "It couldn't be traced. They knew how to bypass MDS security."

"Who was it, what were the calls about?" Cleo used her sleeve to wipe blood from Agent Hooper's mouth. She was probably going to be unconscious soon, her good eye had become unfocussed in seconds. If information was coming, it had to come out soon.

"It was those *Truth for Life* people. They told us things about MDS. They have intel on everyone, *you*. Current stats, confirmed kills...told us if you died we could take your place but...work for them too. Double agents," she coughed. Blood sprayed Cleo's boots, "They wanted us to tell them your weaknesses."

"Did you?"

"Yes, sir," Agent Hooper whispered. Her body stiffened and she coughed again, "I told them you have no weakness."

Agent Hooper smiled faintly. Cleo didn't smile back. Treason was treason. That and the blood smeared over the other agent's teeth was ghastly. There was nothing Cleo could add to the commiseration, damage was done, information already exchanged. No point taking it out on Agent Hooper now.

Cleo looked down at Agent Hooper's hand lying palm side up between them with skin hanging off, gory and ripped to pieces. It didn't even look like a hand anymore. Cleo could see through to bones in some places and Agent Hooper was missing her right index finger, hacked off halfway down so there was a stump from the second knuckle.

Cleo knew what it meant. Rogue agents who went AWOL did similar to stop being tracked by MDS, some did it for their own safety. Anyone who knew agents carried a TC chip with their vitals and stored credits took their fingers to remove the chips and convert them to money on The Outside. Opening the finger up and digging around for the chip would have been extra work but they hadn't had to hack the hand to pieces too, what the hell? It would have to be amputated, Cleo was sure.

"What happened to you?"

"We agreed to meet them, unarmed. They took us out...hunted us like animals when they got the intel they wanted," Agent Hooper said, continuing in her straining and disjointed voice, "They took our TouchCash chips...stole our money. Funny, after offering us so much money for information."

"And now?"

"Now we're in this truck to be thrown out...coyote meat. It's what we deserve."

"I can get you out of here," Cleo said. She frowned the second the words left her mouth.

She didn't know if she could or even if it would be worth it once Number One learned the other agent was a traitor. Agent Hooper was laughing anyway, chuckle out of place in the container and creepy with no echo. Cleo had never been laughed at before. She stayed still, eyes fixated on the other agent, waiting for the explanation.

"I'm not...going anywhere, sir. We both know that," she said, "If I wasn't already fucked...you'd've put a bullet in me for what I've done."

She pulled open her jacket gauchely with her mangled right hand. The bone and skin hung and twisted in the air freely and it should have hurt but she didn't feel it anymore. More blood dripped from her mouth when she dropped her head to look down at her injuries.

Cleo followed her gaze.

Her abdomen was destroyed, a black hole wider than a large fist was leaking blood all over her thighs. Cleo had barely noticed Agent Hooper's left arm over it earlier but keeping pressure on the wound had been useless. She was not going to survive.

Cleo's eyes moved down, racing against themselves to find the next wound in Adonai's shades of green. Two more holes greeted her eyes, oozing thick dark blood mixed with other bodily things. She counted back from ten in her head while she took in Agent Hooper's inevitability and tried not to let it show on her face. She wasn't getting her out, the other agent was right.

"Is there anyone to notify?" Cleo asked. No emotion. The other agent didn't need that shit.

"Just Number One. Agent Stone was the closest thing I had to family. It's another thing I won't get to do. I wanted to, you know, find someone...maybe go AWOL. Live the slave life...nine to five, house on The Outside," she smiled and closed her eyes. Cleo noticed blood coming from her ears before her eyes sprung open again, "Don't trust anyone, Agent Darkrose, okay? *No matter what.* Not civvies, not other a–agents. Not even Number One."

Cleo didn't ask. Agent Hooper was out of time, she could tell by the hoarseness in her voice. Her body was shutting down and Cleo was about to be left in the truck with *four* dead MDS agents. Agent Hooper faced ahead, staring at something unseen past Cleo's shoulder.

"Agent Jennifer Hooper, stationed at MDS HQ," she slurred, "Green Tag CA, age twenty two years, three months and two days. Died a Green Tag...No major kills worth mentioning, nothing great about me...can't all be like you, Agent Darkrose, sir. I was born serving, loyal to MDS. Wish I could've died that way."

The other agent hadn't asked to be taken out with a bullet between her eyes. She wanted to be left to die...and Cleo wanted out. *Now.* The smell of the other agent's blood was making her tastebuds revolt, the scent coating her tongue completely like she had licked wet wounds.

She hadn't even called Agent Starr yet. It was time to leave, the truck was still enroute to its destination and they had murderers to take care of.

10

SO SPADEMAN WANTED TO FIGHT DIRTY, luring dumbass Green and Blue Tags away with his stories and promising money for information. Cleo didn't understand, never thought anyone would sell out MDS like that. It made her guts tight, disgusted at the other agent's treachery.

You were allowed to get fed up and think about leaving, even she was guilty of that, but doing it and selling intel was crossing the line. Treachery was the worst sin at MDS and it never went unpunished. It meant someone like Cleo Darkrose would get given the order to take you out.

She'd been part of the Fugitive Recovery Ops Team sometimes over the years, sent to hunt and Delete rogue agents but most of them were just pissed at Number One and being told what to do all the time, they wanted to be left alone when they split. They weren't trying to sell information to domestic terrorists. Agent Hooper was right, Cleo would have Deleted her if she wasn't already fucked.

Cleo jumped the gap between the container and driver's cab, sticking the landing without as much noise as she'd anticipated. The truck was still chugging. The driver hadn't even noticed the thump her boots made above his head and she was on her stomach instantly, grabbing the side of the cab on the passenger's side and sliding her body to the edge.

She leaned far enough over to see the side mirror and confirm the driver was the only one inside. *Heavy-set, white t-shirt, curly black hair, looking straight ahead.* His dumpy shadowy figure was only lit by the console in front of him while he ate something from a white wrapper and nodded his head to soft music.

Cleo pulled the throwing knife, razor-sharp blade glinting once in the moonlight before she put it between her teeth. She flicked her tongue along the back of the blade, tasting the metal as she slid just enough to hang over the side of the cab, before centre of gravity would kick in and send her completely over.

The window was open and disappeared all the way down into the door. *Perfect.* Cleo gripped under the window frame inside the cab and flipped over the side of the truck, ass-first, just fingertips and strong-ass core muscles to shoot herself backwards through the open window and into the cab, landing on the passenger's seat.

She snatched the knife handle from her mouth and hurled it over her shoulder before the driver could push her back out. The next sound was a dull squelch rolled in a whimper. Only half her blade was visible, the rest embedded in the side of the driver's throat when she swivelled to face him.

They made eye contact across the car seat and console then she smashed her boot into his face and ground his head up against the window, forcing a thin fracture to start snaking down the glass. She stomped his head twice, his jaw threatening to break under her sole.

She grabbed the CRONE from her belt and leapt for him, jamming it in the side of his neck beside the knife handle. She'd planned to miss arteries with her knife and it had worked out, now his eyes were darting from her face and to the front of the truck and back with the blade taut in his flesh. He still had one hand on the steering wheel like he was worried about crashing into something, unused to the nothingness of the desert.

His breathing was heavy and audible when his head went back, shiny-eyed when he looked sideways at her. They were close and she could smell his skin, her face inches from his while she held his other hand down to stop him extracting the knife. Her heart rate climbed when her eyes roved his expression, thoughts of Deleting him rushing behind her eyes, a flashing montage of all the fucked up things she could do to leave him a corpse and splattered on the upholstery. The thought of squeezing the trigger on the CRONE made her finger shiver.

"Why are you transporting dead MDS agents?" Her breathy tone was probably better suited to some kind of sexual suggestion, not an interrogation, and it threw him.

"They're a gift for the people up ahead," he stammered.

"A *gift*?"

She pushed back a little and watched his face change. His chins were sweaty under at least a dark four-day growth all over his face right up to his cheeks. He was low on the food chain, a peon SpadeMan was probably paying peanuts and hoping he wouldn't shit himself during the mission.

"They didn't warn me about an ambush."

Cleo shrugged.

"They gave me a lot of money to drive in here and ignore the signs," he glanced ahead even though there was no road to stray from, "They said when I got to the camp I just had to tell them some of the people in the back had chips in their fingers, we could split the money. They said money's important, it's why you people take down towers and blame the towelheads. You need piles of it."

Cleo shoved the end of the CRONE deeper in his skin and ran her right index finger up his neck through wiry black hairs. The skin on his arms was goosebumping when she glided it over his chin, brushed it over his lips and held it up in front of his eyes. He shuddered, staring at her finger before he looked to the windscreen again.

"People are killing us...for fingers?"

The driver snapped back into some kind of tough guy persona by the time she finished the question. Being so close to her chip made him refocus. He wanted his damn money and he wasn't afraid of some young female from the desert anymore, despite the blade hanging from his neck. He pursed his lips, defiant. He wanted to bite her finger right off. He wanted her money...and just by her touching him, he wanted to fuck her too, in some other circumstance.

They were close to the campsite now and details were clearer; *four people standing around the fire.* They were glancing over their shoulders at the truck and then facing the other way again, unperturbed. It made the driver put his foot down harder on the gas and Cleo went for his nearest hand, jerking his index finger from the wheel and twisting it backwards so bone split. He yelped and jumped away, squashing fat rolls against his door.

She wrenched the knife from his neck and he grit his teeth and made hissing sounds but he didn't scream. Sweat was beading on his temples as their eyes met.

"I want to get my money and go home and you need to get out of my way," he snarled.

He stepped on the accelerator again and sprang in her direction. The CRONE hit the floor somewhere and left her with just the knife in her hand. *Fuck.* She slashed it across his face awkwardly and shoved her knee up into his chest but his fingers were reaching her throat. He was tall enough to still have his foot on the accelerator as they struggled, the truck lurching each time he pushed down to get closer, spilling drops of his blood on her chest while they sped towards the campsite.

His head was up near hers and she had fuck all leverage when she slashed with the knife again, this time across his meaty shoulder. He threw his head back and screamed anyway, his monster howl ringing in her ears, telling her she should have just leaned in from the fucking roof earlier, fired the RavenEye and dealt with a face full of blowback.

The truck let out a high-pitched screech right after then metal grinded metal. Their truck clipped the stationary one and veered in another direction. Cleo and the driver were airborne in the near capsize. Yells erupted outside when she slammed her head on the window and landed. Women outside were scattering and screaming in twisted harmony.

Bodies hit the front of the truck and rebounded off. The driver's hands were tight and squeezing Cleo's throat as a woman got airborne and smashed the windscreen somehow, almost caving it in completely, then she was gone; on top of the roof screaming and rolling across the container at the back.

Everything shuddered. The truck jack-knifed on the flat sand and slid through the fire and over all the shit thrown on to keep it burning. Cleo elbowed the driver in the face, his orbital bone crunching while the cab groaned around them and he leaned in for a tighter grip to break her neck. Then the truck bowed and more screams were cut short as tyres steam-rolled people.

She reached one arm down and found the CRONE in the footwell. It came up clumsy but quick, a charge ready when her thumb flipped the switch on the side and she fired into the driver's bulky chest. *Checkmate.*

His foot slipped from the accelerator and they rolled to a slow stop, Cleo on her back looking up at the ceiling and the driver crushing her as he lay on top. Some of his blood speckled the roof above her like a kid's fingerpainting and he was heavy as fuck and leaking more blood before she shoved him to the side and let his body fall half in the footwells.

She could hear fire crackling outside when she reached over and killed the engine. The bonfire was almost as high as the driver's side window, thick heat penetrating the cab, stiflingly hot and just far enough away for flames not to be touching the door. They'd come through the fire and out the other side without igniting before she'd CRONEd the driver. Now the truck was curved in two, jack-knifed and sitting on the sand clinking.

She stayed low waiting for someone to open fire or order her to get out of the vehicle but nothing happened. Maybe they were all dead. She slid the blood-covered blade along the driver's shoulder to wipe it off then slipped it away kind of dirty and pocketed the CRONE. There were still no voices or orders heard when she drew the M9 for her exit.

The air held tangy sharpness, tasting like the junk cooking in the fire when she scanned the other truck outside. The other road-train was right up next to her door, sitting mostly dark and untouched, the way it had been when she was up on the dune earlier.

She slid onto the sand in one fast motion, minimizing the time her body was exposed to potential shots at vital organs, and hit the dirt to crab-walk the spaces between the sets of tyres. They were cover and momentary rest stops as she moved through the shadowing sand while it reflected swing-dancing flames from the other side.

Heat wafted under the truck like someone had slapped a hot towel over her face. Her temples were leaking sweat while she was stationary at the back end of the trailer watching the tents for movement from across the fire. *Nada.* Once blinked on, Adonai's Thermal said her position by heating fuel tanks wasn't a smart place to spend a lot of time unless she wanted to be part of her own personal barbecue.

She counted four bodies strewn around the fire, two female, two male, dead or severely injured enough not to yell for help let alone stand. She watched for movement but nothing changed among the contorted limbs and blood splashed on the sand.

The tents across the fire and beyond the bodies were spotted with orange sand and dust, apart from the dark one in the middle. It was taller than the others and she'd seen it earlier but her new location meant she could see that it stretched back several feet and had a flimsy six foot door at the front, flapping open and shut again when the breeze changed.

Some guy wearing a white tank shirt was moving around inside. The firelight was bright enough to show her his arms were sleeves of green artwork when he stopped just past the opening and leaned over a stool, desperately trying to load a large black rocket launcher. *Great.* Using the trucks for cover seemed like a *really* shitty idea now.

The other tents didn't throw up any heat sources, his group was down and now it was just the two of them set for a magical evening. She got low when he was concentrating on his weapon and ran around the fire then hit the ground on the side of the dark tent.

She stole another look at the carnage around the fire, still waiting for someone to jump up after her but those people were very dead, it was just another view of vague red mess and shiny things glistening in firelight. The guy in the tent was an arrogant bastard. He hadn't even come out to try and help his friends or call for backup or even run.

She could hear him pushing metal pieces together inside the tent, right near the entrance, separated from her by a thin piece of fabric she hoped didn't show him her silhouette. She was going to breach the front and if he was intelligent enough to operate an RPG, hopefully he'd know she was too close to fire on unless he wanted to blast his own ass to pieces too.

He was still bent over the stool, hands on the weapon and fumbling around in the amber light when she came in. He stopped moving when she cocked the M9 and straightened up to face her.

He was younger than she'd thought he'd be, probably her age and only slightly taller with a stubbled head like a bowling bowl and that damn RPG in his grip. Cleo aimed the M9 and skimmed him for any other weapons but his tank top clung to his body, didn't allow for concealed weapons and his pants didn't have pockets. He hadn't prepped, despite the rocket launcher and those handguns on the table at the back of the tent with the civilian radio equipment.

He wasn't getting to the guns and mags laid out beside them before she opened fire and he couldn't use the RPG so he put it down and raised his hands in the air, pale eyes reflecting orange fire outside.

"MDS?"

"MDS," she said, "*Truth for Life?*"

The guy looked thrown but he caught his expression and tried to look cool again. Yeah, they were SpadeMan's people and he didn't expect her to know anything about him. The fact he was mostly right

60

about that was something she was going to keep to herself.

"Some of you agents are all right," he said, "Some of you know your shit."

Cleo didn't lower her weapon but the guy dropped his hands anyway like he wasn't nervous with a gun on him. She could smell alarm in the air though, he hadn't anticipated her arrival in the tent so soon or for the truck to mow his friends down first...and for her to not give a shit enough to help them or call it in.

"We were supposed to meet a few MDS agents here tonight, they didn't show."

"They didn't show up because they're dead, in that truck back there," she said.

The guy shrugged and turned his back on her to touch the RPG gently and make sure it was stable on the stool. His hands were out waiting to catch it in case it rocked and fell but it found balance and stilled. When he turned back he was smiling.

"I haven't seen a lot of MDS agents in the flesh. You're one nice looking bitch, you know?" he nodded, "I thought you were all feminist, fat dyke man-haters. I'm Evan. What's your name, agent?"

"It doesn't matter," she said.

"Probably not, unless you want to give me some information about MDS, go on record as the source?"

"You want to tell me why you're trespassing and how you got this far inside? Why are those agents dead?"

"I guess security here isn't as good as you thought. We didn't know we were '*far inside*' and we don't need them dead agents anyway," he said, "Everyone knows what goes on around here with underground bases, weapons races and stuff. So, lady, am I being detained?"

"Probably."

"Well, good luck with that. I don't go anywhere with strange women."

"I doubt that's true." Cleo said.

Evan didn't look at her gun at all anymore like it didn't bother him but if he was planning to attack her, it wasn't his finest idea. She would deflect, control, *counter*. All legal and authorized. She was only letting him run his mouth because now she'd figured he needed to be interrogated, not Deleted. No one got through security outposts, let alone killed MDS agents. Everyone at HQ needed to know how they'd accomplished it.

The fire cracked loudly outside, probably jumping and spreading up on the truck and Evan looked over her head, wanted her to follow his gaze but she kept her eyes forward and the gun on him. He sighed and shot towards her suddenly, faster than she expected.

She twisted her body before impact, pulled one of his wrists down fast to bring him closer then slammed the gun up into his nose and threw a knee to his groin. It only took one to send him to the ground, then she was waiting with the gun on him again and feeling it beg for her to take the shot, both of them catching their breath, eyes locked into each other's and getting their shit together.

"Who murdered those agents?" She prodded while Evan squirmed with a hand on his balls and blood dripping from his nostrils.

"I wouldn't tell you, even if I knew. Unless I'm being detained, I don't have to tell you shit. Fuck you."

Uh, huh. Screw it. Cleo was going back to the car to radio it in, get some other patrol to pick his ass up. She knew their co-ordinates, she could request someone else take him to HQ for processing. There was no point hanging around, he wasn't getting anywhere on foot or even in one of the smashed trucks if she left.

"So what do they call you, your name?" One of Evan's hands was covering his nose to catch blood and the other was still resting over his crotch as he lay on the ground trying to get the words out. Groin strikes were funny things, "I'm going to report you."

"My name is Agent Cleo Darkrose and I don't care if you report me. Get on your radio, tell whoever sent you that your team is dead. Tell them deadly force is authorised this close to a classified installation."

"*Cleo Darkrose?*"

"Did I stutter?"

"You killed my friends." Evan said.

"You'll have to ask your driver about that."

Evan pulled a knife from nowhere and tried standing. Cleo flicked the safety off the M9 and both of them froze when a sound cut the air and a yellow spark erupted. Evan's knife catapulted behind him in the sand.

He looked confused. She was too before she remembered Agent Starr was backup outside somewhere and the tent flap was open. She let Evan think she was a magician for a second, observing the confusion slapped across his shaving-knicked face.

"What the fuck, girl?" He hissed.

The shot was a warning, from an M9 or some other small caliber gun. If Agent Starr wanted Evan dead, he would be lying on the sand bleeding out already. A snipe from the rifle would have shattered his head into a thousand pieces and covered her in a stew of skull fragments and blowback. Agent Starr was letting her handle it her way but he was close, nearer than she'd expected if he'd been able to make that shot in lowlight with a handgun.

"I told you to get on the radio and tell them everyone is dead," Cleo said, "If you try anything else, you will die."

Evan was looking at her over and over while he walked to the back of the tent. He picked up the intercom piece on the table and started talking, a few low words about people being dead and the *'lethal forced authorised'* signs they'd all passed on the way in but chosen to ignore. The rest was whispers she doubted the person on the other end would even hear clearly through the static.

She stepped across the threshold to go back outside and leave Evan to his pile of corpses and rocket launcher. Yeah, she was turning her back to a suspect but he was still speaking his transmission and she'd hear him go for the weapons on the table if he made the move. He couldn't shove a magazine up into a gun without giving her a warning.

All superiors at HQ would want to know how a five person team managed to set up a tent city and bring in two giant trucks right under their noses, she was sure of that. It was *impossible* for that to happen, a breach of that size had never happened as far as she knew. They had aircraft flying over every day, constant patrols and drones running the perimeters...It didn't make sense and it was the only reason Evan was still breathing, but if he wanted to push his luck, that privilege would be revoked.

She watched a strip of flames run the length of the truck she'd been inside, licking from the front tyre and stretching back to the end. Acrid rubber peppered the air while Evan put the intercom piece on the table. He tried to be quiet when he reached for the RPG but the metal parts scraped on the stool.

Cleo didn't turn. Even with the few steps she had taken outside, they were still too close to each other for him to be stupid enough to fire the thing and risk serious injury. But she felt him stalk her anyway, struggling with the launcher as her eyes rested on the trucks across the bonfire and then the bodies in the foreground.

Evan pushed the tent flap out of the way behind her. She kept her M9 dangling in her left hand but she could hear him mess around with the launcher. He couldn't miss her at that range, not with a weapon of that size and he was going to fire on her despite the danger to himself. She guessed he really didn't want to be interrogated later.

He mumbled something about all-seeing eyes and '*bullshit secret societies*' while he hauled the launcher up onto his shoulder, cursing under his breath with the weight. Then a familiar crack split the air and echoed back from all sides. Cleo looked over her shoulder and saw a lot of red. Evan was lying shrieking under his giant RPG.

His left arm was missing from the bicep down. There weren't even pieces of flesh strewn across the area, just huge splashes of red on the sand. He was screaming, kicking his legs and shoving the RPG away, smart enough to fly into action and start undoing his belt for a tourniquet before shock set in. Cleo watched him for a few moments then she started walking back to the dunes.

11

CLEO HEADED FOR THE SUV IN SILENCE. Agent Starr was matching her pace without trying, carrying his modded sniper rifle with ease and probably glad he had it with him instead of the weapons they'd made him use overseas. He didn't say anything to her, he just walked with a silent purpose similar to hers, never once stumbling on the uneven and slipping sand.

She didn't thank him for shooting Evan. If she opened her mouth, questions were going to fall out instead. She hadn't turned around to neutralise Evan, she'd given Agent Starr the chance to Delete him when he came out of the tent and made it clear he wasn't worth keeping around. It was a gesture of goodwill, a 'welcome home' gift. It wasn't every day you got to Delete some civilian asshole and he'd refused it, he'd actually fucking *refused* it. They had authorization too, it was nice and legal to take the bastard's head off but he'd settled for half an arm.

"You still trust me with your life," he said suddenly.

"Always." There was something too pregnant in their pause and she added, "You're a Red Tag."

The POD was waiting when they climbed back in the car, staring at them like it should have had arms crossed asking who the fuck they thought they were going on their own adventure and leaving it behind. Yeah, they had to keep to the times loaded on it or they were screwed. Seeing it reminded her they had to get back on the road, let some other patrol sort through Evan's scattered friends because they had some conspiracy theorist wannabe-bomber to snuff.

Cleo opened the driver's door and grabbed the radio receiver to notify Perimeter Patrol. Agent Starr opened the door to the backseat and slid his weapon and bipod in and then went to the passenger's seat across from her. He raised a leg to step up and get in but stopped short. Something big exploded.

The noise was impossible to pinpoint–*ringing from every direction*–threatening to rupture eardrums and maim and kill. Cleo hit the sand, half stunned by the sound. She pushed backwards, up against the car for cover, and reached down for her M9. She only got the chance to pull it halfway.

Another sound burst overhead, high pitched and screaming. Engines. An aircraft losing altitude at dangerous speed. Icy wind rippled along her shoulders, violently tousled her hair. Her uniform clung to her skin like it was wet. Something else exploded over the sand dunes a moment later. Fire blasted into the air.

Confusion melted to relief. The attack was happening over the sand dunes, at the tents. *You're okay. This is home. Limbs are still attached, vision intact.* She could see a glow from over the dunes when she pushed herself up and dusted the sand off. The commotion was aircraft sent from HQ, arriving after all the hard parts were over, probably to destroy the evidence. Looked like they weren't interested in investigating or interrogating.

Her door was open enough to see through the car to Agent Starr's side but her look over to him for his thoughts was fruitless, he wasn't looking back. He was crouched outside and getting up slowly, hands empty and his eyes fixed on the upholstery of the open door in front of him. He hadn't looked up to figure out what the sound was or even drawn his weapon. He swallowed hard when he finally met her gaze.

Cleo pulled herself up into the car and didn't say anything. She knew that look. She'd just never seen it on an MDS Red Tag before. She kept her eyes down while he shuffled into the passenger's seat beside her and shut his door.

Cleo's hand came down on the gears and her boot moved to the accelerator. She couldn't remember either of them deciding to move the car but they were speeding alongside the dunes to where they were less steep so she could drive the car up and through a gap between them to get a better view of the campsite.

Everything was in flames when they stopped on the other side, far enough away to observe safely. The camp had disappeared into a spluttering ball of orange and yellow fire, striking vibrancy against the night and weaving in and out of climbing black smoke while it merged with the sky, billowing like a fucking space launch. The air was thick with sulphur, cordite, something like a combination of the two that Cleo didn't have a name for.

The truck she'd been in was a blackened frame against angry fire. She only caught a glimpse before lighting flashed overhead, zapping across the sky and changing night to day for a blinding instant. No, *not lightning*, green spitting electrical charges splintering the atmosphere. The flash only lasted a second but it was bright enough to shock her eyes and leave images of zigzagged beams across her vision when she blinked. Then the sky was murky silence.

Cleo looked at Agent Starr, he looked back this time. Another explosion blasted around them, bigger than the others. Reflex slammed her boot on the brake even though they were stationary. It sounded like a hellish storm; lightning first then rolling thunder and unescapable devastation. Whatever was left of the campsite erupted and flew in all directions, chunks of debris shooting into the air and fragments spreading for miles.

Body parts and tent poles were hauled up and obliterated, dusty remnants gusting across the windscreen. Others plunged after long arcs like flares through the sky. Flashing reflections lit her face while her ribcage vibrated, the drumming inside almost strong enough to disrupt her heartbeat. She recognised the deep heavy sensation, MDS aircraft were hovering somewhere above them using anti-gravity propulsion systems, pulsing and sending waves of pressure through the air as they annihilated their targets.

It was only the second time she'd ever seen them destroy a target right in front of her, probably something she wouldn't get used to. They called the ones with radar-reflecting surfaces *Ships*. Matter became almost nothing when they fired and all she knew was they caused mini nuclear explosions without the radius of deadly fallout, something people on The Outside still thought was impossible. The fact the aircraft were coated with mirrored surfaces so they couldn't even be seen was a cross between ingenious and disturbing.

She reached for the radio to identify their car because friendly fire was a bitch and she didn't want to end up charred carbon if they tried to drive away and drew the wrong type of attention. She tapped the screen on the GPS fast and brought up their exact co-ordinates to call them in then she was repeating the location twice, resisting the urge to rush her words while she used the phonetic alphabet in feigned calm. She began reversing the car slowly while the operator on the other end did his work.

Agent Starr's eyes were down when she glanced over, he was staring at his lap, skin pale as stripped bone and reflecting the blasts like a strobe light.

"*Agent Starr.*" Cleo said. Not a question.

She repeated the co-ordinates to the operator one more time and hung her head out the window trying to get a look at the practically invisible MDS aircrafts. The vibration in her chest was subsiding then absent in seconds, leaving her watching scattered fires and shadowed objects on the sand all over their field of view.

Agent Starr was facing his window, turned away from her and getting his shit together. Call it a hunch, but she was reasonably sure the destruction in front of them was just the icing on top of the shocking things he'd seen lately. She didn't know what it meant for her success record.

12

ENTERING OTHER STATES HAD BEEN EASY. Border Patrol saw the uniforms, scanned the licence plate and asked no questions like good little peons. Now she and Agent Starr were speeding down another road with nothing for miles ahead, just sporadically passing cars coming the other way and old gas stations at long intervals.

Driving the state lines was standard, most assignments started about eight hours out from HQ where dense civilisation began. Having Agent Starr next to her this time tinged the journey with *Déjà vu*. They had swapped seats a few hours back and he was sitting on driving duty without complaint. Cleo rode shotgun, filling him in on what she'd found inside the shipping container, talking to the side of his head.

The road splayed in an endless grey tar line parting shrubs and sand, stretching back into the distance, all nonchalant and watching them shoot by in a black blur. The sun wavered the horizon behind persimmon hills under wisps of cloud in a robin egg sky. The whole backdrop was postcard-worthy or fucking eye-watering, depending on how jaded you were. Guess which one she was. Half a day whirlwinded past in a haze of desert and rock and her primary concern was avoiding taking her dark sunglasses off. She had no idea how Agent Starr was coping without his pair.

Arid air breathed through from her window and flicked her hair before gushing out again as they picked up speed. It was good to be a passenger and it hadn't happened for a long time. She didn't trust anyone else to take the wheel except another Red Tag and Agent Starr knew her well enough to feel comfortable in her silences.

He was busy proving he wasn't dead weight too, doing the pointless shit agents were supposed to but agents of their rank usually didn't bother with. She'd watched him keep track of signals they picked up over the radio as they passed various pockets of civilisation, recording them and storing the locations on the GPS system, pressing buttons and pinpointing the information for future analysis in case Number One required it.

The only times he'd spoken were to throw in a random *"oh yeah?"* and *"right"* while she described the carnage in the truck. She'd thought he was decidedly aloof until he'd asked if they needed a bathroom stop as they approached one of the sparse garages. The considerate request was probably only for her benefit. She knew he could hold it for longer than any normal human being she'd ever met. Now it looked like his skills were bordering on supernatural. Maybe running around the deserts in the Middle East had trained him better than anything at HQ could.

She'd heard the military made piss tubes out there in the deserts, long repurposed tubing shoved into the ground so they could take a leak and not ruin their camp. Whatever the reason, he was able to hold it and she was envious. When they had finally stopped to use a bathroom and stretch their legs, he'd mostly jogged a few laps around the car while he waited for her, then they were back on.

The POD beeped the notification in the afternoon when they were a state and a half from HQ. New information downloaded and updated when Cleo flipped it open and accepted the files. The POD scrolled disclaimers and beamed up a hologram in front of her face; 3D and taking over her side of the car, showing instructions in large plain white text over a black and grey backdrop, floating midair.

She could see through the image to the windscreen and beyond to random rocks beginning to appear either side of the road as they drove but the plainness of the white font in her face demanded attention. The next objective was to board an MDS boat in a place called *San*

Freedom, some fishing dock a few hours drive south of their current location.

The words faded and the next projection showed a detailed topographic map, bird's-eye view. It flipped slowly and settled, coming down level to her viewpoint then the view zoomed in to a long highway lined with different sized rocks, shades of greys and coffee-brown and orange stacked up on each other almost like the way sand dunes created solid waves around HQ. It was the road they were traveling on, the vision they would have an hour into the future.

She saw Agent Starr look over and frown before he turned back to the road. Yeah, there was a shorter route to San Freedom than the one the POD was advising. If the information had come sooner, they probably would have voted to ignore it and go another way instead.

Now they were heading south through Baha, thanks to the POD, apparently spending the night somewhere, then going hard east to San Freedom the next day to catch a ride across an inlet of water they could have saved a few hours and *driven* around. She didn't question it out loud. If they were given the instruction, then there was a reason she was too stupid to understand right now and she would do it Number One's way...but reading further warned that if they weren't standing on the boardwalk the next day at 16:00 with their shit in-hand, they could kiss SpadeMan's protest rally and seminar goodbye.

He was going to speak at a hotel in a city called Menas on the other side of the bay. With a four hour approximated journey through the water, it was going to be tight, ludicrously tighter if she made them turn around and go back the other way. Agent Starr was still looking at the road, leaving it up to her to make the final call.

The POD beamed up a wooded area next, some offshoot from the road they were driving. Rocks and boulders either side had become trees reminiscent of the types that grew tall in national parks and stretched to the sky-totally out of the ordinary for their climate-but she knew there were government projects going back decades where they'd tried to change the landscape. There were even private organisations trying their hand at man-made oasis landscapes for business or religious retreats. She'd seen them before, but not this one.

A dirt track led from the road into the scrub, then the view changed again and shot towards a dark motel in the middle of it all while white font explained that it was their only scheduled rest stop before San Freedom. Agent Starr needed it. He was a good agent and putting discomfort aside for the sake of making good time, keeping the ETAs accurate and attainable but he couldn't do it forever.

He would have spent the last day in the Middle East getting his belongings together, being debriefed then jumping on a plane back over to their country. *Then* he would have caught a private plane to MDS HQ to get extensively interviewed by Number One before being prodded in the Infirmary. It was probably after all that he'd rigged an elevator and asked to be part of her assignment. Yeah, the guy was a machine but he needed rest or he was going to be completely useless to her when they got to Menas.

She was already questioning his merit after the way he'd acted the night before. It could have got them killed in another situation. He hadn't mentioned his freak out at the campsite, probably wanted her to assume it was error caused by fatigue but she was getting to think he hadn't frozen when the Ships went over just because he was drowsy. She remembered the look she'd seen on his face. You couldn't fake that shit.

They had no time for the excuse though, whatever the real story was. If he was a liability, his ass was going home. It had to be that way. Her one hundred percent success record couldn't be jeopardised; religious-like mantra that enabled her to survive and funnelled her focus from anything else, including hanging out trying to understand another agent's mental state.

Yeah, he had the night in the motel to sleep it off before she made the final call on whether he was staying and if he fought her about stopping for the night, things weren't going to end well for him.

"There's a motel in some woods between here and San Freedom," she said, taking out the Adonai contact lenses to put them away, "If we reach it before twenty three hundred we can rest there til zero eight."

Agent Starr nodded and Cleo let her stare get heavy, daring him to look back again but he resisted. He knew what she was looking for, didn't want her to see just how tired he was up close in the daylight and without sunglasses. He was on his 3rd wind and there was no sense in swapping seats now so he had nothing to worry about. She would let him drive while she took a break before she had to take first watch at the motel.

The civilians evaporated behind her eyelids while she stirred later. They had probably been located by now and she couldn't catch the details before they dispersed but the dream had been about Number One hiding every piece of *slightly-more-advanced-than-The Outside* technology from view; the standard smarter Smartphones that were able to be crushed and crammed into a pocket and the variations of Adonai contact lenses some agents wore permanently. She almost cracked a smile imagining what Number One would think of Tanya Pierce's mouth.

It was dark out when she sat up, snatching the sunglasses from her face and grabbing her thigh and arm. The RavenEye was in its place, the throwing knife still secure. Her seatbelt was strapped across her chest where she had snapped it closed earlier and her watch confirmed she was missing two fucking hours.

Agent Starr glanced across at her, face lit up with the console and bathed in green tinge like a space alien. He looked like shit now, fatigue blanketing his features while he watched her get her bearings. The important thing was his boot was still down on the accelerator and they were probably making good time.

The rocks on either side of the road were gone and giant dark blurs were shooting past the car in their place. Powerful headlights from their car lit up the narrow coffee dirt and gravel path ahead and warned there was no way they were getting through the surrounding trees if they had to change direction. The woodland was far too dense, only one way forward and one way back. If someone was coming the other way, one of the vehicles would have to pull over to let the other pass.

An eerie soundtrack crackled from the radio to match the scenery, picking up faint chatter and quiet frequencies from invisible campers on civilian walkie-talkies, coming in spurts and whispers from the darkness. There were people out there but they couldn't be seen and it left her unexpectedly uneasy as they passed through and left them behind.

"I was just about to wake you, we hit the woods five minutes back." Agent Starr said.

She felt an impending something, like something was wrong, but there was no sense in raising an alarm just because she'd woken up unnerved by the change of scenery outside the car. It took a few seconds of blinking and looking around to figure out that it wasn't just the dark trees that had her spooked. She settled for resting her hand over the thigh rig, ready to draw the RavenEye if she had to. *Because her guts were a jar of butterflies having an orgy.* She scanned across the front of the car, eyes going from one side of the road to the other.

"Are you all right?" Agent Starr asked. He looked at her then back to the road.

"Why do you ask?"

"You feel something," he said," Got it written all over you."

A hot breath of anger flared under her skin as his sentence ended. She didn't need to be analysed in his nanosecond judgement, but he was good. Yeah, there was a feeling in the air, she just didn't think she'd done anything to make it noticeable. How close had he been watching her?

"I don't see anything up ahead...but I know your intuition is better than my sight," he said, "And I trust it. Tell me what to do."

He glanced at her again and back to the road. The car was still traveling at the same pace, waiting on her order.

"Keep driving," she said

"Keep driving?"

"Keep driving."

She looked over into the backseat, to the back window and then down to hers and Agent Starr's rucks full of ammo and other supplies in the footwells behind her. Everything was in reach if they had to stop the car or they were driving into an ambush. It was all sitting there waiting on the floor like second class citizens while Agent Starr's rifle bag lay across the backseat in comfort. Damn thing. If she'd thought of it earlier, she would have moved it and dozed off there instead.

She was turning back to the front when she caught a quick black blur that sprang up then down again behind the backseat. It wasn't a trick of light or shadows from passing trees. Maybe they'd hit something that flew up as the back tyres ran over it? A glance to Agent Starr told Cleo he hadn't seen a thing and her theory perished.

She faced the back again, concentrating on the air and trying to tap that sense deeper than sound, difficult over the hum of the engine...but it wouldn't be in a few seconds. Her heartbeat slowed enough to match her breathing, calm and rhythmic and one. Focus shifted and concentrated. Agent Starr and the car disappeared into black and she felt something right away, someone else's energy.

There was somebody in the back of the car.

Her arm was a snake stalking prey, sliding along her left leg until her fingers reached the retention button on her thigh rig. She pressed it slowly and released the RavenEye. Agent Starr's face changed, hearing trained to the sound. He'd owned one too and the small click made something in him shift and gear up.

He looked at her with just his eyes, asking her what was going on without using words or turning his face from the road. Cleo strained her eyes in the direction of the backseat and trunk and he looked at her properly then, turning his head and dipping one dark eyebrow like she was crazy. Cleo's eyes told him to shut the fuck up and do what he was told.

She watched the car eat up the road again in front and just breathed. The trees whooshed past both sides, black and green smeared into a mash of dark colours like a moving abstract painting. Agent Starr was the one driving, another glance to him told him he had both their lives in his hands. It was his cue.

Twenty five seconds and Agent Starr slammed on the breaks. *Hard.* The car *screamed* like it was in pain. Gravel disintegrated under the tyres, dust flew up all around the windows. They fishtailed wildly, threatening to tip and roll despite all the reinforced axels, shuddering from everywhere with the strain. Cleo pushed back in her seat and watched trees hurtle towards them before Agent Starr wrenched the wheel back the other way. The car teetered and threatened to roll again...then everything stopped.

Cleo ignored the seatbelt trying to squeeze her insides out of her mouth, unclipped it and spun quickly in her seat, her arm around the side near the window to use the rest of it as cover. Her RavenEye was pointed to the back of the car. Agent Starr armed his M9 beside her.

Dust and smoke floated around in their peripheral vision, ghostly blue and grey mist outside in the moonlight. The smell of burnt rubber took over the air.

"*Identify yourself,*" Agent Starr commanded the back of the car.

Cleo waited for a response, eyes focussed on the top of the backseat, ready to take out the threat and wary of a gun barrel coming over and shooting them in the face before she could get off a shot.

"This is a Majestic Defence Syndicate vehicle, you have committed a felony by being aboard without prior permission. Identify yourself immediately. We have authorization to shoot to kill. We will give you a count of five to surrender then we will open fire," he said.

Cleo staged the trigger on the RavenEye. Agent Starr wasn't playing around, any countdown he gave was going to be more of a head's up for her to get in the zone to open fire, make sure her Firing Glove was tight to counter the shattering recoil of her gun. They were about to destroy the backseat and anyone behind it in a Canadian-accented *five, four, three, two...*

Instead, two sets of shaking hands appeared. When their heads came up one waved. Agent Starr started laughing.

"Oh...shit."

13

CLEO WAS PISSED. No, she was more than pissed. If Julia or Tanya moved from the backseat she was going to find it hard not to kill them herself. She paced fast and hard in front of the car like she could crack the earth with her boots, one side to the other, blocking the burning headlights and then passing them only to repeat the motion over and over.

She knew Agent Starr was standing further up between the car and the treeline watching in silence, blinking each time she moved away from the headlights and they momentarily blinded him. She didn't care. She wanted to kick the shit out of him too. It wasn't funny. The civilians had done something so incredibly stupid...and he'd *laughed*. She stopped pacing when he walked over to her and stared him dead in the eyes.

"This is not amusing, this is disgusting," she said, anger cutting her words.

"Excuse my error, for not taking this seriously, sir," he said, "You are my superior on this assignment and what I did was wrong."

"We have to go back to HQ, we have to take them back to Number One."

"The orders don't allow time for that, it's in the POD, sir. I assumed it's why we didn't double-back earlier and go around the water instead of driving down through to San Freedom. We don't have the time."

"You think it's safer for them *or* us if we let them stay?" She hissed.

"Not safer, no, but if you and I fail this..."

Fuck. He was right. There was no way they could go all the way back home and still reach the hotel in Menas at the right time to catch SpadeMan's seminar. She would lose the target and her hundred percent success rate would be worth shit.

If she called HQ for a pick up, they would still have to wait for a transport vehicle or helicopter...or leave the civilian cargo in the woods unguarded. It couldn't happen, Julia and Tanya had been important enough to break decades of protocol so it was obvious Number One needed them protected at all times. It wasn't the type of thing a Red Tag with her reputation could fail.

The only other choice was to leave Agent Starr with them at that nearby motel while she went on to San Freedom and then Menas alone. He wouldn't want that, and it was probably going to result in her sneaking off close to dawn with him still asleep and assuming they were all going to leave together in the morning.

Cleo bit her bottom lip until it hurt. There was a saying for situations like this, something about a creek without a paddle. She couldn't remember the specifics and Agent Starr was standing in front of her like a hyper dog waiting on her next instruction.

"They have to come with us," she said, "And since this is so humorous to you, Agent Starr, they will be your responsibility."

Because fuck babysitting.

"Yes, sir, I understand," he said, clear green eyes suddenly dark with seriousness, "Will you be informing Number One of the...situation?"

"No and no one else either, including the agents when we board the boat in San Freedom. They will believe it's part of the assignment, we'll tell them it's all to plan." *Not that you're going to be there to give your side of the story.*

Agent Starr liked her answer, she could tell from the stupid look on his face. Neither of them wanted other agents to know they'd managed to miss two stowaway civilians in their vehicle and they didn't want to fail Number One. You didn't confess to the higher-ups that you were fucked unless you actually were and technically they weren't *yet.*

"Another search for them at HQ will take a long time before they suspect they're with us. We should be in Menas by then. Agents on the MDS boat should know the location of a safehouse in the city, we could make a detour for it if we arrive on time," he said, "I'll, uh, let them know they won't be staying with us long, advise them to co-operate as much as they can."

Oh. He wanted to tell the civilians the details alone and field all their stupid questions without her in earshot. She watched his back while spotlighted and standing alone in the headlights as he went to one of the back windows in the car to relay the details to Julia and Tanya. He'd thought she needed a moment or twenty, otherwise people were going to get hurt...and he was mostly right, again.

She couldn't hear what he was saying but she got the bass in his voice, all the low buzzing murmurs until he stepped back and laughed. It actually seemed genuine, maybe his part of a Good Cop/Bad Cop routine he thought would help. She guessed she knew which role she'd been cast.

She walked to the driver's side feeling eyes trail her from the backseat and yanked the door open to get in without looking back at Julia and Tanya. Agent Starr climbed in to ride shotgun without questioning the arrangement. Good for him. He didn't need to be told he'd blown it by laughing at the situation, she wasn't letting him drive anymore.

Unease made everyone else still when she shut her door and belted up. Tanya and Julia were staring from the backseat, waiting for her next move until the tension grew too much for them and Julia cleared her throat in some polite lady-like manner that sounded fake as shit.

"Agent Darkrose, I'm sorry. *We're* sorry," Cleo watched her blankly in the rear view mirror, "It was too quiet at your HQ and I felt helpless. I just thought that maybe you didn't have to hurt anyone, I could talk with Alan instead and we could all just reach an agreement. You know, maybe both sides have a point."

Cleo's eyes moved over Julia's face and down. She was wearing a jacket now, big and black and bulky over her clothes. It was MDS-issue. The nameplate on the side of the chest said *"Starr"* in white capitals. Cleo made eye contact with Julia in the mirror.

"You have risked your lives on an irresponsible whim," she said, "Both sides are *not* correct. Alan James Pierce has caused civilian unrest, inciting others to perpetrate acts of terrorism on government facilities in a so-called *'war'* he has created in his paranoid mind."

"That's my dad." Tanya said.

"That's my target."

The next time Cleo checked the dash clock it had been half an hour since they had discovered the civilians stowing away. She was thinking about HQ. She thought about Number One and the aircraft and all the grains of sand in the vast orange desert shifting with the hot wind. She went over drills and cadence in her head and tried to plan a workout routine for when she got home–*anything*–to stop involuntary focus on the bad jokes, singing and general civilian bullshit coming in high-pitched frequencies from the backseat.

Tanya would not shut the hole in her face. It just kept coming. Agent Starr had spent the better part of the travel time sideways on his seat, seatbelt almost choking him out, leaning through to the back to talk to the civilians. He was entertaining them too, giving them his best PG-rated stories about funny things he'd seen on assignments and the places he'd been.

Half of her wished he would shut his fucking mouth and stop encouraging them. The other half was morbidly curious about his ability to fit in so effortlessly. He talked about streaming Hollywood films on some video site on the internet and plots to episodes of shows from television networks on The Outside, all without stumbling once.

He knew what he was talking about with their celebrities and music, who was dating who and who sung a particular song. She assumed it was because he'd spent so much time with military personnel in the Middle East, she didn't know where else he would have got the information. MDS HQ rarely allowed music or films from The Outside.

81

All the music at MDS parties or functions was beats and sounds put together with no lyrics. Films from The Outside were a rarity, only shown if they had relevant content or pertained to an assignment somehow.

She listened to him for sarcasm, or feigned interest. Nada. He was actually enjoying the conversation. Julia was leaning forward towards him, chest straining against her seatbelt like he was a flesh covered magnet. Glimpses to the rear view showed Cleo the woman's eyes were lit up and shiny in the dark, enamoured with him. His conversation wasn't that stimulating, really wasn't.

Civilian women liked Agent Starr, something she'd duly noted some time back while on assignments together. He had *"it,"* whatever *it* was. Julia kept reaching out to touch him too, a hand on his arm mid-conversation. She must have liked "it" because she'd coughed up more information about herself than what Cleo had been able to extract when she brought them in the first night.

It was 21:20 when she pulled up on off-white powdered and crushed gravel beside the road and turned the car off. Tanya needed a bathroom break and she couldn't hold it. Clinks echoed as the car settled and everyone exited the vehicle to Tanya asking if there was another jacket she could borrow. Her stupid pink tank top was suddenly insufficient after seeing her mother get to wear an official MDS jacket. Cleo let her have hers from the back of the car, mostly because she knew Number One would want the civilians healthy and not returned to HQ with Pneumonia or some shit.

Tanya and Julia walked hand in hand off the dirt path into the trees across from the driver's side, stepping over shrubs and sticks awkwardly and giggling about it. Tanya put her hand backwards and grabbed Agent Starr's, pulling him into the scrub with them. He looked over his shoulder at Cleo. *Yeah, no, thanks.* She leaned against the driver's door instead and watched them cross the treeline, joined together like a trio of circus monkeys.

The sky provided enough light to see without a torch and she had a clear view to the stars. Everything was vibrant without buildings and pollution and the woods were good...but there was nothing like the night sky over HQ. It was crisp and clear and surreal. Walking over the sand was like strolling through another planet's landscape. Sometimes she'd look up and wonder how many satellites were peering back at her and all the data being recorded from all over the world. Then she would remember her next assignment and stop the pointless bullshit.

She could hear parts of the conversation between Agent Starr and the others as they disappeared. Nothing interesting, something about an action film Tanya had seen the week before and complaints about the MDS jacket doing nothing for her figure until they were far enough out that Cleo didn't bother straining to catch what they were saying.

She'd told Agent Starr to take fifteen. She could have allowed thirty but she was catering for the civilians to slow them down at another point in their journey, and they would. It would be another bathroom break or that they were hungry and didn't want the supplies in the back of the car because MREs were shit. If she was honest, she couldn't fault them on that.

She recalled reluctant chitchat with agents in different agencies when they were security for their respective superiors at global meetings. They had told her transporting civilians was the worst gig. She never thought she'd ever have the displeasure. Technically she *had* body-guarded civilians in the past; high profile ones like diplomats and presidents but she'd never had to babysit a soccer mom and her brat before. They weren't going to be her problem for much longer though. She hoped Agent Starr could just get them home after she left the motel and before Number One burst too many blood vessels.

14

CLEO WAS STILL ALONE AFTER THE NINE MINUTE MARK. There was no more scratching of branches shifting above her or scurrying of the odd animal. The woods were waiting in some kind of anticipation that she could feel on her shoulders. Half of fifteen minutes was less than nine. Agent Starr and the others should have been on their way back, she should have been able to hear them and their bullshit discussions.

She should have gone with them. If Agent Starr couldn't get them back to the car on time what made her think he'd be able to defend them against anything out in the woods? *Dammit.* The civilians knew they weren't safe, they'd been packing their shit to vacate their house even before she'd got them out. People wanted them dead and she shouldn't have left them, even if they were hours away from where they were last threatened.

Cleo's boots squelched dirt as she stepped into the woods. The environment changed instantly like she'd walked through a doorway, dense shrubs and vegetation crunching under her boots accompanied by an eerie drop in temperature. All she could think about was wringing Agent Starr's damn neck atop his freakishly tall body so she ignored the change to stomp weeds and head straight.

She didn't see any traces of her partner or the civilians, no tell-tale snags of clothing on a branch or footprints on the ground, lighting was too bad for that anyway now. It was like the civilians had been swallowed whole and everything else was watching her from a dark corner to see if she'd get scared and back out.

Her only concern was getting lost. If she did, then they were fucked. She couldn't think of anything worse than having to call Agent Starr's phone for directions back to the car knowing every call was recorded and saved back at HQ for routine audits. It meant there would be witnesses to their clusterfuck of an assignment, nevermind the dent in the ego.

Moonlight didn't want to follow when she trudged further into the dull green foliage vortex. Adonai was sitting neatly in the storage box back in the car and her torch would have been handy but it was probably lying on the backseat from when Tanya had asked to borrow it to make stupid faces in its beam. Visuals were down to how fast her eyes could adjust to get a read on which way to go.

She looked around logs and parts of fallen trees, straining her eyes for anything significant. Agent Starr was putting them in overtime. She wanted to find him fast but she didn't yell because she wouldn't have been able to stop herself using an expletive instead of his name.

Tanya was sitting in dark bushes to the right, like a garden ornament, as she cleared another group of trees. Large leaves surrounded the out of place teenager, draped over her shoulders like a dark green cape when she looked up at Cleo. For a moment the two of them were stopped still, eyes meeting across the small clearing. Great. Agent Starr had left her alone in the middle of fucking nowhere.

Cleo drew the M9. She hoped Tanya wasn't injured. Number One needed her returned in one piece. She glanced around the scene, over Tanya and either side to check if it was some sort of trap. Tanya watched her movements without an expression. She was just *there*, glaring back at Cleo from the ground. Her bare legs were crossed long white sticks against the dark, the rest of her was hunched up inside the MDS jacket, cold and probably regretting that cheap-ass hoochie mini skirt. Cleo walked over to her and put the gun away.

"Where's Agent Starr?"

"He's with my mom," Tanya said, "They wanted to talk."

Cleo frowned before she could catch it and Tanya shrugged her response. What the hell did he and Julia have to talk about? An immediate consideration injected itself into her head and caught her off-guard; *it was possible they were they doing more than talking.* He'd been in the Middle East for a long time...his and Julia's conversations in the car had come too easy and she'd been fucking touching him at every chance she got. Maybe they were somewhere taking advantage of the chemistry.

Number One wouldn't be impressed he'd been doing the dirty with someone he didn't have permission to date, worse if it was a civilian *and* on an assignment, with witnesses. He'd left half Number One's collateral alone in the woods while he was off doing God knew what with a civilian woman. He was screwed, more ways than one.

Fury pulsed while she looked at the other feeble civilian sitting in the dirt. She struggled for something to say, assure Tanya it was all part of the plan and this shit happened all the time, respected MDS agents just left civilians they were in charge of alone in the fucking woods in the middle of the night, to hell with their partners or assignments.

Julia and Agent Starr were heading back like magic as the thought ended. Julia's voice ringing on cue like they'd read her mind and chosen to appear before she could decide to have Agent Starr written up. Cleo watched the trees and Tanya got to her feet and mimicked her, staring in the direction of the voices with the same hand on her hip. Cleo put her arm down.

Agent Starr emerged from the trees first, pushing moonlit bushes aside to get through. The other hand was holding Julia's, helping her to keep her balance as she stepped over shrubs behind him. She was still wearing his MDS jacket, smiling at him when he turned to make sure she was okay.

The look between them forced a scowl from Cleo. What Agent Starr did in his personal life was his own business, had been for a while, but if it endangered the success of the assignment he had to go. *If she couldn't trust him, he had to go.* Whatever sexual activity he'd had with

Julia in the short period of time away from Tanya couldn't have been worth risking the assignment for. Surely.

Both of them slowed their steps when they saw the look on Cleo's face; two teens sneaking home after curfew. Agent Starr glanced over the scene, to Tanya and back to Cleo and swallowed.

"You left her here, alone," Cleo said, "Those were not your orders, agent. Do you want to be written up and sent back to HQ?"

"No, sir," he let go of Julia's hand, "You have my word it will not happen again, it was a stupid decision."

"Yeah, you keep making those." Cleo grunted.

She turned and walked into the brush, taking point fast so she didn't have to speak to anyone. She had the M9 out again as they walked back toward the car but it was unarmed, mostly only drawn because she was leading the group and it made sense. She would have loved to be holding the RavenEye instead but rules were rules and she'd already broken them by drawing in the car. Someone had to keep their mind on the job.

She could hear the others stumble on twigs and rocks as she forced them to catch up behind her. Tanya whined her teeth were starting to chatter and it was going to attract silverback gorillas. She was still wearing Cleo's jacket so that was bullshit, that jacket was a sauna when it was zipped up, and gorillas? Cleo didn't even know where to start. The brat was just being annoying. Even the other two hadn't bothered to reply.

Cleo trod over the last row of bushes bordering the treeline and stopped, one boot on the gravel, the other still in the woods. The air was weighty and the scene was changed to a *'Spot the Difference'* picture. She scanned the treeline across the road and either side of where she stood. The SUV was a few feet in front of them, in the same position they'd left it and nothing seemed out of the ordinary. Logic fought instinct in her head while the others caught up, giggling the end of a conversation.

She turned to face them, searching the silhouettes for Agent Starr's.

He was holding Julia's hand again. Cleo didn't want to analyse the way their fingers were positioned or how tight the grip was, whose hand was on top. Agent Starr read her face in the starlight and dropped Julia's hand like it was a grenade.

"Everyone get low, we're going to head to the car but we need to wait for Agent Darkrose to clear it," he said, looking from Tanya to Julia and ushering them back to the trees for cover. They all squatted down and waited among the shrubs silently. Julia and Tanya exchanged worried glances, the same way they had when Number One's bodyguards wanted to take them from Cleo back at HQ.

Cleo put the M9 away and drew the RavenEye. Yeah, the tension in the air was so strong now she suddenly didn't care about the rules anymore. She pulled the suppressor out from her right hip pocket and attached it as she walked, eyes all over the scene, fingers working to secure the parts together without looking down.

She was glad the RavenEye still had subsonic ammo loaded from the other night, and things would be even quieter if she fired with the MDS-modded suppressor. She didn't want to be creating more noise than she needed to. Something was going down and Agent Starr felt it too, she'd heard it in his voice. She could feel his eyes fixed on her, ready to back her up if she needed it.

Cleo approached their car slowly. If anyone was stowing away in the back this time, they were going to get their face blown off. No warnings, no optional surrenders just *face-gone.* She got low and circled the car slow, checking in the windows carefully and sliding her fingers under the car and near the tyres, feeling for any obvious civilian-made tracking or explosive devices.

She flung open one of the back doors and searched the inside, RavenEye cocked and ready to fire as she checked the backseat and compartment Julia and Tanya had hidden in earlier. She signalled for Agent Starr to bring Julia and Tanya over when she came up empty.

She moved to the passenger's side and opened the door for cover, standing between the body of the car and the door, keeping watch as

Julia and Tanya climbed in the back of the vehicle. Agent Starr was bringing up the rear, weapon drawn when he headed for the driver's door without saying anything. Cleo kept her back up against the car and the RavenEye sweeping over the treeline across the road again and again.

The heaviness was still hanging in the air but she couldn't pinpoint the source. It was thick on her skin though, sliding over it as she stood there waiting for the others to shut their doors. They needed to leave the area, start the car and get the hell out, even if she was wrong somehow, even if it was just some paranoid mistake.

She glanced across the front seats at Agent Starr and shoved the RavenEye back in her thigh rig. Their eyes met as she stepped up to get in and a feeling sparked between them, something they weren't fast enough to say. They both ducked.

Something punctured the car—*localised, not very big*—still enough force to chip paint and bend steel on his side. They slammed their doors shut. It was a round with their names on it. Another shot hit the car immediately, one then two, then it was raining bullets.

Rounds pinged off the mirrors and hubcaps. Some embedded themselves in the car body. Agent Starr was ducked low in his seat, Cleo was sliding further to the footwell telling the civilians to get down. She didn't know if they were obeying the order behind her. Her eyes were on Agent Starr's side of the car, she couldn't see the ignition over the steering wheel but if there were keys in it she should have been able to see them dangling underneath. They weren't there.

"*Keys*," she said. Agent Starr's face changed when he reached for the ignition.

"Not here, sir."

Cleo brushed her hands over the floor then the dashboard and consoles, still crouched and squashed against the bottom of the driver's seat. The position didn't give her much leverage, the thigh and shoulder rig were digging into her muscles, strained at the movements in the confined space.

Julia started crying. Tanya began firing a million questions, demanding to know what was going on, asking if they were really being shot at. More rounds drove themselves into the car. *Gunfire and confusion.* Cleo could feel the car shudder as Julia and Tanya started scrambling over each other for more cover. No one had anywhere to go. They were stuck, trapped in their metal bubble until the proofing failed and someone took a hit...and Cleo couldn't find the damn keys.

She could hear Agent Starr's frenzied movements beside her as he searched too, trying to keep low. *Where the fuck were the keys?* She couldn't remember what she'd done with them. She'd been so glad to get rid of Tanya for five minutes she hadn't bothered to keep track of where she'd put the fucking keys when they all got out.

A bullet smashed into Agent Starr's window, lodged in a dangerous halo of ruptured and cracked glass a few inches from where he was bunched up below. Bulletproof was subjective, depended on caliber and other factors. Cleo wasn't going to tell the civilians that but it was definitely time to bail. She started feeling around on the floor again, fingers rushing over each other like legs on a dying spider. *No keys.* Nothing on the mats. Just dirt and carpet and something sticky. When she glanced at Agent Starr he was struggling to keep low now, far too tall to stay cramped much longer.

They couldn't tell when the car was going to be pelted until it was happening. Rounds came at random, bursts of five or six, shocking the civilians into screaming every time. *Semi-Auto.* Cleo was reasonably sure there was only one shooter. All the shots were coming from the same direction, ending up on the driver's side of the car where Agent Starr was.

Time between the series of shots indicated the attacker was pausing for a reload, and it had to be an amateur because they hadn't even tried to kill the fuel tank or take out the tires to prevent an escape. If they had, then they were a terrible shot, a bonus for Cleo while she ran through their dwindling options.

Another spray of bullets perforated the car body and Tanya and

Julia screamed again, shuffling until they were lying side by side and sardined on the backseat, heads behind Cleo. Tanya was almost falling off onto the floor. Their high-pitched squeals drilled her brain, made it difficult to concentrate. Agent Starr told Julia and Tanya to stop moving around and get as low to the floor as possible. He had to tell them twice.

"No keys," Cleo slurred as she scrunched further down to the floor, "I'm going out there."

The keys weren't getting found anytime soon. If someone had taken them out into the woods and dropped them then they were likely missing forever. Agent Starr's face changed when he digested her words and he frowned, ready to argue.

"Number One wants them alive. I need to get to Menas." Cleo said.

"The vests are in the back, we can't get to them. This isn't worth it. The keys've got to be here somewhere, he'll have to re-load again soon. He'll stop," he said.

He was full of shit.

Cleo shot him a look. The sound of gunfire was making him nervous enough to make a fool of himself in front of the civilians. She could see that look on his face again, unfamiliar anxiety that belonged to a civilian, not a damn MDS Red Tag.

"Even with body armour it's—you don't have a vest, Cleo."

"I don't have a *choice*," she snapped. He'd used her first name in front of the civilians, probably petty in the circumstances but fuck, "Be quiet, Number One needs this done."

Three rounds burst into the back window and shivered the car. Julia and Tanya were jumping and squealing their terror. Cleo's eyes locked on Agent Starr's.

"If you find the keys, get them out of range. I'll catch up."

Julia and Tanya shrieked in unison when Cleo opened the door, like they thought it was the shooter somehow getting inside the car. She wanted to tell them to shut their mouths but she didn't bother, it wasn't going to happen. She took the RavenEye, pushed the handle on the door then kicked it further open. It swung and shuddered, tried to bounce back at her as she waited for the next break in the shots.

She got a glimpse of the side mirror while she slid out and saw a black blur. Someone ran across the path further up behind the car. The shooter was trying to get to the other side to set up a good shot at Cleo's side of the car. She held her fire, didn't want it to turn into some sort of firefight, not with the civilians so close.

It was too dark for an accurate ID but the shooter was male, sprinting into the treeline across the road, instantly disappearing into the woods to find a new vantage point. He had a long-range weapon, a big-ass sniper rifle he was barely managing to run with. He wasn't going to come up to the car for a kill. He was going to find a new spot and wait them out.

She didn't have time to turn back and search for Adonai, she was going old school. She looked at Agent Starr once, the full stop to their argument, then she ran for the trees after the shooter. Agent Starr's face flashed behind her eyes as she raced, he didn't think she'd make it.

15

CLEO WANTED THE KILL. The feeling was just *there*, some kind of thirst dominating her senses. She could feel it ride her blood while she became hyperaware of everything; her body, her moving limbs, warp-speed thoughts and so many 'what ifs' around unignorable thirst in the dark. There was *nothing* like hunting another human. It didn't feel like anything else, morphed things inside that never changed back when it was over.

She could feel her heartbeat thud in her ribcage, her hands cutting the air as she ran. The soles of her boots crushed the small rocks on the path and then the dull damp groundcover. Adrenalin exploded into her bloodstream as she cleared the treeline and crouched between the first clump of thick bushes she saw.

She was only a few seconds behind the shooter so it was going to turn into one of those *'shoot on sight, shoot to kill'* things. Whoever set up a decent shot was going to come out on top and the loser would be splattered red, dripping from branches flanking some hiking trail. He had the bigger firepower and a scope, probably NightVision too...but he'd still need to set it up before a Double Banded Red Tag located him. *Advantage, Darkrose.*

Her eyes strained in the lowlight, surveying angles, looking for her next move. The place was darker than the other side of the path and the moon didn't want to help her out, it had moved away to another corner of the sky and left her wishing she'd put the damn Adonai in. Her vision was 20/20 but that didn't matter if lighting was *shit*.

She could smell the dank earth under her boots, almost taste the bark on the trees carried on the air as she moved forward. So many trees, close together as if some ancient had planted them within inches of each other hundreds of years ago even if it wasn't the case. The effect was creepy, made her feel like she was walking through an obstacle course designed to slow her down.

Overhead branches scratched each other, shamelessly warning her to get out or slyly calling her towards them. Some lit up weakly because Agent Starr had turned on the high beams back at the car, probably trying to make it harder for the shooter to target a specific occupant behind the ball of light. The scene was only partly visible from her position now but the car was side on and the lights were pointed up the path. She didn't know if his idea was going to work.

She had the RavenEye, the M9 in the shoulder rig, two spare mags in her side pocket and no one to answer to, unmistakable bloodlust gliding over every thought and pushing her to get that kill. It wasn't a virgin voyage for the pulsing in her veins as she hunted in the unfamiliar terrain, trying to avoid stepping on anything that would give the shooter her location.

She was headed up an incline, prowling for the sniper bastard among dark trunks and dirt and sticks. He was probably getting to the higher ground, it was what they liked to do, so he was going to be close by. She stopped behind a thick tree for cover and double-checked the RavenEye was ready to go the second she thought she sensed him. He felt so close so abruptly that it was eerie.

Three rounds tore the air and exploded into the side of the car. Tanya screamed, ragged and full of pain. *She was hit.* Cleo recognised agony, knew what it was like to catch a bullet, the scalding burn that seared flesh and couldn't be quelled no matter how much you grabbed at it or danced around or yelled. The scream was so *clear*. There had to be a window or door open in the car. The round had come right to her. *Dammit, Agent Starr.*

She traced the probable trajectory for the rounds, imaginary lines lighting up like a laser pointer in the dark beyond her tree and further up the incline. She headed for her eleven o'clock, nice and low. Her eyes were trained on anything that moved. She could tell the approximate location of the sniper and she was going the opposite way, to climb the hill a little more, circle around and come down behind him.

She was going to kill him. *So very dead.* One of her civilians was probably bleeding out so he was going to pay up big. She pushed through random and wayward bushes before a sound came from the road and paused her steps. It was manipulated and changed due to distance, but it was a car door being shut. Someone else had got out of the SUV while the shooter went for a reload.

A magazine being dropped nearby switched her attention back into the woods. The shooter was shifting position again. He'd fired his last few shots to lay cover and possibly hit Tanya by chance but whoever got out of the car wasn't going to be as lucky.

The guy came into view after Cleo slipped around the next tree. He was squatted behind low bushes, parted in the middle with a clear path to aim at the car. He didn't even have to be a great shot, everything was set up perfectly for him like he was looking down a funnel to his targets as he moved to lay prone.

He was a few feet away, lower on the incline, diagonal left past the next tree. The urge to put a bullet in the back of his head percolated against her vein walls and she felt the smooth coolness of the RavenEye in her fingers, sexily daring her to grip its good parts and blast a hole through him while she stood.

The shooter was probably near six-foot, medium build, tough to tell for sure when he was so close to the ground. He was facing the other way, wearing pants and a jacket, with a hat placed on the dirt next to him. His balding head caught slices of moonlight when branches moved overhead. He was just *lying there*, no attempt to make himself unseen by eliminating a typical human profile. That was lesson 1.01 for snipers, she was sure.

The firearm was probably one he'd picked up in a civilian store but she couldn't see the details or tell the distance it could make an accurate hit from as she closed in and saw him line up the next shot, eagerly manoeuvring the gun for a new target. When she followed the line of sight with her eyes she saw Julia outside the car, swapping seats and getting in the front? *What the fuck?*

The shooter looked over his shoulder the same time she launched her boot into the side of his face, jerking his head to the side like it should have come off. He fell on top of the gun and took the bipod to the dirt with him.

Then he rolled on his back, clumsily reaching for his belt, probably for a stashed handgun she never let him get. She fired the RavenEye, no warning. The shrieking was instant, ricocheted right back from the trees, overtaking the orgasmic whoosh from the suppressor and bouncing off a million things in the dark.

The shooter was holding his arm up in front of his face, right hand missing. Cleo didn't tell him she could see the side of his palm and three fingers glowing behind him on the ground in the moonlight. She didn't know where the rest of his hand was, maybe he'd be able to pick up all the pieces when it was light, like some kid on an Easter egg hunt.

She shoved the RavenEye away and stepped towards him as he struggled in the dirt. He was coming at her, low, still trying to get to his feet, armed with one and a half hands and forgetting about any other firearm in his possession. She slipped out of his way and kicked him in the back when he stumbled past.

She was going to demand what the fuck he was doing, who he was working for as she ran up after him but she hit the ground instead so they were lying parallel, eyes on each other's, his bewildered as fuck. She told him to stay the fuck down when she went for the RavenEye again and he obeyed.

Her five senses were on fire and her sixth one was an inferno. Someone else was headed their way and they were both waiting like they were on a stakeout together. He understood though, he wanted to keep quiet too if someone else was coming but he was recovering in the silence. He was sizing her up while struggling to hold in whimpers and wrapping his hand in a bandana she'd watched him slide from his pocket cautiously in case she opened fire on him. Her concentration split between his movements and watching for their approaching guest.

Agent Starr appeared a few trees down out of nowhere, M9 in his right hand, moving towards them like he was floating over the uneven soil and tree roots, never having to slow his pace to look down. His weapon was aimed at the man on the ground the whole time.

"How many?"

"Just this one," Cleo said, "What happened?"

"Tanya's hit."

Cleo pushed herself up, trying not to spew a stream of profanity.

"She didn't shut the door properly and leaned on it. The round bounced off the doorframe, took some sting off. She's alive–caught it in the calf with an exit wound– it's like a graze, surprisingly small caliber. I'll do a proper exam when we're clear, but they're all right. They have the medkit, we're still good," Agent Starr reported then he smiled, "Julia's amazing, knew exactly what to start doing."

Well, wasn't Julia the hero? She supposed she should have been pleased they weren't all dead. Admittedly, she'd barely got to the shooter in time to prevent him doing more damage. She looked down at the guy on the ground while he was frantically reaching around in his waistband again. Agent Starr kicked his good hand and then stepped on it, crunching it under his boot and grinding fingers against the tree roots and dirt while he spoke, ignoring the groans spraying from the shooter.

"We're still good for time too. Motel-wise," Agent Starr said, "We might even get there around twenty three hundred like we planned but we'd have to leave now because–"

The shooter squeezed his hand out from under Agent Starr's boot and grabbed his ankle. Agent Starr coolly fired the M9 down and the round struck the guy in the left shoulder. Non-lethal, perfect precision.

"You were saying?" Cleo raised her voice over the shooter's screeching.

"Because Tanya needs medical attention. We need better lighting and maybe a bed or something for her to lie on so I can check the wound properly."

The shooter's good hand was outstretched and straining to grip his bleeding shoulder. Cleo noticed something on the second last knuckle, where a wedding ring would go. It was black in the lowlight but it wasn't dirt. She stepped closer for a better look and he recoiled in horror, spitting at her, freaking out like an injured cat. Okay.

"Show me your hand," she said.

The shooter spat again, the white wad of saliva missing her by inches. She didn't know what she would have done if it landed on her but it would have concluded in a lot more blood loss. He was pushing his luck.

"Show. Me. Your. Hand." Cleo forced the short blunt words through her full lips.

Agent Starr gave it a second for the guy to comply before he bent, grabbed the shooter's bleeding arm and twisted it upwards into a joint lock, no consideration for the bullet in his shoulder. The shooter's screams blasted into the night as he was hauled halfway to his feet. His arm was over-extended, tendons about to split at the elbow. Cleo bent closer to him. The black mark on his knuckle was a Spades symbol tattoo.

"You're not going to get to Menas, you know. I know that's where you think you're going," The shooter said, bitter and snarled, "And you're not going to shut us up. I pay my taxes, I see where my fucking money goes. Us regular people know more than you think...I want you to know something. Come here, girlie."

Cleo didn't want to catch his next gob of saliva with her face so she didn't move. The shooter nodded gingerly; there was no hidden motive, it was okay to get nearer. She glanced up at Agent Starr. He aimed his gun at the shooter again, if things went to shit he would break his arm and put a bullet in him, an instant kill shot.

Cleo knelt in the dirt slowly as Agent Starr loosened his grip on the guy so they could be closer. The woodland floor was cold, damp on her legs through the uniform again but the double padding in the knees took the brunt of it. She gave Agent Starr another glance, reminded him of his unspoken promise to shoot the guy if necessary before she pushed some hair behind her ear and leaned forward carefully.

The shooter whispered so softly she had to strain to make out his words. They were tense, pain flowing through them as he squeezed out each syllable. He didn't try and grab at her or pull her, maybe due to blood loss. The bandana around his half-hand couldn't have been enough to halt the bleeding.

His words slithered into her ear slowly, wrapped themselves around invisible things that made her chest tight. When he was done, she stood up and brushed the dirt from her legs. She tried not to look at Agent Starr, he would read the look on her face and then she would have to discuss what some Crazy had decided to impart to her and waste even more time. She looked at the shooter instead.

"Ain't that a bitch?" He whispered.

Agent Starr was watching her, glancing to the guy on the floor and back, wanting to be let in on the private conversation.

"Would you ever miss a shot like that?" She gestured with her head, direction of the car.

Agent Starr turned and surveyed the path of trajectory through the trees from their position. He thought about it for less than a second; the distance between the gun and the car, the higher ground, the access to a tire or fuel tank or Julia when she'd got out and moved to the front seat. He dipped an eyebrow.

"No," he said, "I'd never miss a shot like that."

Cleo turned away then back with her RavenEye. She fired a round into the shooter's head and watched it burst.

16

PAINKILLERS WERE GREAT. A pill or a shot could make you think everything was okay, shut off pain receptors and make the body think nothing was wrong. MDS issued some damn good ones, sometimes too good and agents became addicted. The ridiculous high left your head stuffy and thick, thoughts travelled slower, dancing on a swirling breeze with leaves and other debris and shit caught up in it.

She had experienced them a few times in the Infirmary but she didn't like it. Hence she usually took her pain as it came. There was a saying they used for that; *take it like a Red Tag.* It was like the saying "*take it like a man*," only more hardcore.

The *Nano Field Shot* they'd taken from the Medkit worked instantly, the injection of nanoparticles delivering analgesic and a variation of Fentanyl into Tanya's bloodstream to calm her down and shut her mouth. Agent Starr was correct, her wound wasn't serious and packing it with gauze stopped the bleeding but getting the auto-inject syringe into her leg while the car was moving again was all kinds of dramatic, wails and tears. The blubbering teen even asked if she was going to die when Agent Starr said he was going to stay in the back and monitor her breathing despite only administering a fraction of a dose.

Cleo was glad it was him back there, she would have put Tanya out of her misery about an hour back when the worst of the ear-piercing shrieks were happening. Now it was annoying whimpers at intervals. Small victories.

The scent of drying blood hung on her uniform even with the

window down. Yeah, she hadn't thought that far ahead in the woods and they were paying for it. Using the RavenEye had consequences for everyone, not just the person eating the round. The momentary memory lapse meant she'd had to wipe bone fragments from her own uniform and blood off the side of her face. Agent Starr had been a good sport about the chunks of meat splashed across his pants but he couldn't have been happy about it. The shooter had thrown her off her game for a few seconds and now they both smelled like a butcher's shop.

It was close. There was no way to tell if other shooters were stalking them or how the one she'd blasted had managed to locate them but he'd seemed to think he knew a lot about MDS. Like Agent Hooper fading out in the truck, he alluded to more going on at HQ that she'd been too busy basking in her notoriety to take any notice of. *Of course* SpadeMan had connections on The Outside, she'd just forgotten because of all the stowaway civilian shit.

She should have made the decision to drive straight to San Freedom, ditch the motel idea because they didn't know if they had a tail now but Agent Starr let her call it and they were still going to stay the night there. She needed to lose the other three, stopping for them to rest while she made off with the car was the only way it was going to happen. Selfish as fuck, but getting Number One's target and herself another confirmed kill was more important than body-guarding collateral. Agent Starr had that part *more* than covered anyway.

Julia was in the front passenger's seat, a lock of hair wound around a finger, neck craned to the back to make eye contact with him while she explained why she'd vacated the car. She'd found the car keys and wanted to get Tanya out of range like she'd heard Cleo say. The revelation was a surprise, the woman hadn't just fled the car on some weird civilian freak out...but Cleo wasn't about to throw her a parade. Agent Starr had already thanked her too many times, telling her she was a 'goddam hero,' when he probably should have been telling her she was a fucking idiot for exiting the vehicle.

Tanya was dominating the backseat, hastily bandaged leg across most of it and leaning up against Agent Starr while he sat behind Cleo. The teen had her eyes closed, listening to her mother's conversation with the MDS agent she found just a little too fascinating. Their conversation flowed like they were elsewhere and without an audience. Cleo didn't want to think about their exchange before they thought it was a good idea to leave Tanya alone in the woods so they could disappear and...

Fuck. She guessed Agent Starr had changed. The refusal to kill Evan back at the camp, all the deer in headlights stuff with the ships and then fucking a civilian he'd just met? That wasn't the agent she remembered, not the man she knew. She blinked the thought away when she saw the motel coming up between the trees on the left. The dash clock blinked 01:27, blue green light drawing her attention back down. She didn't want to check her own watch, if it agreed, she didn't want to know.

It was looking like she was going to have to skimp on sleep and leave soon after they set up in the motel. There was no way she was missing that boat in San Freedom, even if Agent Starr was still awake to hear her drive off in the SUV and leave them at risk and stranded. He was just going to have to call it in, take the blame for not returning the civilians sooner and get them an EVAC or request one of those other Red Tags he'd said were home and on call to escort.

He'd probably have to do it quickly too, before Number One pulled some quirky shit like killing their phones just to shake things up. Poor Agent Starr, he didn't seem to be up for that stuff anymore, at least not on a mission by himself. Yeah, well, he should have thought of that before he started playing prom night with Julia.

17

CLEO SIGHED OVER MASHING OF TIRES ON THE GREY STONES as they parked the car. Small motels meant other guests remembered faces, staff recalled how much luggage you brought in to numbered rooms etched in their brains. She didn't like it but she followed the orders. Number One's judgement was better than hers—*she knew that*—but if it was up to her, she would have found somewhere else to stay, where they could blend in and hide the screaming child with a bullet hole in her leg.

Twin splintering wooden poles made up the signpost, a flickering neon sign between them standing out against the night like they were near Vegas. Spluttering hot pink cursive letters were alternating which letters were lucky enough to have electricity filtering through, exclaiming the motel's name; *Still Waters*. Uh huh. Cleo could barely make it out from inside the car, the I, A and T were dark when she looked up.

It looked like a place civilians went to cheat on their husbands and wives among the odd felon on the run. That thought made her feel better, chances were the people running the joint wouldn't mind fetid, bloody people carrying a whinging child through the doors near two in the morning as long as they could cough up some money.

Cleo pushed the car door open and left Agent Starr with the civilians. He didn't need instruction, he'd get them ready to cross to the motel doors once she'd cleared the area. She stood outside the car and surveyed with her eyes, listened for anyone hanging around but the air wasn't carrying the weight of a lifeforce and they were alone. It was just the pink light from the sign buzzing and flickering to her left and a whole bunch of dark trees.

She could practically smell the too-old creaking beds inside the motel when she glanced at the doors. The next few hours were not going to be fun but it was safer than sleeping in a car with compromised window integrity. The vehicle looked like they'd been in driveby.

She pressed the release and took the RavenEye out then unclipped the thigh rig and threw it backwards into the car where she'd shed her M9 and shoulder rig as they'd pulled in. She pushed the gun into her waistband, wincing at the cool metal up against her skin before she tucked her uniform over. She usually brought a bellyband with her somewhere in her ruck but they were already short on time.

The gun was bulky on her guts but civilians rarely looked for concealed weapons. *As long as the RavenEye was hidden from plain sight.* She hoped Agent Starr hid his gun when he came in too. Despite the bloody black uniform, she'd hoped to tone it all down and appear less...MDS and no, she didn't have permission to go in armed with the RavenEye but she was not leaving *that* gun behind in the car.

Still Waters Motel was a giant two-storey log cabin without the logs. Long flat slats of dark wood made up the walls instead, near black in the night, like a haunted house and only lit around the porch courtesy of the two lamps hanging either side of the front door and a dull glow from inside. The few steps up to the porch creaked and threatened under her boots. She hoped she wouldn't go through them, they didn't have time for that.

The front door was a crooked piece of wood with a cracked frame that had blown shut once too often. It moved easily, making way for a smell to ghost its way into Cleo's face with dizzying strength; some potent blend of sweat, beer, urine and...some sort of fish? It wasn't her bloody uniform and it wasn't a dead body or animal rotting away in the corner, she knew what those things smelled like, this stink was different. Her heart sank when she realised the source was living.

He was thick-necked, overweight and heaped behind a dark pine reception desk opposite the door. A wide staircase flanked his right, leading to where the rooms were, lined on both sides with wooden banisters all the way up and blocking her view to a hall running across at the top. She looked left to a short alcove at the end of the lobby to small black stick figures stuck high on the wall, indicating bathrooms back there somewhere.

The walls were all wooden, no windows apart from the two small ones either side of the front door. The ones she'd seen from outside were all up on the first floor. Guests liked to see outside, not just get an eyeful of shellacked and sealed wood. Lamplight made the room seem like it was lit with candles and she guessed it gave a cosy vibe, got people to ignore the lack of windows. She just felt stuffy as she took mental pictures and noted escape routes.

The guy was reading a magazine spread out flat on the desk in front of him. It didn't take a genius to figure out what it was. He kept his balding head down, staring at the pages in front of him with his mouth half open and saliva glittering on the end of his tongue. Either he hadn't seen or heard her come in or he didn't care, favouring the perverted 2D images.

Stubble around his mouth looked days old, dotted with remains of food long gone and his stretched white t-shirt was complete with almost-clichéd stains across his saggy chest. She couldn't see under the desk but she hoped he was wearing pants.

He wasn't armed, she could tell. His shirt was so worn it was see-through. There was no way he could have concealed a weapon unless it was stashed under one of his rolls of fat and keeping it there probably required skill he didn't have. Agent Starr wasn't the only one who could turn on the ghost walk when it was needed, Silent Stepping was second nature as she made her way toward the pungent mess hoping the experience wasn't going to be what visuals predicted.

She stood on the other side of the desk and considered slamming her hand on the service bell nearby but she didn't want to risk any other smells escaping from the guy if he got a fright. He sensed her then, jumping to his feet, clumsily grabbing at his magazine before finally getting a grip on it and throwing it over his shoulder. Anger flashed across his lined face then he smiled and exposed his yellow goalpost teeth.

He ran his nicotine fingers through waning brown hair and shot her a wink. She could see the sweat shining on his scalp when he leaned forward and introduced himself as *Frank* in a voice a few octaves higher than she'd expected. He mumbled something about an available room, he always had one for someone like her. She didn't smile back, too busy holding her breath even when he told her it was going to be half-price because she'd made his night, showing up out of nowhere like she'd stepped out of his magazine.

He looked like he wanted to lick her after that. She was good at deciphering that look, she'd seen it a lot in the giant cesspit on The Outside. If she'd been an unarmed civilian wanting a room, his expression may have worried her, bothered her so much she would have left the motel and spent the night in the car instead.

Frank's eyes moved over her lips then down to her chest and back again. He wanted to say something else he probably thought was suave and witty but he didn't get to. Agent Starr came through the door carrying Tanya in his arms.

He was wearing a long black MDS-issue trenchcoat. He would have First Aid items somewhere in the deep pockets and he'd be strapped under it and maybe even have an extra magazine for her RavenEye like he was her personal caddie. He walked through the lobby and stood next to her at the counter, glancing down asking what the deal was with only his eyes while Tanya stayed quiet up against his chest.

"He's going to give us a room, half-price." Cleo said.

"No, no," Frank shook his head, "That was when I thought it was just you, not your boyfriend too."

"He's not—we're not—" Cleo started.

"I can't just *give* people rooms, you know," he winked again and let his eyes repeat their scan over her chest, "Unless you got something to trade?"

Julia came through the door behind them and severed the tension with a door slam. Agent Starr glanced over his shoulder and Cleo followed his eyes, saw Julia smiling like she was on a fucking vacation and give a stupid little wave. Agent Starr smiled back and dropped it as he turned to Frank again.

"I don't like the way you're looking at her," he gestured with his chin at Cleo then back, "Show some respect. This girl needs medical attention. We need two rooms total but we're going to pay for *one* because otherwise I'm going to get angry."

Tanya wailed on cue, high-pitched like a squeaky-toy, arms tightening around Agent Starr's neck. The money didn't matter to Cleo and it sure as shit didn't matter to Agent Starr. Together the two of them could probably have funded a war between two small countries. Agent Starr was playing and it was okay, good even, civilian dirt needed to respect MDS, know the order of the food chain and stay out of their damn way.

Frank was clearly intimidated by him. She could tell by the way he was looking up and swallowing. Civilian women got flirty when they came face to face with Agent Starr. The men just stared in something like jealous awe. Hey, whatever got them into a room ASAP without her having to roll up Frank's dirty magazine and beat the shit out of him with it.

18

THE HALLWAY AT THE TOP OF THE STAIRS WAS DARK and stretching in both directions. Small lamps lined the walls, jutting out from between room doors but the place was still dim, worse than the lobby. The lobby had clearly been decorated to lure people into paying before they saw the type of service they were going to get. Walls were peeling either side in the hall as they walked. If it was daytime, Cleo guessed they would have been pale pink. She couldn't tell for sure though, it just looked like shit.

Frank waddled ahead of her holding two candles on a china plate. She didn't know whether he couldn't afford the electricity bill or he just wanted to create atmosphere. Either way it was annoying as fuck. They were in single file; Frank then Cleo, Agent Starr carrying Tanya and Julia bringing up the rear. Cleo couldn't help it, she looked down the crack of Frank's ass peering out from the top of his over-stretched white shorts. She didn't want to but she had to watch the hairy flabby mass closely because he was stopping suddenly every few seconds hoping she would run into him.

He led them to a room down the hall and pushed the door open watching the candles in his other hand in case they blew out with the motion. Predictable squeaking hinges greeted their ears as the door revealed the interior of the first room. Frank felt around the other side of the doorframe for a few moments to turn on the light before he found the switch.

Everything in the room was worn and dull like they'd travelled back in time a few decades. A large bed sat crammed up in the corner, covered in merlot-red sheets, diagonal from two arm chairs in the centre of the room. They were covered in faded pink upholstery patched with dark green mould. Both chairs were askew like two people had been sitting across from each other and thrown them backwards to stand up for a fight.

The carpet on the floor wasn't much better, brown with faded red patterns and swirls pathetically staring up at her. They were soiled and stained with food and, in some places, blood maybe. She couldn't be sure and bending over to get a closer look wasn't an option. Not with Frank in the room.

Her eyes slid to Agent Starr's. He didn't say anything when he looked back, his way of telling her to let it go, it didn't matter what state the rooms were in because they just needed to get Tanya's leg elevated and rest up before the next part of the assignment.

He pushed through everyone and headed for the bed to put Tanya down. She was still grunting and complaining about her leg and feeling cold, even while wearing Cleo's jacket zipped right up. Her words were slurred from the painkiller but they could still understand her drivel as he lowered her to the sheets.

Julia followed and dragged a mouldy armchair bedside. Cleo and Frank watched from the doorway, side by side. Cleo ignored Frank's glances from Agent Starr to the side of her face. No, she was not going to look back at him. He could fuck off.

Agent Starr shed his trenchcoat and started taking things from the pockets, forgetting his shoulder rig and weapon were in plain sight but Frank didn't seem to notice. Cleo saw Julia's face light up at the first aid items, impressed before Agent Starr had even done anything with Tanya's leg. Big deal, Cleo could do what he was going to. She'd done it a few times over the years, mostly for other agents, once for herself.

He was going to do a better job cleaning up the wound than he had in the car and then probably start suturing. He was doing it in a warm room with a bed too, she'd had to do it out in the middle of nowhere once with rain pelting down in her eyes. The round had been lodged in her left calf and the positions she'd had to sit in just to reach it with good leverage had pulled muscles she didn't even know humans had.

Frank gave Cleo another wink when she looked over. He was more repulsive close up, even candlelight didn't help him. His stubble was poorly hiding bad skin and drool stains from whenever he'd passed out last and his brown eyes were small and birdlike while he checked her out, blinking too much then motioning for her to move along the hallway to a room two doors down.

Déjà vu hit when he opened the second door. It was a mirror image of the other room but a long faded red loveseat in place of the two arm chairs in the middle. Frank smiled and let her know that if she was bored during the night he was willing to keep her company in whatever way she needed; it was all part of the wonderful service at *Still Waters*.

Cleo walked into the room and shut the door in his face. She slid the metal security chain across and waited, leaning against the brittle wood until Frank's heavy footsteps trudged down the stairs and out of earshot.

She could hear Julia's voice down the hall, murmurs and laughter, talking with Agent Starr while he stitched the hole in Tanya's leg. He had to stay in the same room as them all night, *procedure*. It was the safest option and it made sense but she wondered what the final sleeping arrangements would be like. It sounded like Julia and Agent Starr couldn't wait for Tanya to drift off.

She stepped away from the door to wait until her escape but the loveseat was out of the question and so was the bed in the corner. She didn't want to think about what had gone on on top of either piece of furniture. She stood in the middle of the room for too long before she gave up and sat cross-legged on the carpet, RavenEye to her left. The carpet was the lesser of two evils, she'd take dirty shag over other dried bodily fluids any day.

She pulled at the Velcro down the left side of her chest and peeled back the Kevlar panel on the bloodstained uniform shirt so it was hanging and she could see the zip running down the centre of the second layer clinging to her body. She dragged the metal tag down then slid the shirt backwards over her shoulders and arms to drop it behind her.

The MDS tank top underneath was comfortable without the uniform and it was as naked as she was going to get in a room that was probably hooked up to some feed Frank jerked off to downstairs. The straps on her tank top were thick and soft either side of a wide neckline that left most of her chest bare and the tight MDS bra underneath kept everything close to her body. It was unflattering but functional and she'd welcomed the way it minimised her chest.

It wasn't unheard of that a female MDS agent could walk around in just the tank top, pants and no MDS uniform shirt but it was rare. Technically, it was classed as underwear in MDS circles so she usually felt uncomfortable without a shirt. On The Outside, it looked like something Tanya would wear walking down the street, and in the motel room, it was necessity because the stale blood splashed on the uniform shirt smelled like it was beginning to fester.

She could still hear Julia talking in the other room when someone knocked on her door and she stood, RavenEye in-hand, to pad towards it slowly. She got up against the wall, approaching it from the side. Frank was making a big fucking mistake.

She pulled the door open a crack, expecting to see the smelly bastard with some kind of proposition for her. She even had a comeback ready, sharp and dangling on the end of her tongue but it was Agent Starr. He leaned close to the opening to speak quietly over the chain lock. She could only see the left half of his face and one of his Aurora-green eyes.

"Are you all right?" He asked.

"Why wouldn't I be?"

"You've been quiet since the woods, since the shooter."

"I'm always quiet," she said.

"I know." He looked like he wanted to say something else but he didn't.

"You should get back to Julia." The words fell out before she could stop them.

Agent Starr frowned a little then wiped it from his face.

"Uh, yeah...she and Tanya shouldn't be left alone, eh," he said, "Are you sure you want to stay in here by yourself?"

"Yes."

"The motel owner's a degenerate piece of-"

"I've noticed. If the lock on the door isn't sufficient, I'm sure the RavenEye will be."

"Heh. You did good tonight, Cleo."

"Thank you, *Agent* Starr."

"No problem, Agent Darkrose," he said, "Goodnight"

Cleo shut the door and the security chain relaxed but Agent Starr didn't leave right away. He was standing on the other side of the door probably trying to figure out her taunt about getting back to Julia. *Stupid.* She didn't know why she'd said it, some bitchy thing she should have kept to herself. It was a few seconds before she heard him breathe out and then walk back to the room he was sharing with the civilians.

19

0440 AND CLEO'S LIMBS WERE STIFF. She yawned trying not to take a deep gulp of the sour air, reminding herself it was only the journey down the stairs and to the car before she could change into another shirt and move out. She was going to leave the motel immediately but nature was screaming and it didn't care if she was MDS's version of practically half naked or not. She had to make a bathroom stop on the way out.

She needed one more check on Julia and Tanya too, to see if Agent Starr was still up on watch or if they were all out. It was no big deal if he saw her awake, she was headed to the bathrooms and they were downstairs...where the car was. But she hoped he was sleeping. She wanted to see where he was lying too, the proximity to Julia and if she had to worry about him running off with the civilian woman and leaving her to face Number One's wrath.

Cleo's bladder turned off the warning sirens and permitted her walk to the other room without threatening an accident. Their door was predictably shut and she took her room key out and tried it in the lock for the hell of it. The damn thing clicked instantly and unlocked without trouble. Guests at *Still Waters* could get into everyone else's room as well as their own. *Great.*

Vague pink glow came in through the window blinds across the room, ambient from the sign outside and gently illuminating corners of objects in the room. The chain lock hadn't been on when Cleo pushed the door open further and waited, familiarizing herself with where the furniture was again and then made her way to the bed in the corner, passing the two empty armchairs on the way. She didn't see Agent Starr in either of them.

Were all three of them in the same bed? Dammit. *Really?* How the hell was he supposed to get up, get his gun and set up a shot from there? If it was her, she would have been sitting in one of those mouldy-ass chairs, ready to blast anyone who breached the door, key or not. She was disappointed not to have a barrel shoved in her face the second she entered the room.

When she was near the foot of the bed she saw it was only Julia on the left, her arm hanging out over the side of the mattress, face hidden under her hair and Tanya on the right. Tanya's eyes were open, catching the pink light while she stared at the ceiling.

"I want to go home," she whispered, "This is stupid. I wish we didn't sneak into the car. You hate us, you don't want us with you, we can tell. The only person that's been nice to us is Agent Starr."

"Where is Agent Starr?" Cleo asked quietly, she didn't want to wake Julia and have to talk to them both.

"He's downstairs. You're lucky you know, at least he's nice to you," Tanya's bratty tone managed to ride her hissed words clearly as she sat up on her elbows, "He came all this way to see you, I wouldn't have, you're mean. He did something very bad and got sent home and now he has to get noticed again, even if he has to work with *you*."

"What do you mean?"

"He probably wants to be the best again, better than you."

Oh. Cleo didn't need to hear anymore, the info Tanya had given up was enough. There had been conversation and it sounded like Agent Starr had told them both more than he'd told her about why he was really home. If he wanted to be the best then she had to watch her back. Yeah, he was a different now, like those traitor agents dying in the truck back at HQ.

Hooper and Jimmy Stone had confirmed she wasn't paranoid, other agents were after her reputation. Some of her own people wanted to take her place. She could barely believe Agent Starr was one of them though. The only way he was going to be the best was if he killed her soon then carried on and completed the assignment alone or sold out to SpadeMan and became a double agent. Yeah, well, he was going to wish he was back in the Middle East, in that living hell he'd described. MDS did not tolerate treachery and neither did she.

She heard footsteps downstairs in the lobby when she was out of the room. It was still lit up down there, the same cosy glow she'd first seen Frank bathed in. Cleo backed up at the top of the staircase and she didn't have to wait long. Agent Starr came from the bathrooms slowly. His hair was tied back and he had been outside to the car and changed his uniform because it looked clean. He also had another new uniform folded in his hands.

When he reached the stairs he walked up a few then sat, back to Cleo. He didn't know she was there. He put the spare uniform down next to him and leaned his elbows on his knees, head in his hands. He was in some deep thought right away or maybe just exhausted. She didn't know, she didn't care. She heard him breathe a long sigh.

She placed each boot down slow, distributing weight, clearing each stair silently on the way down. He was on the step below her when he finally sensed someone coming, just about making the turn to look over his shoulder when she snatched the RavenEye from her pants and smashed the butt into his skull.

20

ADRENALIN WAS PEAKING. Time moved too slow. Agent Starr was lying face down on the ground. Cleo had kicked him in the back and sent him off the stairs to the floor after the blow from the RavenEye. He was out cold. She wasn't sure if she'd hit him hard enough at the time but now there was no question.

She sat on a step halfway up the staircase and waited. If he came at her suddenly, she'd have a couple of seconds to respond. She watched him, sitting, legs apart, boots on the next stair down and the RavenEye hanging from her hand, begging to be used.

A full three seconds passed before he stirred and blinked his eyes. She saw the moment his mind clicked, when he realised he'd been knocked out. He reached down for his gun, found it missing, and pushed himself up anyway. Cleo cocked the RavenEye.

Agent Starr stopped, half-standing. He was facing away from her, raising his hands slowly and trying to look over his shoulder. Cleo could see a little river of red slither down the back of his neck between his hairline and the collar of his uniform. *Good.*

"I have your weapon." Cleo said. She stood and glanced down at his gun beside her on the step.

"*Cleo?* What is this?"

"My name is Agent Darkrose. I'm an agent, loyal to MDS and those who serve as agents." She said, disgust peppering her words, "*Unlike some.*"

"What are you talking about?" He tried to turn.

"*Don't move.*" She warned, "You're dangerous."

"Say again? Cleo, I'd never hurt you."

She walked down a step so she could get a better range if he decided to run to his left, past the reception desk to the front doors. He was fucked. Even if she missed his vital organs, she was using the RavenEye and she was wearing the Firing Glove so she didn't give a shit about the painful recoil or how many times she may have to fire to put him down.

"Why did you come back?" She demanded at the back of his head.

"I told you, Cleo."

"Agent Darkrose."

"Agent Darkrose. I was sent home, sir. I messed up where I was stationed in the Middle East.

I'm on this assignment because they don't want me near the labs or NovaRose data until there's been an investigation into my actions and an extensive psychological screening...sir."

Cleo wasn't expecting *that*. He was on the assignment with her because Number One couldn't stand to look at him right now and they wanted to give him a complicated psychological screening? *Interesting.* He turned to face her very slowly and she let him make the move but the RavenEye was fixed on him. She would kill him if he stepped wrong.

"I know something's wrong with me because I don't want to Delete," he said, "I will, because that is what you need me to do. You are my superior on this and I will follow every order you give me without question...but I don't think I can kill anymore, if I don't have to."

The expression on his face was stuck between realisation the words had left his mouth and apprehension he was trying to hide while he waited for her reaction. The confession was gigantic and the fallout, if he was serious, was going to be devastating.

"Do you mean that, agent?"

"I think so. I wasn't *randomly* drafted. They didn't utilise my skills there, said they didn't recognise MDS Sniper School. I only did a handful of missions, prone position twelve hours a time with their guns, picking off enemies they told me were threats. Found out they just wanted *me* there because I knew how to use it, where to drop it, how many people it would...*kill,*" his words were hushed and running into each other, "Number One wanted MDS represented, wanted the deadliest weapon in the fight to come from us."

"You mean NovaRose."

"I was in their aerial frigate with it. The other guys weren't told what it was, it was need-to-know. It was next to me the whole time, I could see it through the window in the cylinder...*so much* of it, enough to kill thousands. The cylinder was five feet long, a foot and a half wide," he shook his head, "I sat there...stared at it for hours, the whole trip over, watched it for cracks or leaks."

"And?" Cleo walked down another step, RavenEye still on him.

"And when things were bad, Number One and the others wanted us to use it. I said no, argued on the phone until Number One threatened me with Deletion! I'd seen so much death already. Human skulls completely crushed, severed limbs, intestines hanging out," Cleo saw him hard-swallow the memory. His mostly straight eyebrows were bent in a frown now and he took a few seconds staring at the floor before he continued.

"We'd driven over IEDs, vehicles were destroyed, then my whole squad was wiped out on a BDA. Me and another guy got injured. Some other guys were sent back if they pretty much had a *papercut,*" he said, "I was in the Infirmary for *months.* Number One wouldn't let me come home because they were planning to deploy it in different provinces and '*required my consult.*' We needed a win but I wasn't going to unleash NovaRose on those people."

"And that's when you made your mistake?"

"Number One is the only person in command of NovaRose now. Number One doesn't care about the UN, all the rules and the paperwork about the use of chemical munitions. Everything we both signed means nothing, they're probably using it over there right now. So the other day I stole the original hard drive and hardcopy data when I got home," he shrugged, "It's under the driver's seat in the car."

He said the last sentence like he could have been talking about anything else. The RavenEye wasn't aimed at him anymore, loose in her hand and hanging by her side having made the move without her realisation. Something cold washed over her body. One of the deadliest weapons known to man was able to be created from the information on a hard drive and two folders he had just casually sitting *outside in the fucking car.* First things first.

"What happened there?" *What happened over there to make you do something so stupid?*

"I don't know," he said, like he'd gone over it a thousand times and still come up empty, "I felt kind of disrespected, after all I'd given this country, all I did for MDS. I remember being deployed, engaging the enemy. I know I, uh, called your phone from the Infirmary a few times then...nothing."

"What do you mean nothing?"

"I don't remember."

"Nothing." She stated.

"Just small flashes, right up until I was in that office being discharged. They kept saying, *'service no longer required'.* I get small flashes, nothing solid...and the things I've seen myself do, they're...the worst things."

"Like what?"

"Things I would never've done, only I did them." Agent Starr's gaze drifted to the floor again, "I hurt people and I heard guys from my unit were doing things to kids in front of their parents, pimping out *children* for five bucks American. A pack of cigarettes!" He swallowed hard again, disgust taking over his face, "You don't harm the little ones, Cleo. You just don't."

"You didn't."

"I was there and it's enough," he said, "Even before I went over, I'd done the worst thing you can do, take someone's life. I do it so often for MDS it means almost nothing. Imagine if somehow I was judged for that, if someone asked me why I'd done those things and all I could say is '*because I was told to.*' I tried to stop the things they were doing to those people at the start but then I couldn't change anything so I didn't try anymore."

Cleo didn't have comforting words, even when he looked so miserable. Her opinion on civilians differed too much from his for anything that came out of her mouth to sound sincere. People fucked up in warzones, didn't think straight—*self-preservation*—tribal and pack mentality, or so she'd heard. She didn't know for sure though, she'd never been part of a real war of course so hearsay was the best she had to draw on and it wasn't going to cut it.

All her assignments were suburban; take out ex-agents, make sure a specific political figure didn't see their next birthday, neutralise the bodyguards and get out before anyone sees you. Agent Starr had done things she couldn't comprehend, the guy couldn't even sleep properly and on top of it all, he was back home to be punished for something he couldn't even remember doing. Yeah, he felt bad enough without her telling him to "*Red Tag up*" or pretending she knew how to sympathize. She took a few steps down toward him until they were standing almost face to face.

"I can't explain why I'd just stand there and let things happen to civilians, Cleo, like it wasn't even me. What if—" He shrugged and shut his eyes for a long blink before he looked at her again, "What if I was discharged for—what if it was worse? What if I did it on purpose?"

"*You didn't.*" Cleo said. No space between their words.

She put the safety back on the RavenEye and slid it in her waistband then pulled her shirt up over it, made sure everything was secure so the gun wouldn't fall. She'd caught a RavenEye on the foot a few times over the years, it hurt like a bitch.

Agent Starr's eyes were fixed on her, stare heavy while she pushed the gun further in. When she glanced up he was frowning again. He looked at her in the face, silently asking her the question once more.

"You didn't do it on purpose," Cleo said, "I know you."

21

CLEO WASHED HER HANDS IN THE SINK under a small toothpaste-speckled mirror. Her reflection looked worn, coming back at her from between tiny white, minty dots. Frank's bathroom facilities matched the bedrooms upstairs. Old and dirty, practically alive and moving with the germs. The plumbing made clanging sounds when she turned on the tap and the water had come out brown before running clear but when you had to go, you had to go.

She hadn't heard Agent Starr go back upstairs. He was probably sitting on a step in the other room, gun in his hand and clotting the scrape on his chin, trying to figure out whatever the hell got him sent home from the Middle East. Stealing the NovaRose data was not good, Number One was going to have his ass for treason unless he returned it before it was found missing. Sure, it was his creation but that didn't matter. It was treachery to remove it from HQ. Number One had to be severely pissed at him already for refusing orders and not deploying it overseas, if the data was found missing, he was screwed.

Cleo didn't pretend to know what he felt. The only part she truly understood was when he'd said he felt disrespected after all he'd given MDS and the country. She got that part. She'd taken it further than just feeling that way.

It all hit two years ago, right before Agent Starr was drafted out. She'd been staying with him at his house on The Outside most of the week, going from there to HQ and back, getting the medical screenings and checkups and passing all the security checks so they could get five minutes alone when their schedules allowed. She was managing assignments, career objectives and their relationship and she was a shitty juggler but clever enough to figure none of the effort was going to matter in the end.

Being a Red Tag meant she'd probably come to an end where they'd need a trowel to scrape her off a sidewalk somewhere. Being in a relationship with another agent, particularly another Red Tag, meant it could never eventuate to anything more than an intermittent fuckfest. The risks of death were too high to plan anything past the next day and she'd begun to hate that the same time she realised she honestly cared about him.

Dread kicked in her guts when they were on separate assignments and she lived always uneasy he wouldn't come back, hoping both of them would survive enough to see each other again. It drove her fucking crazy, stole her focus from assignments. MDS was the priority *–there was even a bunch of documents with her signature to prove she understood that–*so it exhausted her. She didn't know if he felt the way she did either, if he found it hard to focus or worried about her. He'd never said.

She'd sat alone in her dorm one night and thought about the TC chip in her finger and how she'd never been allowed on The Outside without being tracked and monitored because they owned her. She'd even thought about cutting the chip out, telling them to shove it, MDS wasn't where she wanted to be anymore. But it wasn't just MDS, it was everything.

Telling Agent Starr it was over had been hard at the time. She'd kept it short; it was no one's fault, she just couldn't deal with it. Then she'd gone AWOL, ditched her phone, watch and anything else MDS would use to track her besides the TC chip. She'd driven around for days in a jacked car visiting dusty places she'd only passed through on assignments and meeting with people MDS would have Deleted her just for associating with.

She'd even tracked down *the* Drew Terra, a wanted ex–Red Tag the rogues went to for new identities because he'd set them up with the works; a new name, passport, social security numbers, a new past they could pretend was theirs. When she saw him, he'd even offered to kill Trent Starr to help her leave nothing behind.

Of course she'd never told anyone that part...or the part about how the crazy sex they'd had left her leaning up against a shower wall with a near concussion...but she supposed that's what you got when you fucked a psychopathic ex-hitman who hated anything to do with MDS. Even when she tried not to think about it, she remembered everything about the nights she stayed with him, right down to the dead look in his slate-grey eyes while they'd had sex.

Then she'd got anxious about being on The Outside permanently and gone home. She'd just needed time to get her shit together, lose the emotional side that Agent Starr and a recent death of a friend had drawn out of her. *Emotion got you killed*, in every way she could think of and some people never came back from it. Learning that was a fundamental part of the training. You never fought angry, you didn't make a decision based on a feeling. It was something she'd conveniently forgotten.

Amazingly, Number One didn't punish her for disappearing, marvelled when she didn't react as they told her Agent Starr had been drafted for an undetermined period of time to war on The Outside. It was like Number One still believed she was strong, *capable*. As cold as she needed to be to serve MDS with her whole ass and not just half. And Number One was damn right about that.

Cleo walked out from the bathroom quietly. It was late, or early, depended on the type of person you were. When she checked her watch, blue numbers flashed 05:10. The plan was to leave ASAP. The drive to San Freedom was going to take almost four hours and when she arrived she had to remember to grab the NovaRose data to leave it with the agents aboard the MDS charter boat.

She strolled through the alcove back from the bathrooms, trailing her hand and feeling the peeling and bubbled wallpaper under her fingertips. She was expecting to come out to the right of the wide stairs in the lobby, see Agent Starr still sitting there and tell him to get some rest. She stopped walking when she saw him standing in front of the bannister instead.

He was watching something out of her view up on the landing. His posture was alert, eyes focussed like he was waiting for an opportunity. *Bad sign.* Cleo slid the RavenEye from her waistband. She knew Agent Starr could see her in his periphery but he didn't look. He was being watched too closely for that.

Cleo Silent Stepped nearly to the threshold of the alcove. She wanted a clear shot at whatever was keeping Agent Starr in suspended animation. She took a few more steps, strafing sideways until she could see someone on the landing at the top of the stairs near the rooms. She recognised Frank the same time he aimed his pistol at her.

"Get out here and put your gun on the ground," he said.

Frank had Tanya. Cleo could see them through the wood palings in the bannister as she approached. He had no body armour on, just that stained white shirt but he had a human shield now. Tanya's arm was bent painfully behind her back, Frank keeping it tight. His other arm had been around her throat but now it was busy aiming the gun at Cleo. Tanya looked like she was shivering. Cleo didn't know if it was from fear or what she was wearing. The girl had the singlet tank top and mini skirt on again, no MDS jacket.

"I had an interesting call about you tonight, Agent Darkrose with MDS." Frank said.

"You know of MDS?" Cleo asked.

"They told me about you, offered me a *lot* of money to make sure you didn't leave. They said if you tried to get away I could kill you, never get caught cos they're coming here to clean up."

Tanya didn't squirm in Frank's grip like half of her didn't believe it was happening. Cleo didn't blame her. She felt the same way only she didn't have Frank's sweaty, hairy arms on her bare skin to remind her it was real life.

So their location was blown. Maybe some *Truth for Life* asshole found the shooter's body in the woods and raised the alarm. If they had, then they weren't far away. She didn't like to run but she didn't know how many they were up against. She probably had less than an hour to get everyone as far away from the motel as possible, if she could get Tanya away from Frank first.

"Is this about money?"

"It's always about money, money makes the world go round," he retorted, "I love money."

"Love of money is the root of all evil," she said.

"And you know that for a fact, do you, Agent Darkrose?"

"I know it to be fact, Frank. It makes good men do evil things, makes countries war, makes people easy to control. *We* know that," she said, "This world isn't run by Presidents or government, it's controlled by people whose wealth is incomprehensible in conjunction with agencies like mine. I've known it my whole life. If they told you that part, it's true."

Cleo watched him think about it. Those types always said the same thing. They knew there was an elite class controlling everything at the top tiers of society and they were right. Cleo had met them, been in their company as they discussed global matters, but she usually just attended meetings to bodyguard in a team for Number One.

Bilderberg meetings were the worst; pompous assholes strolling past her in reams as she stood by doors and looked on, bored shitless. *Truth for Life* people and other civilians were angry because they were the bottom feeders, the type standing outside the event with placards declaring the meeting was illegal. Frank shook it off, another mean look on his face as he pulled Tanya closer.

"Aren't you supposed to be talking me down, saving the hostage?"

"I might if I cared about civilians," she said. Unintentionally too flippant. She even felt Agent Starr give her a look.

"So it's true then, you're henchmen for the *Illuminati*?"

"Whatever that means nowadays. Civilians have made that word into a joke, so the majority ignore history and destiny. It would take too long to explain to you, so I'll make it simple. If you let Tanya go, you can join the *winning* side, Frank. You can have much more than what that caller promised you. There's so much more."

There. She'd tried to "talk him down." It looked like the slaves were only interested in money but what she'd said hadn't been all lies. Her education was one she knew conspiracy theorists would have lost their minds over. Their grasp of history was different to hers, much less detailed.

"I told you to put your gun down," Frank growled. He shoved the barrel of his gun into Tanya's ear and jerked her head to the side. Cleo's breath caught in her lungs. He didn't take the shot but cold hard metal slammed up against flesh fucking hurt. She hoped Tanya wasn't going to end up bleeding.

Julia appeared behind Frank, yelling to let Tanya go, gibberish shrieks that made Frank spin and fire a messy shot at her as he teetered on the edge of the stairs. Tanya was screaming too, the sudden move throwing her into hysterics.

Agent Starr bounded for the start of the staircase. Cleo armed the RavenEye and fired up into the bannister. It exploded loudly, shattered wood and splinters flying in all directions like sharp fireworks. More screaming from the civilians.

She hadn't been aiming for Frank, he was safe because she was worried he'd kill Tanya by accident as he went down. The bannister meant distraction then a clearer view when it was mostly in pieces on the ground. A hole the size of a bowling ball was missing out of the wood next to him.

Agent Starr was more than half way up the flight of stairs but he hadn't reached Frank in time, three stairs from the landing when Frank turned the gun on him. Cleo couldn't see Julia anymore, she was backed up away from the gunfire, probably closer to the rooms, but she was still pleading for Frank to let Tanya go. She wasn't hit, Frank's shot had missed her despite being almost point blank.

Frank shuffled on the landing, moving across to the right so he had a view of everyone. Cleo could have killed to have Julia's position, *would* have killed if she was standing in it. Julia had a direct line to Frank, all she had to do was wait until he was looking their way again and push him down the stairs. Fuck Tanya being in his grip, they'd sort that out when the two of them landed at the bottom.

Julia could do it. She'd gotten out of the car back in the woods, risked her life for her daughter's to move the vehicle out of range. Cleo hoped she got the idea to shove the bastard down the stairs in the next few seconds or she'd have to go to plan B or C...or D, whichever they were up to since the damn civvies had joined them.

Frank glanced between her and Agent Starr and back at Julia. His voice was shaky when he told Cleo to put her gun on the ground again. It was probably mostly because his hearing was fucked from the bannister explosion but he was going to lose it. He had no idea what to do next, going from moment to moment. She could see it on his face.

Cleo rounded the end of the stairs so Frank could see her better, so he wouldn't panic and hurt anyone. She put the safety on the RavenEye and dropped it. It rocked by her boots when it landed heavy on the ground.

"If you pick that gun up again, I'll shoot your boyfriend." Frank said.

"He's not my boyfriend," Cleo said, "That is Agent Trent Starr. He is a Double Banded Red Tag with MDS. He is much fitter than you—*faster*—than you. He will most likely leap the stairs to kill you very soon. If you're going to shoot at him...you'd better make sure you hit him."

Frank's face changed. He knew he wasn't a good shot. Missing Julia was proof and they all knew it. It was why Cleo had broken the rules and given the gun up in impish favour of drama. Agent Starr was letting her play, waiting for a cue. He looked calm, confident he wouldn't be shot, even while battling pain from the blow to the head earlier. He didn't mind that she'd just put him in the shit because she hadn't been lying, he wouldn't even find it a challenge to get up the last stairs, disarm and kill the guy.

Agent Starr put his boot up on the next step like he'd read her last thought. Frank cocked the gun in his hand but it was wavering. He barely knew what he was doing with the weapon, it almost looked too heavy in his meaty grip.

Cleo took small steps towards the stairs, staying wide of Agent Starr. Frank pointed the gun at her then back to Agent Starr quickly in some clumsy move that confirmed they had him. He couldn't shoot them both at the same time. If he couldn't hit Julia from two feet away, there was no way he was hitting anything vital even if he managed to get off a couple of shots at them.

"I'll let the girl go but you get up here instead," he said, motioning with his head to Cleo.

Well, that was a new one.

"And you," Frank said, "Lover-boy, you go down to the bottom."

Cleo trudged up the stairs while Agent Starr began walking down them, giving her a look on the way. Her eyes were on Frank alone. When she got to the landing, Frank shoved Tanya towards Julia and pointed the gun at her instead, mid-line level, solar plexus region. It wasn't great news but he had two hands on the gun now, an attempt to stop it shaking and control his aim as the two civilians fell over in the background, crying and carrying on.

Cleo put her hands up, open palms like she didn't want any trouble but she came forward until the end of the barrel was touching her chest. Frank's shock at the move was priceless before she grabbed the weapon for a twist and disarm. She swivelled her body side on to his, punching him in the face and forcing the gun to point to the floor but her right boot slipped off the landing. Balance was fucked and she was headed down the stairs, Frank still tight in her grasp.

Instinct contorted her body to throw him down before her as the stairs came up fast, the two of them face to face and rolling. Cleo smashed her right shoulder on the sharp edge of a step and Frank's weight jammed it harder. It felt like she'd torn it open but she didn't let go of him, hoping he'd cushion her landing. Either that or he'd crush her. She took her chances.

It hurt. She was tasting Frank's body odour and feeling his sweat splashed on her neck when they hit the floor. The RavenEye skidded to her left and Frank's gun was on the ground somewhere above her head. She lurched for the RavenEye, ready to fend Frank off if he recovered first, her lungs stunned by the impact and screaming for air when she made the move.

Her skull pounded hot shockwaves from the rebound off the floorboards and her ascent was probably slower than it felt but it was fast enough to make her guts churn while she rocked on her feet and waved Agent Starr away.

Frank was lying side on and breathing out angry snarls. She saw blood. His arm was broken and the bone had pierced the skin, a gruesome compound fracture needing medical attention she wasn't going to administer.

Agent Starr was at the top of the stairs with Julia and Tanya in moments, checking them for injuries and asking if they were okay. He let them cry and hug it out in front of him before he said her name like a question.

"I'm fine," Cleo answered. She didn't add the part about how her shoulder felt like it was shattered and grinding on the inside, "We have to get out of here."

Agent Starr nodded once and jogged down the stairs, jumping off the last few and mumbling something about clearing the parking lot. He looked at Frank when he headed towards the front door and paused like he was considering helping him. When Cleo followed his eyes she saw Frank holding his broken bone, passed out from pain or shock. Good.

22

JULIA AND TANYA WERE STANDING CLOSE TOGETHER half in a hug on the landing, practically holding each other up. Tanya was staring down the stairs at Frank like she'd never seen some big fat guy break an arm before and Julia was snivelling and wiping her nose on the sleeve of Agent Starr's MDS jacket in between stroking her daughter's hair.

The clean uniform Agent Starr brought in earlier had remained on the stairs halfway down, untouched like Cleo and Frank had got some air on their descent and somehow skipped over it. She wanted to change into it but she walked upstairs to Julia and Tanya instead, trying to keep her face neutral while her shoulder burned.

"What's happening, Cleo?" Julia sniffed. Her hair was sticking up and crazy like she was the one who'd rolled down the stairs. The woman was a *mess*.

"The motel owner was bribed to keep us here." Cleo said.

"Why? With what?"

"The *Truth for Life* movement offered him money. They know who I am and this location is compromised," she said, "We need to leave before they arrive here to kill us. We don't know how many there will be and we don't have time to ambush them adequately."

Julia pulled Tanya down the hall towards their room. Tanya struggled to keep up, limping and dragging her injured leg, crying that it hurt and it was supposed to be kept elevated. Cleo watched them with her back to the stairs, careful not to stand too close to the edge this time. She didn't know what they had left in their room, maybe just her MDS jacket that Tanya had been wearing and Julia's giant bag but they'd wanted to get their things.

Her shoulder felt like she'd stuck herself with a hot poker when she prodded it. It wasn't dislocated though and she was reasonably sure nothing was broken either but whatever she'd done made her less grateful that she hadn't landed completely on her head. Her skull was surprisingly nowhere near as sore. Her shoulder needed a cold-pack and rest to put out the fire under her skin. *Yeah, Red Tag, maybe you want a blanket and a pacifier with that.*

She stretched her arm out slowly, moving it in all directions to make sure she had full range of motion, listening to Tanya and Julia arguing about something in the other room as they searched for whatever belongings they didn't want to leave behind. It was fucking deja'vu. The two of them were all whispers and fast words again like in their house days earlier. It was all meaningless shit while Cleo assessed her grazed skin and impending bruises until she caught the word '*gun*' and felt her stomach drop. The gun. *Frank's gun. Fuck.*

Cleo turned and the staircase was empty, Frank wasn't crawling up in some vain attempt to slaughter them all but he wasn't lying on the ground where she'd left him either. His gun was also gone.

Cleo ran for the rooms, drawing the RavenEye and kicking open Julia and Tanya's door. They screeched when they saw her. Cleo pointed the RavenEye from the doorway, scoping the corners behind them and running her eyes over every piece of furniture. If there was anyone else in the room, they were dead. She didn't think the fat guy could have snuck past her but she didn't know if there were other ways up besides the main stairs.

Julia and Tanya watched with wide eyes and confusion. She turned side on so she could see out into the hall and reached down into her pocket with her right hand to search for her phone. Her shoulder protested, sending a scorching reminder she'd practically had it crushed only minutes before.

She dialled Agent Starr, switching her focus from the screen to the room and then hallway continuously, her eyes fighting to get used to one source of light then the other. Number One's office had always been the first speed dial, Agent Starr's number used to be the second...she'd have to go off memory and dial it in this time.

Cleo could hear the purr of the ringtone in the silence then he answered with *"Starr."*

Something about him not answering with *"Trent,"* or just *"Hey,"* made her think he'd deleted her number from his phone too and there was a pang of something that hit her in the guts and disappeared as quickly as it came on. Then the phone went dead, no hang up, not even a signal. She blinked at the screen a couple of times and shoved it back in her pocket. Whatever. She didn't need his ass anyway. Julia and Tanya were standing ready, waiting on her instruction.

"Out. Now." Cleo said.

Julia and Tanya passed a predictable glance between themselves and headed for the door slowly. Navigating them downstairs and out to the car was going to suck. Cleo pushed in front of them to take point and cleared the doorway then the landing, straining her eyes and forcing them to focus in the lowlight.

"You need to stay behind me," she told them, "You step into my footprints, *you do not speak, you do not lag behind.* Julia, put your hand on my right shoulder. Tanya, put your hand on Julia's. We move together."

There was no time now, anything left behind belonged to Frank, a souvenir. Cleo stepped towards the stairs again, feeling the stale air lick along her bare shoulders and arms with Julia and Tanya close behind, tentatively walking the path she'd just made. Her shoulder was stinging with the barely-there weight of Julia's hand but she couldn't have anything touching her left side and threatening to fuck up her aim or reflex with the RavenEye.

Wind howled softly around corners outside the building like something wanted them unnerved in every way possible. It stirred up gravel and leaves and made eerie moans tumble down some invisible xylophone and reach into every crack in the wooden walls. Lights flickered like a scene from an old horror film, taunting them and threatening to go out and leave them in complete darkness just in case they weren't anxious enough. Cleo cocked the RavenEye.

The weak lights dipped while they headed to the top of the stairs. Tanya whimpered when they dimmed for a few seconds too long. The kid was spooked. Cleo didn't like the situation either but the stairs were the only way down unless they wanted a two storey trip to the gravel outside when they jumped from a motel room window.

They were easy game from now on. No cover down the stairs or beyond. The plan was to gradually clear the stairs and end up in the lobby area where Frank had broken his arm. Then there would be two areas to watch; Frank could be hiding in the alcove with the bathrooms on the right, with a clear shot at them and it was also possible he'd be waiting in the reception area directly in front of the doors on the other side of the stairs.

Cleo put one foot down on the first step, sighting red smudges below where Frank had been lying. She looked over her shoulder and made eye contact with Julia, silently telling her to keep up and keep quiet because shit was dangerous and she couldn't predict the next few minutes. Then she began to descend the stairs with her terrified conga-line.

Julia's hand re-gripped her shoulder, the sharp pain enough to make Cleo flinch and hesitate the next step. They were moving awkwardly and unsure like a three-legged race. Only her team had six, trying not to make a noise or fall down the stairs.

It took Julia and Tanya a long time to place each foot down carefully. It had somehow become increasingly difficult since they'd realised Frank's body was missing. She'd felt the air change then and Tanya had even stopped walking for a moment. The brat was going to lose it if they didn't get to the car soon. Her breathing was coming in small quiet gasps like she was trying not to cry.

The lights dipped again when they reached the bottom of the stairs and stepped around smashed pieces of bannister. The alcove off to the right was empty. No fat man waiting to take their heads off from near the bathrooms as far as she could tell.

"The door." Cleo whispered over her shoulder.

Julia's eyebrows dropped low, her face tight and concentrated on getting her daughter out alive, committed to whatever Cleo was going to have them do. *That* part was still unplanned though, Cleo had to go first towards the front door and reception or bring up the rear and protect the civilians from the bathrooms side in case Frank showed up from that direction after all. *Dammit, Agent Starr.* It was a two-agent operation and he still hadn't returned from the parking lot.

Everything around them turned more than real, like walking through a life-sized pop out picture, bad guys about to jump out from every corner. It felt like the VR ranges at HQ, only Frank the fat-ass had *live* ammo and she couldn't just bail on the program and request the range be reloaded later when she actually felt up to running a gauntlet.

She pointed the RavenEye back towards the bathrooms then headed for the front door hoping that if Frank made an appearance he couldn't fire his gun on account of the broken arm. The RavenEye was armed and thirsty and didn't want to fuck around waiting anymore. Adrenalin started emptying buckets into her veins without permission, a thick and hard drumbeat that made her hands tingle and told her to make her move.

She could feel that low heavy feeling in her guts too. *Someone was going to die.* Her fingers re-gripped the gun and Frank pounced from the reception area with his mouth wide open, eyebrows high on his forehead. Cleo spun and fired. Julia screamed somewhere behind, begging her, *"Please don't use the RavenEye!"*

Frank's smashed arm burst. The RavenEye round caught it above the elbow and severed it halfway so it was hanging by threads of thick red meat. Cleo fired again and hit him in the same shoulder. It could have been a kill shot but she wanted him to know he was fucking dead—watch the unstoppable blood flow and see the flesh missing—*know* she'd hit an artery and he was going to bleed to death in his shithole motel.

He looked down surprised at the hole in his shoulder and the stretching red goop. Sometimes sudden trauma was too much for brains to register a limb had been partially blown to pieces. People only knew it when they saw it. Then it was a rush of everything all at once, the pain, the panic hitting worse than the actual RavenEye rounds.

Frank threw his head back and screamed then his eyes were on the blood spurting like a broken fountain. His eyes followed the path of blood in strange awe and he dropped his gun. Arterial spray hit the walls and splashed down on the floorboards but Frank chose not to search for a towel or a belt to make a tourniquet. He pulled a short knife from his pocket and ran at Cleo instead, his shoulder pumping his blood straight into the air.

Cleo tried to kick him away but it was stifled by his rolls of fat. His blood flicked across her cheek when he slashed with his mini blade, messy from the bloodloss.

Frank's charge backed Cleo up against Julia and Tanya, all of them stumbling to escape his reach when Cleo went to throw another push kick but she was stuck. Julia's arms were tight around her waist. *Frank was still coming at them with a blade!* Cleo wasted nanoseconds grabbing at Julia's hands, trying to prise them apart and keep hold of the RavenEye—*push the crazy bitch off so she could finish Frank*—but the damn woman's grip was too firm, hands may as well have been made of steel.

Cleo slammed her elbow back into Julia's chest and twisted, forfeiting balance for possible escape. They both fell. Cleo landed backwards on top of Julia, felt the air shoot out of the civilian's mouth against her neck when they hit the floor. Frank was still coming, looming over them yelling something about being a sacrifice to the Illuminati while his blood rained.

He would pass out soon—*had to*—but he was still holding a knife. He was staggering too close, yelling his nonsense and covering them in blood as someone else slammed through the front door behind him.

Cleo fired the RavenEye point blank. *Fuck it. She'd been covered in worse.*

The round tore from the gun and ripped through Frank's stomach, splashing them all with globs of flesh. He collapsed towards them with his blood spilling onto the ground near Cleo's boots like the holes in his body were vomiting at her. The smell of his ruptured stomach flooded the air.

Cleo held her breath for the second it took Frank to crash down between her legs, head landing on her left thigh right up near areas she'd rather have kept to herself. She looked for the next target in the shocked silence then Julia cried; *hysterical*, mashed together words and sounds and screams all coming at different pitches like there were five crazy bitches behind Cleo, not just one.

Frank was dead. Cleo didn't know how he'd lasted so damn long but his face was a mask of horror, frozen and staring ahead when she looked up and saw Agent Starr and not *Truth for Life*. His gun was on Frank, waiting for him to make another move while his eyes roved the scene.

Cleo stood up awkwardly and pushed Frank's head off onto the floor. She stepped around the blood, RavenEye still in her hand, speckled and sticky. Agent Starr shoved his gun away and cleared the distance to her in a second.

She watched the frown on his face as he looked for obvious injuries, checking the blood smears on her face and hands were only spatter and transfer. His jaw was gritted inside his mouth, hands cool from the air outside as he ran them over her arms and hands then her collarbone where a shitload of blood had landed. He stopped when she took a shaky breath in, his temperature clashing with hers and sending goosebumps over her skin.

"*What the hell is wrong with you? Check them.*"

She pushed him off and stepped around him to grab her clean uniform from the stairs and head for the front door. She didn't want to stick around while Agent Starr assessed Julia. She didn't need to see that shit.

She tried not to take full breaths as she crossed the floor. The smell coming off her shirt was making her gag already but she knew she wouldn't be able to get away from it, even out in the fresh air. It was already burying itself into every single thread in her tank top and through splashes of blood on her face and neck. Yeah, Frank had marinated her in a disgusting cocktail of blood and intestinal things that weren't coming out on Laundry Day.

Julia was standing behind the dead man on the floor when Cleo pushed open the door and glanced back. Agent Starr had an arm around her, his other hand on the back of her head, stroking her hair in some overly-close hug. She was still crying. *Loudly.* Her words were gibberish partly muted in his uniform, her face in his chest.

Agent Starr was looking at the bloody floor somewhere between Frank and Cleo before he snapped his head around and told Tanya to back up and not to come closer. Cleo could see her hanging around behind them, she had seen it all anyway. She'd just taken it with some kind of silent acceptance, better than her mother had. Maybe she was more mature than Cleo gave her credit for. Or maybe she just didn't need Agent Starr's attention as badly.

23

CLEO CAME UP QUICK JOGGING FOR THE DRIVER'S SIDE. Everyone else was already in the car. She hoped Agent Starr was in the back with Julia and Tanya or in the passenger's seat. She wasn't in the mood to fight over who was going to drive.

Dragging Frank's body out back to where the industrial sized bins were had been a huge pain in the ass. Actually, it had been a huge pain in the shoulder and she was damn tired. Dead weight was the worst. It never went where you needed it to. It had a mind of its own and even taunted you, purposely going the opposite way sometimes, moving without consequence. You couldn't hurt dead weight anymore, you couldn't threaten it or kill it when it defied you...but you could still kick the shit out of it in frustration.

Maybe she should have taken Agent Starr up on his offer, let him deal with Frank's shitty corpse instead and just guarded the civilians until he was back but she'd wanted more time inside the motel too. She'd taken the new uniform out to the car, made sure it didn't get dirty, then come back for it when the messy part was over and she'd moved Frank.

It was the standard female Red Tag uniform; wrap over Kevlar front and buckles and super-tough velcro down the side of the chest, complete with the double band on the right bicep to display her rank. Agent Starr had obviously searched hard through the rucks to find it. Points to him for that one because she had no fucking idea where she'd put it when they packed and it felt good to be wearing it, new and equipped for duty like Frank never happened.

No one spoke when she sat in the driver's seat but the feeling in the car wasn't tension this time. It was the come down, silent shock and inability to think about what was next. Julia and Tanya were sitting in some quiet hypnotised state staring ahead. Cleo was okay with letting them be zombies when she turned the key and stomped the accelerator.

Truth For Life people were on the approach and her team was still catching up the time lost in the woods chasing the shooter. It was why she'd dumped Frank's body near the bins like the piece of trash he was instead of making a welcome banner with his insides in the reception area for their pursuers.

"Why did you do that?" Nearly half an hour into the journey before anyone spoke and it was Julia. It wasn't the first thing Cleo wanted to hear.

"Why did *you*?" She snapped back.

Who the hell stopped someone from taking out a threat when it was headed right for them? *Frank had a fucking knife.* She looked in the rear view mirror and made eye contact with the angry civilian, challenging her to keep their exchange going or shut her giant mouth altogether.

"What happened to you to make you like this, Cleo?" Julia's words brimmed revulsion.

Cleo felt Agent Starr watching her from the passenger's seat, undoubtedly noticing Julia use her first name. It was his fucking fault she knew the damn thing in the first place and everyone was hanging on her response, seeing if she would take the bait. She kept driving with her eyes forward. It was only a few moments before she decided the best answer was probably none at all but she had something else for Julia.

"You knew what the RavenEye was called, you knew what it could do before I took the shot. I've never told you what it's called," Cleo said, "How do you know its name?"

"I didn't know."

"You shouted for me not to use it when I fired at the motel owner."

"I saw you use it before, on the stairs."

"No, you didn't see me fire into the staircase, it could have been Agent Starr who fired. You came out afterwards," Cleo said, "How did you know what *my* weapon would do? How do you know its name?"

Cleo took a sideways glance at Agent Starr. Yeah, she had his attention, one hundred percent. He was half turned in his seat, wearing suspicion on his pretty-boy face and wondering what she was getting at.

It seemed like they'd passed a million dark and moving trees. Everyone was gradually forgetting the conversation in favour of their bullshit thoughts but she and Julia kept meeting each other's gaze in the rear-view mirror and it didn't feel like it was over.

24

SAN FREEDOM LOOKED GOOD. Cleo wouldn't have lied if someone bothered to ask. She had even slid her sunglasses up over her hair to see it all in blinding technicolour as they approached. The water was visible at the far end of town when they drove up over a hill to cut through the city centre and head for the dock.

The road had transformed back to being lined with rocks after the motel and woodland then it was desert again like they were near home. The flat land towards San Freedom was dotted with a few diners along the way, taco caravans and then some giant crocodile-shaped sign Tanya had wanted pictures of before woefully remembering they'd confiscated her phone back at HQ. Bathroom breaks were minimal on the stretch and they were making better time than she'd expected so Cleo didn't complain about the brat's bitching.

Catching the edge of a step in her shoulder wasn't good. Cleo had stayed mostly silent on the journey, keeping the cold-pak from the back of the car resting on her injury until it turned warm. It was some kind of shock after it happened and she was lying at the bottom of the motel stairs surrounded by parts of the splintered bannister. She couldn't believe that fat pervert Frank had caused her an injury she was still carrying. She hadn't felt physical pain for a while, usually fast or smart enough to get out of the way. The result of the impact was some fiery throbbing reminder that she could still get hurt. The other damage sustained seemed to be an equally as bruised ego.

She'd pilfered an hour or so sleep after she and Agent Starr switched places and he drove but the poor bastard had to be more than exhausted now. His eyes were bloodshot testimony, and not just because he'd forgotten the sunglasses he usually had glued to his face. She gave him a moment when they stopped the car, let him shake it out and stretch then instructed him to walk a perimeter and back into town for recon; a three hundred metre radius in every direction but the water.

The wooden dock extended out from the mainland in a hollowed out rectangle, nothing in the centre so people had to walk around the empty space on a boardwalk or fall into the water if they wanted to get to the furthest point on the pier. The wood was wide enough for them to park the car on the far edge to be close to the MDS boat when it arrived but it meant being vulnerable to attack from either side while they waited and it left the only escape to be the water if they got trouble.

Moving the car to that position was something Cleo planned to do only right before the MDS boat docked in case SpadeMan's *Truth for Life* people caught up. Until then, it was going to sit on the mainland by all the broken down kiosks and fishing nets, *mostly* blending in despite the bullet impacts and dents from the night in the woods.

She cleared the dock before allowing Julia and Tanya to exit the vehicle because there weren't many people; two middle-aged Mexican men fruitlessly casting rods from the edges of the dock by a handful of other non-descript younger civilians sitting in the sun. All were unarmed and barely noticing her or the others, favouring low-level unrelated conversation she only caught snippets of. Good.

According to the POD, they had three and a half hours to kill before the MDS charter's ETA, which had surprised her given all the delays, and things were calm but it was a fucking long time to be sitting ducks out in the open. Yeah, it was sort of her fault. She'd just wanted them to be a dot on the horizon since Frank told her about the phone call he'd received. She'd freaked when she'd learned they were co-ordinated, those *Truth for Life* suckers, having a guy in the woods and then another group approaching the area. She didn't put it past them to make the distance and catch up in San Freedom.

She'd always found it interesting when civilians had the clout to recruit bounty hunters and general assholes who wanted opportunities to put bullets in people's heads for money. She used to have some naive notion it was only agencies like hers who had that kind of power but domestic terrorists were proving all the time that they were improving tactics and worldwide contacts. There were many people around the world who hated her country and those who they perceived ran it. Hell, it was why she was taking one of them out as soon as she arrived in Menas.

Cleo breathed in salty air and let it out slowly, observing the old boats swaying and bobbing nearby and below the boardwalk, all moored and surrounded by bright blue. She just needed to keep the civilians happy and alive for three hours, *easy.* She could do that in a place like this with sun reflecting off ripples and flashing silver gleam as small waves broke on the wooden supports holding up the pier. Yeah, civilians liked days like this, the smell and air and scenery. They'd soak it up and behave until the boat arrived.

Julia and Agent Starr were standing beyond the dock and car, on the mainland back near the kiosks and a hotdog stand that made up the edge of town. Tanya was close by, eating something out of a paper bag and throwing pieces to gulls that had ventured away from the water. A family of four people walked by them cutting her line of sight for a moment, holding hands and laughing like a living postcard. Well, shit.

Cleo didn't have the thigh rig attached and the RavenEye wasn't in plain sight, lodged in the waistband of her pants. Agent Starr wasn't armed either, at least not visibly. She tried to pretend she didn't have her weapon at all, wondered if she would have fit in without the gun and uniform, looking like everyone else hanging out on the dock. Fuck, he did it so well.

Julia was talking to him in the shade under the hotdog stand awning, only just close enough that she could see they were both eating and smiling. They looked like some couple out with their kid. The only odd thing was Agent Starr's uniform, stark black and standing out in the midst of all the colour and shades of white and blue but the admiration they had for each other was clear, even at a distance. It made everything else flatten into the background.

Julia touched his arm when he laughed. Her hand lingered for a few seconds longer than it probably needed to and he smiled down at her like they were lovers. It was another element to the assignment that was a first, besides escorting civilians. Cleo had never had to work with some lovesick, horny partner before, never had to work so closely with an ex-boyfriend and watch him flirt with someone else while she tried to act the way a Red Tag should and keep them all alive.

25

AGENT STARR TOOK OFF THE MDS SHIRT facing the back of the car because Tanya had spilled icecream on it. Cleo didn't ask. He'd laughed it off, said he didn't mind, that he'd been a lot dirtier before but Cleo knew he also didn't want to meet the crew on the MDS charter looking like a slob. Chances were they would have heard of him and he probably wanted to match his reputation. She didn't hold it against him.

The civilians had spent time eating and exploring the dock, all in her line of sight as commanded, without argument. Cleo was hanging back while she pushed the POD in a pocket after her latest check on the ETA for the boat told her they had two hours left. Julia's eyes hadn't wavered, stuck on Agent Starr as he removed his clothes. She watched the muscles in his back and shoulders catch the sunlight when he reached into the back of the car for another shirt.

The chain from his ID tags was visible on the back of his neck sitting above some other necklace on a thin black cord. It was against the rules to wear any jewellery besides MDS ID tags and Cleo couldn't help her eyes roll. She'd remind him of the rule when the others weren't around but what was the fucking point? He'd done worse in the last twenty four hours.

Her attention flitted back to Julia when she heard stifled laughter. Her eyes were still scanning Agent Starr like he was edible, they went to his ass and up to his biceps and back again. Tanya nudged her then the two of them giggled some more.

Yeah, Cleo got it. Agent Starr was good to look at, only she'd done more than look. She'd touched, tasted and bought the t-shirt. Her pocket buzzed on cue, saving her from any other mortifying thoughts to follow the last one; the POD was updating with new content. She pulled it out and squinted, holding the compact up to her face to try and make out the screen.

It wasn't good news. Cleo read the words, "*approaching your current location*" in between the flashes and reflecting glare. She guessed Frank had been right, *Truth for Life* wanted them dead so she didn't get to SpadeMan's rally and seminar and stop him detonating his bomb...and they had caught up.

She felt the weight of everyone's stare while she digested their new reality. Agent Starr was facing her and pulling his new shirt on, Julia and Tanya were statues with eyebrows raised and expecting the explanation to send them into familiar panic. Cleo didn't have to say anything when she made eye contact with Agent Starr. He went around to the other side of the car to get his rifle bag without a word.

When he appeared again he was carrying the bag like it weighed nothing, walking past Julia and Tanya with no acknowledgement, like someone had put up a curtain between them. *MDS CA mode.* He came towards Cleo quickly, wide strides and eyes only on hers.

"ETA?"

"Apparently we have approximately ninety minutes before a contingent of the *Truth for Life* movement arrives," she said, "Intelligence says they know I'm here, that means–"

"They'll be armed to the teeth and trigger-happy like camel jockeys on New Year's," he murmured. Military slang picked up while he was overseas maybe. He kept skimming the dock with his eyes, over and over, looking for someone who may have identified them and called the enemy.

"You'd better be careful," he said, "I'm going to set up on the perimeter, play lookout for a while. It's all we can do until the transport gets here."

Cleo nodded once and he did the same, goodbye and good luck, then he walked away fast, rifle bag swaying as he moved, handles wound around his right wrist. He didn't look back. Their partnership had to split, like the old days when they were on an assignment together. Whatever he did on the perimeter was his business as long as he backed her up. Whatever she was going to do to safeguard the civilians was hers.

She watched his back until his form wavered in the heat coming off the cement further up near the hotdog stand. Julia and Tanya were standing where he left them, still waiting for her to relay what was going on, what they had to do to stay alive *this* time.

Cleo reread the content in the POD and scrolled down. Spademan's *Truth for Life* movement had paid their way through some telco's satellite roaming system and triangulated Cleo's position using the GPS in the car. *Stupid.* She knew GPS wasn't scrambled when they were away from MDS airspace unless requested. It wouldn't have been hard to snatch the info out of the air.

Number One hadn't been kidding, SpadeMan knew his shit. He had money and enough supporters to make things happen. Not all domestic terrorists could obtain explosives like he had. Agent Hooper and Stone being in on it shouldn't have surprised her when she found them dying in the truck. SpadeMan was ex-MDS, he was able to infiltrate their minds, knew what to say to twist the truth. Even Agent Starr had considered some of his group's theories while he was deployed in the Middle East. They were dangerous.

Cleo walked to the car and started pushing rucks and bags around inside. She was looking for something besides shit-tasting MREs and Adonai, and when she found it, she was going to have to get it out past her civilians without them seeing and asking their prying questions. She knew what Julia would think and she didn't want a repeat of the earlier freakout, bitch had arms of steel.

"Get in the car," Cleo's voice came out typically low and ominous and she didn't turn to look at Julia and Tanya. She waited, bent over and leaning into the car, until they decided she was talking to them and did as they were told.

She couldn't take any chances now. SpadeMan knew how MDS worked, that Red Tags were highly regarded and permitted to do things their way, operate solo or with little help. He knew she was mostly on her own. Frank had told her back at the motel that the people coming knew who she was. Well, she was going to show them what that meant, just who they were fucking with. You didn't try and take on Cleo Darkrose. Things had changed since SpadeMan was serving and she was fucking untouchable.

26

CLEO'S BOOTS SQUELCHED IN GROWING POOLS ON THE DOCK. The brightness made it a vastly different dimension to the dull pungency of seawater and bird shit underneath. She hated getting wet. It was almost the worst thing in the world and standing there with a damp uniform sucked. Besides taking a shower and drinking, water was unnecessary and she avoided it. She liked the sand and heat of the desert. Go figure.

There wasn't much space between the pier and the water but they'd managed to put another jetty directly below the one on top so people could moor their smaller boats and fish from another beam perilously close to the water. The whole structure had strong steel girders keeping it all up but it was just wood and it was perfect for placement...

Gold had C4-like properties; plastic based, almost mouldable. A pack usually came with sixteen blocks and detonators, plus the remote. All she had to do was press a button to start the timer, wait forty five minutes then a current would build and the first detonator could blow. Gold would convert to compressed gas and produce a big-ass shockwave to tear through anything around it and send it sky-high.

She'd hung like she was busting out a chin-up to place the Gold blocks on the higher girders underneath, consequently only her boots and pants were wet from spray bouncing off the supports. The sublevel adventure had also seen her drop her fucking cell phone in the water too. Relying on barely-there upper body strength since her shoulder injury had been hard and the phone had been scrunched into a ball in her pocket and then rolled out when she climbed back up top. Losing it posed a whole new set of problems but the main thing was the *POD* had survived and it was probably more important.

She passed the two men fishing and the group of people nearby still sitting and watching gulls lazily skim the water but there were fewer civilians around than before. It looked like all the fun had happened and it was time to head home. Or they'd somehow felt the anticipation Cleo did and bailed on the joint before shit went down.

It was almost 16:00 when she checked her watch again. Being under the docks making placement ate time, the MDS charter was supposed to be there now. It should have come up while she was underneath and swinging on the girders like a wounded monkey but she couldn't even see it on the horizon, nothing to do with the tint in her sunglasses. The MDS team was late and that meant trouble.

Agent Starr wasn't back either. She couldn't call to inform him that they were on their own until the MDS charter arrived, *Truth for Life* approaching and, oh yeah, she'd pressed for detonation the moment she'd placed the Gold thinking they'd tell the locals in the area to get the fuck out and then be long gone. It was all going to go up in under forty five minutes and blow a sizable hole in the whole waterfront.

Tanya was strapped in the backseat when Cleo got to the car, nodding her head to some garbage civilian song on the radio. Julia was up front in the passenger's seat hunched over reading a small notebook. Cleo approached her side, seeing her do a double-take then start frowning down and reading furiously. Oh. She didn't want Cleo seeing the contents of her notebook, trying to get as much out of it as possible before she had to put it away.

"What's that?" Cleo shot a fake smile when she stood by Julia's window. The glass was all the way down, she could have stood on her toes and looked over into the car if she wanted.

"They're notes on clients of mine. I'm a clinical psychologist, I help people who have personality problems," Julia flipped the notebook closed, maintaining eye contact while she spoke.

"Personality problems?" Julia must have had it on her since they left her house, stashed in her oversized bag of clothes and photos. If it had made it past security, then she'd hidden the notebook during screening. Hidden things posed risk to MDS.

"I help people with disorders," Julia said, "people who need help dealing with things that have happened to them."

"Do you think I have a personality disorder?"

Julia swallowed, hooked and ready to spill her opinion. Cleo put her hands on the window frame to listen.

"I told you I know all about you and that's what I meant. I think you've been through a lot in your life and it's changed who you are," Julia said.

"Changed me from what to *what*?"

"You're an agent...cold, aggressive, dominant but maybe years ago you were a young woman not so jaded. Someone who had sincere feelings and was warm and–"

"You're wrong," she told Julia slowly, "I'm just an agent. I've always been just an agent, beginning to end."

"Well, that may be so but there are things you can't fake or change, things we all have inside us as human beings. Feelings like regret, curiosity..."

"What about them?" Cut the shit, lady.

"You're not *'just an agent'* because I can see them in you when you look at Agent Starr."

Great.

Cleo looked away then back again and snatched the notebook. It was outside the car in less than a second. Julia had been a good little civilian and locked the car door as told so she wasn't fast enough to reach for it back. She kept her eyes on it in Cleo's hands, making sounds, half words like a baby, excuses and reasons.

Cleo backed up away from the car and opened to a random page. The handwriting was small with some sections highlighted in fluorescent marker and messy words scribbled sideways in the margin. She pushed her sunglasses up over her hair and squinted. Her eyes watered, shocked at the brightness and refusing to focus until she saw her name in a sentence halfway down the left page. It was surrounded by a handful of other scrawled words but there it was; *Darkrose.*

Julia had her car door open now, leaning out gingerly and trying to find words to explain. She slid out and started walking towards Cleo, shrugging with her arms out and rambling excuses. Cleo backed up again out of Julia's reach, a bully with another school kid's lunch money.

The writing mentioned customized weapons, the RavenEye and others. The next page listed martial arts and fight techniques written in a long list going down the page. She'd trained them all off and on over the years, and someone thought it was a big enough deal to document.

She turned the page to a hand-drawn picture of a woman's body next, front view on the left, back view on the right. Circles looped various areas with lines coming from them, the same untidy handwriting describing knife wound scars and the bullet impacts; a bullet scar on the left shoulder blade, knife scar on the back of the right hip and a pellet scar on the left calf.

Cleo couldn't stop herself looking to Julia for the explanation. All the wounds on the sketches matched the ones on her body. Whoever had drawn the diagrams had either spent a lot of time around her to notice the scars on different occasions...or they had seen her naked.

"What is this? Does this belong to Agent Starr?"

She was holding the notebook out in front, keeping her voice calm like it wasn't creepy as fuck. There was *no way* Julia could have accurately depicted her injuries and scars...and absolutely no way she could have known about the fighting styles.

"This is how you knew what my weapon was going to do the other night." Cleo said.

She flipped to another page halfway through the book and she was staring at a well-drawn diagram of the RavenEye, complete with point form notes and specs about the gun. It detailed structural angles, the velocity it fired at and how many years MDS had provided its Red Tags with the weapon at the time the notes were written.

She looked at Julia again for an answer, a raring lioness and a gazelle in the brush. Cleo wanted to pounce, rip her to shreds for not only knowing the information but having the nerve not to turn it in. She was doing her a favour, getting her and her brat daughter to safety and Julia was reading up on her from secret notes written in a sick diary by some pervert.

"Yes, that's how I knew about the RavenEye. It's the reason I told you I knew about you," Julia said.

Cleo didn't look when Agent Starr approached them with his packed up rifle bag. He said something about his phone being killed by Number One and he couldn't use it to call anyone or some shit. Cleo didn't bother acknowledging him. He'd get his turn when she was done with Julia.

"Did Agent Starr give this book to you?" She pressed.

Agent Starr didn't answer for Julia. He stood watching the scene confused for a moment then with quiet confidence he'd done nothing wrong. *Fucking infuriating.* Julia didn't look at him for a cue before she answered either.

"He didn't give me the book. It was my husband's, it belongs to Alan Pierce. *SpadeMan*," she said, "He had a few of them, about different agents. He didn't make them digital, said they were less likely to be hacked or stolen this way. He told me to take them to independent news stations if he was ever in this situation."

"Is that what you plan to do?"

"No, I just wanted to read it."

"The pages show he's been documenting my life for a long time."

"He probably knew they'd send you after him one day because of your status."

"Did you have this with you back at HQ?"

"Yes. I had a few in my bag, he wrote about all the prominent agents...but I threw the rest away," Julia's eyes were on the ground, "I kept that one, I hid it when I knew your name."

Cleo pushed the book into Agent Starr's hard stomach and shoved him as she passed. She was done. Anger was pulsing so hard through her veins she wanted to punch someone in the face. She settled for pulling her dark sunglasses over her eyes so no one else could see the look in them. *Fucking civilians, the slaves!* She marched to the back of the car, picked up the thigh rig and headed for the pier. Her left fist clenched up like it was craving the RavenEye.

She didn't know what she was going to do when she reached the middle of the pier where she'd climbed up earlier. She wanted to run, get the hell out of there as she stepped dangerously close to the edge. Was she going to jump? Swim far, far away and forget the assignment ever happened? Fuck, she hated water. She still had a one hundred percent success record to maintain too. She breathed out until it hurt, then strapped the thigh rig back into position, clipped it up on her belt and tried not to kick the shit out of something nearby.

Agent Starr called out a few moments later. He was jogging up, eager to be the voice of reason as usual, probably wanting to enlighten her with some Buddhist philosophy or quote; things were going to be okay, what Julia had done was no big deal in the grand scheme of things. But SpadeMan's *Truth for Life* people were coming, the MDS charter hadn't arrived yet, and the place was rigged to blow. They had to be away from the dock within the next twenty five minutes or—*kaboom*—civilian confetti.

Agent Starr appeared beside her looking over the view in silence. The MDS charter would come from the right, doing a circular route from Menas, to pick them up and take them back but he wasn't watching for a boat. He was just watching the gulls, taking in the scene like they had hours to waste. It was at least a full twenty seconds before he spoke.

"Did you read the whole book?"

"I didn't have to," she said.

"I destroyed the pages about Number One's office."

"There were pages about Number One's office?" She looked at him and back to the water.

"Yeah, a few, mostly the location at HQ and the clearance needed to get up there."

"That's–"

"So classified it's not funny."

"Yes," she agreed.

"This guy made a lot of notes. Julia says there are about five more books like that, written on other Red Tags."

"On you?"

"She doesn't know...but it seems I'm mentioned quite a lot in yours, as it were," he said.

"Great."

"Yeah. There's even a hardcopy of one of our relationship permission slips pasted in there, the ones we had to carry around when we were–"

"*I know the ones.*"

Agent Starr took a few steps back from the edge, almost out of her periphery but he was still looking at her. The weight of that bright green stare had always been damn heavy. She kept her eyes ahead on the water through her dark sunglasses, willing him to go back to the car.

"It was your half of the permission slip," he said.

"It was? I wouldn't know, I lose things."

"Yeah, it's yours. I still have mine," he added, "Took it with me."

She looked over her shoulder before she could stop herself, glad she was wearing sunglasses so he couldn't read her eyes. He took the permission slip with him...*over there, to the Middle East.* He'd taken it *with* him, over deserts and oceans, kept it through blood, combat, injury.

She hoped he didn't say anything else because her face felt hot and she had nothing but unease. He gave it another second then just shrugged and started walking away. She watched him go, unable to turn back to the water, pushing for focus on other things before she was stuck in the moment any longer.

"They're in danger, Agent Starr. We need to be out in the water in fifteen minutes, max," she said, "You need to find a vessel for us. Now."

27

AGENT STARR RAN FOR THE CAR LIKE A START GUN HAD GONE OFF, despite the probable throbbing from her blow to his head the night before. He'd recognised the tone in her voice and moved his ass with no indication he was in pain. Good for him.

Cleo followed, thoughts coming faster now. She'd been stupid to squander the lead they'd had on a tantrum about Julia's book of secrets. So the woman had a handwritten dossier on her, it didn't matter. It was just reaffirmed documentation of how dangerous Cleo could be if Julia didn't follow her instructions. The stuff with Agent Starr and the permission slip had to wait.

They had to get the civilians on a boat with the rucks, the ammo and anything they were going to need or shouldn't leave behind, including the NovaRose data. Fifteen minutes probably wasn't enough time to get it all out in a boat and far enough so they wouldn't be hit with debris when the dock blew but she wasn't turning back to go through the city. She wasn't going to miss SpadeMan's seminar because she'd run in the wrong direction. The only option *was* to push forward.

Agent Starr flung open the driver's door and Cleo jumped into the passenger's side right after. She hadn't told him about the Gold but apparently she didn't need to because the car was moving before her ass hit the seat. He jerked the wheel to the right and accelerated to an instant barrage of questions launched from the backseat. Julia and Tanya fired them one after the other, getting louder, more panicked as they watched the scenery whizz by.

The water came up nightmare-fast, like they were going to go over.

Cleo kept her back up against the seat, hoped the others didn't notice the look on her face. *Dammit, Agent Starr.* He screeched the car around, side on to the edge and stopped, leaving a couple of feet between Cleo's side of the car and the edge of the dock. When he turned it off he glanced over the scene for an easy target, some boat that wouldn't take him long to jack.

Small boats were moored from the second level, five all grouped together, matching white paint peeling under the sun. It didn't matter which one they chose or who was going to be behind the wheel. The MDS charter boat still hadn't arrived and they couldn't sit on a rigged-up pier and wait. Cleo wasn't going to call it a mistake yet, but she shouldn't have relied on their boat to get there on time. She'd bet all their lives on it.

Agent Starr pulled up the brake and swung the door open. It meant Cleo had to get Julia and Tanya organised, make sure they understood they had to move their fucking ass unless they wanted to die. The middle-aged fishermen watched her bark orders for the civilians to grab the rucks and supplies when she jumped out and went to the back of the car.

She pushed her sunglasses on top of her head to see inside when the back doors were open and moved the lightest bags to give to Julia and Tanya. Julia was wearing Agent Starr's jacket again, zipping it higher when she came up even though it was hot out. Cleo held out the bags so she would stop fucking around but she kept her head down, focussed on prying the zip further so Tanya pushed in front of her, hands out for Cleo to pass her the bags instead.

They were across the dock in seconds, faster than Cleo thought possible, bags and all. The civilians did it without protest too, clutching the rucks and cases awkwardly and looking over their shoulders like they expected they were in immediate danger. They were, but it would be friendly fire if they got hurt now, Cleo's fault. The Gold was strapped to the beams below and ticking away into final countdown.

When they got to the edge of the dock Agent Starr was a few feet lower, standing in some boat that was barely going to fit all four of them and the junk from the car but he had control of it. Hey, she'd take what she could get. He stood unnervingly stable while it bounced in the water, balancing effortlessly, like some sort of man-cat *thing* watching them come over. Julia pulled Tanya towards the edge first so she could drop her bags down to Agent Starr and Cleo brought up the rear.

The boat was small and white, short walls coming up a little past Agent Starr's shins. The controls were all within reach of the passengers and only protected from the elements by some window shield that wrapped around the front of the boat and halfway down the sides. The thing had no seats, just a damp floor. Cleo read the words "*El Pato,*" faded and half-eaten away on the side. Yeah, that sounded about right. She wondered if Agent Starr had read it. If he had, he'd chosen not to risk her wrath by laughing about it.

The engine was already started, moorings unattached when Cleo dumped her stuff on the edge. Agent Starr reached up and took the bags from Tanya then Julia, catching them and throwing it all behind him on the deck to repeat the same motion for the rest. Then he helped Julia over the watery drop into the boat.

Cleo headed back to the car for the last of it. She had to pick up two bags, her shoulder rig and M9 and the POD. Agent Starr's rifle bag was still on the backseat and the hard drive with NovaRose data and the two folders—*the formulas to make an airborne bio hazardous death-bomb*—were underneath the driver's seat. She had to get that damn thing too. It was going to be at least two trips, probably three.

She could hear Tanya whining to Agent Starr that it was impossible to jump the distance to the boat with her leg all shot up as she grabbed the shoulder rig and gun and then the POD while the dispute went on behind her. She shoved it all in her deep pockets, some of it half hanging out when she walked back to the edge with the other bags in her hand.

Agent Starr's face was calm as if Tanya wasn't annoying the shit out of him, like he'd been ready for the brat's drama. He didn't shield his eyes from the glare or act like being in a strained position, hands out waiting to catch her, was taxing while she danced around trying to convince herself to jump.

Cleo made the call to shove Tanya off the pier if she didn't jump in the next few seconds but she did. She sat down on the wooden precipice then scooted right to the edge and pushed herself off into Agent Starr's arms down on the boat, leaning on him hard to get stable when it rocked violently and threatened their balance.

Cleo dropped the gun and rig into the boat and passed the last of the bags to Agent Starr one by one. The second one was heavy and she got to her knees to lower it to him. He missed the strap and grabbed her hand instead, eyes lit by reflections off the water and surrounding hulls. She could see herself mirrored in his pupils, bordered by impossible green...then his face changed.

Loud cracks popped and echoed across the dock. *But it was too early for the Gold!* No, they would know if *that* was happening, there wouldn't have been time to think before Hell unleashed. She looked at her watch and detonation still wasn't for another ten minutes. The sound was gunfire.

She dropped the last bag and threw herself backwards, rolling on her shoulder and landing up against the passenger's side wheel of the SUV. She pulled the RavenEye. Agent Starr was low in the boat now. She couldn't see him but she heard him yell for Julia and Tanya to lie on the floor. Then he called her name, "*Agent Darkrose.*" When he stood up again she could just see his face and neck before the edge of the dock blocked her view. He was gesturing for her to run back to the boat, looking like he was struggling to breathe.

She didn't know what his issue was. His rifle was in the car, he was going to want that back. *More shots.* Cleo pushed herself up harder against the tyre. She still didn't know where they were coming from. That was a problem. She didn't look at Agent Starr anymore.

She heard him say her name again as she reached up to open the car door and pulled herself into the seat. She left the door open, didn't want a limb blown off when she got the hard drive and the rifle then ran for the boat. The passenger door panel meant slightly less exposure before the jump, or so the logic went.

The shots were coming from four guys approaching in front of the car, handguns out and live. They were civilians as far as she could tell, wearing baggy pants and tank tops and no body armour. Clichéd wannabe-gangster types in it for whatever money they'd been paid. Their lame-ass look didn't make them less dangerous though. They were still there to kill and Cleo knew enough not to mess with loaded guns she wasn't behind.

The civilians remaining in the area were running with their hands in the air and screaming. She couldn't see the ones in the shops and the hotdog stand further back, everything looked dead and closed up. The two fishermen were now hobbling towards her car to hide, looking over their shoulders in terror.

The gunmen were walking in a V formation, maximising their shooting range and looking like they were trained. She doubted they were, but they were already firing precise shots at other people, taking them down as if it wasn't against civilian law and they weren't going to be caught; systematically blasting holes in other humans like they had time to create as much carnage as possible.

More armed civilians joined them from behind out of nowhere then broke off into groups and headed into the buildings lining the edge of town. It was like watching marching ants pouring out from every alcove and corner. Some of them shot at gulls but most went after people already fleeing. Weren't the *Truth for Life* movement supposed to be against the government and agents, not other civilians? Maybe the blood-thirsty gaggle of psychos hadn't got the memo. It was a short thought before Cleo ducked down in the car when she figured she was in range.

"*Cleo,*" Agent Starr said, "Let's go, come on."

She reached across the driver's seat to the floor. The NovaRose hard drive and folders were there somewhere. The RavenEye felt bulky, almost unfamiliar in her right hand as she searched for the hard drive with her left. When her fingers ran over a smooth plastic corner she grabbed it up awkwardly and put it on the driver's seat.

The gunmen were running towards the car when she stole another look. It was too late to move to the boat without being noticed but if she could get the shit out of the car in the next few seconds, she'd risk the gunfire and spring for the boat. If not...well, Agent Starr and the others had to leave without her. And if *that* happened she was going to turn the car on and drive straight for the *Truth for Life* gangsters, flatten them all and hope she could keep going so the Gold wouldn't blow her up too.

When the Gold went up it was going to be a National Incident for sure. Number One would be *pissed.* But she'd wanted to send a message to SpadeMan, Alan Pierce—*whatever his name was*—that he couldn't fuck with Cleo Darkrose. *She was MDS,* she hadn't abandoned her post like he had, she believed in the greater good, like Number One said...Her message was just going to be a little more dramatic than she'd originally anticipated.

"*Cleo?*" Agent Starr sounded too uneasy, "Forget the hard drive. What are you doing?"

She squeezed half her body through the space between the front seats to reach the back. The handbrake dug her hip when she leaned, trying to keep an arm free to fire the RavenEye while she pulled up the rifle bag. She didn't know if she'd get it over the console in the centre, the angle was shit and she was already risking her ass by having her back to the action.

She yanked the straps on the bag but it didn't come up. Fourteen kilos on a smashed shoulder wasn't going to work. Her muscles waged war when she tried again, painful twinges in her neck sharp enough to make her gasp and drop her grip on the straps.

Another look over her shoulder told her the gunmen were even closer. She could make out their ugly faces now. The two fishermen darted in front of the car and blocked her view, yelling at her in Mexican, commanding her to start the engine but they caught a bullet each and dropped past her vision before she could respond.

She turned for the bag again, twisting her body further this time, using both hands and throwing the RavenEye near her knees on the passenger's seat the same time a round hit the car and cracked the already-compromised windscreen. *Fuck. Come on.*

More shots to the front of the car. She'd been seen. The bulletproof glass splintered and tried to hold off an onslaught one last time then it burst inwards with firework patterns, blocking most of the view and shedding tiny daggers of glass before it shattered over her back. She made a final grab for the rifle bag before she saw numbers light up the watch on her wrist. Detonation was imminent. *It was over.*

Time had run out and between her and her watch, she'd just made the decision of a lifetime. No getting the gear to the boat now. The only option was to start the car, mow down the assholes coming for her and hope to make it off the dock before the Gold exploded and hurled pieces of buildings and boats in her direction.

She hoped Agent Starr got their boat away from the dock, out of range of the gunfire and debris, when he heard her start the engine. The civilians were in danger and so was he. Paranoid gangsters and an impending explosion, if Agent Starr hadn't left when she looked back the next time, she was going to find it hard not to fucking shoot him herself.

Three more rounds hit the car, one after the other—*big caliber this time*—rocking the car as she swivelled to face the front again. Two more rounds blasted the open door. Another big one hit low. Cleo smelled fuel instantly. *Fuck no.*

Nine gunmen were headed right for the car in that same controlled V shape, eleven men and women marched behind them like reinforcements. They were a makeshift army with Special Forces-looking gear they shouldn't have had access to. She didn't know how they knew to walk like that either but they'd known enough to hit the fuel tank and she was fucked.

Frantically twisting the key in the ignition wasn't helping. Juice was gushing out the bottom of the car, spreading over the dock like a dark wave. The smell dominated the air. There was no way the car was going to move with a severely ruptured tank even if she was stupid enough to keep trying. She caught herself and breathed out slow. It really was game over, even with the RavenEye. There were only so many rounds in a magazine, not enough for everyone coming for the car.

The NovaRose hard drive. It couldn't end up with the *Truth for Life* movement, she had to use the RavenEye to destroy it. When she shot it to pieces, the rounds would penetrate the seats and go beyond. The car was going to go up in flames and take her with it, then Gold would vaporise everything else. She breathed in and felt it shiver on the way out. The notion felt like it drained the blood from her limbs. She was dizzy watching the gunmen approach the car, seeing the sweat shimmer on their faces and specks of dirt being thrown up from the ground as they ran.

She reached for the RavenEye on the seat, grabbing nothing a few times before she looked down. Her gun was gone. Agent Starr was standing outside the car, behind the door, a tall black figure suddenly just *there,* like an angel of death.

He held her RavenEye in his right hand and opened fire. Time faltered. She watched it in some kind of slow motion, following his long arm down to his hand and seeing the recoil slam the gun back into his palm and bounce out again. He wasn't wearing a Firing Glove, his arm shuddering violently with the kick.

His face was blank as he fired again and again. His rounds hit targets fluently, clean head shots with incredible precision, taking men and women to the ground. The couple that missed were kill shots to the chest. He was Deleting anyone who had them in range and anyone with guns pointed in their direction, skilled enough not to take out random civilians in the crossfire. His aurora eyes were lifeless, tranced and cold. Sadly beautiful in the chaos.

Shots peppered the door panel, denting it and threatening to rip through metal into his flesh and she wondered how long the vehicle could stand another barrage of gunfire. She was slow to realise his left arm coming towards her and yanking her from the seat but she went with the motion, his grip too tight to resist even if she'd wanted. She held the hard drive and folders tight as she slid from the car and he moved so she could pass behind him and head for the boat. You didn't argue in certain situations, even if you were *Double Banded, Red Tag Agent Cleo Darkrose.*

She jumped the gap between the dock and the boat and hoped it didn't seesaw Julia and Tanya into the water when she landed. Julia was reaching out to her, still lying on the floor, asking if she was okay while she held the hard drive up and made sure it didn't hit the deck or bounce into the water.

Agent Starr was on the edge of the pier behind her, one hand low with the rifle bag twisting in his grip, the other firing cross-body at the last few *Truth for Life* gangsters with the balls to still be running towards them.

He made it onto the boat and landed in a squat, dumping the bag and the RavenEye and messily running for the controls. Cleo fell backwards, rolling into Julia and Tanya as the boat cut the water and took off threatening to tip them all out.

Agent Starr turned back and watched her trying to find her balance, on all fours attempting to get to her feet and pathetically losing the battle. He looked anxious, even annoyed when they made eye contact, his hand in his shirt, feeling around his neck and chest before he said, *"Request, you don't do that to me again, sir."*

28

CLEO WAS SITTING UP AGAINST THE BACK WALL OF THE "EL PATO," watching *Truth for Life* gangsters clamber onto the moored boats under the dock. They were getting smaller as Cleo and the others sped away but they were going to chase. Whoever was paying them was paying them *big*.

The dock was going to blow. Her watch said there was one minute left and she still hadn't told Agent Starr about the Gold. He'd known they'd had to leave the dock ASAP and he hadn't questioned the order but he didn't know the reason. He'd just followed instruction. She had expected him to take the civilians and leave the moment he smelled fuel escaping from the SUV, following protocol; leave an agent behind if his life was in danger. The explosion wouldn't have been an issue because she'd be dead and never have to explain the Gold...but she'd survived and that meant she probably owed him an explanation.

They had cleared the docks and were mostly out in the open on the water, anxiously watching *Truth for Life* struggle to start the boats they were jacking. Agent Starr was back near the controls, one dark eyebrow low and trying to figure how much time they had before their pursuers made it out into the water.

Julia and Tanya sat half-crouched on the floor near his boots when Cleo glanced over her shoulder. Julia's arms were around Tanya, some tight motherly hug. They were whispering again, fear and confusion plastered on their faces. It was becoming their regular look. Cleo guessed they weren't used to spending hours in a car or being almost skewered by crazy fat guys running motels in the middle of nowhere. That kind of thing stayed with civilians.

Julia had lost all her makeup and the unnecessary strong perfume had faded, probably into Agent Starr's jacket. They both looked like they hadn't slept in a week and Julia believed it was Cleo's fault. Yeah, well, at least they weren't fucking *dead*.

The Gold blew. Julia and Tanya yelped and let go of each other and Agent Starr hit the deck between them. Cleo felt the explosion in her chest. The sound was piercing sharpness from every direction followed by deep booms. She moved low to the floor and wood from the dock sprayed up in broken shapes and speared the sky to rip clouds open. The boats near the dock flew into the air. Bodies became rockets. She couldn't believe the trajectory of the human rag dolls, limbs flailing and bending at nauseating angles as they somersaulted.

Flames and fireballs bellowed out in heavy breaths across the dock and water. Then it was impossible to see anything but red and orange and black smoke as fuel and gas were added and everything went up. Cleo saw the monstrous dark wave creeping out towards them, unfolding over itself and picking up speed. All the blackness and debris was coming at them, consuming the perfect sky. She swallowed hard. *They weren't far enough out.*

Agent Starr told Julia and Tanya to get closer to the controls. The fibreglass windshield wasn't going to help much, but it was better protection than nothing. Cleo stayed where she was while they scrambled. The sky glowered and turned black over San Freedom...and then it propelled a deadly hailstorm of glass and wood at them.

The sound was the worst. Cleo was squatted, arms over her head as falling glass slashed and stabbed the boat, chunks of the dock dropping from the sky to crunch dents in the floor of the El Pato.

She looked past the debris to the civilians and Agent Starr, trying to protect them from the worst of it, on the floor and kicking the burning pieces of wood away. He and Julia were both covering Tanya's head. Then he was telling Cleo to get over to them but she didn't, even when the raining glass and wood subsided to make way for body parts.

Pieces of flesh smacked the floor, impact absorbed by skin and muscle in each severed limb. A forearm hurtled down between her and the others, thieving everyone's attention in the chaos. The skin was burnt back so they could see tendons and muscle inside near the ripped elbow joint. The hand was in a fist on the other side and covered in blood. It rolled and stopped in front of Tanya's foot.

More parts fell from the sky after it like a sick airstrike. Cleo saw fingers, feet and things she couldn't identify but she knew came out of human beings. Organs splattered around them and speckled their faces with blood.

A chunk of wood smashed her injured shoulder. The pain was instantly sobering, jolts and pins and needles through her body enough to shock her still and hold in a cry. She grabbed her shoulder trying to make it stop but it was fucking raw like the wood had been on fire.

Julia and Tanya had mouths open, screeching, eyes darting all around and Agent Starr was trying to cover their heads and faces but they were uncontrollable and squirming in his arms. He looked at Cleo through the blood rain and all the movement. The expression on his face told her he had a suspicion who was responsible.

Julia and Tanya were in shock and struggling to breathe as the last of the body parts and wood came down, one more insurgency against the boat like the explosion was vomiting whatever was left. Agent Starr pulled them closer to each other again so they hugged and cried in their own little ball. He looked so concerned, worried they weren't okay when he stood up awkwardly and walked to Cleo, stepping around severed body parts and fiery shards of wood.

"What was that?" He asked quietly but his face changed as she opened her mouth, cut off any bullshit answer she might have given, "Cleo, I can smell it in the air."

Her eyes rested on a charred human finger, trying to ride out the boat's manic bouncing created by the explosion. Her shoulder felt like someone had hit her with a fucking sledgehammer. She wasn't in the mood for his Holier Than Thou shit.

"Was it us, Cleo? Thermite, *Gold*?"

"Yes," she murmured.

She took another look back at the dock and it was shell. Most of it was gone, collapsed down into the water. There was nothing left where the *Truth for Life* gunmen had tried to hijack boats to come after them. The Swiss cheese MDS SUV was gone too, the wooden pier it had been parked on wasn't there anymore and the sky was still black and red over the dock and the water.

She had to squint when she turned to look back at Agent Starr. The sun was going down sort of behind him, bright orange sky vibrant and blending from blue to orange. The waves were a mix of the two colours, rolling over each other, shimmering on top. It was like their boat was a halfway point between Heaven and Hell and she was on the evil side, surrounded by all her death and devastation. He stood haloed by the sun, staring down at her for a second then he looked at the floor.

"There were probably still innocent people up there..." He whispered.

29

THE MDS CHARTER ARRIVED TWENTY MINUTES after they were out on the water. It had come out of nowhere and pulled up alongside them at dusk. The crew was mostly Green Tags and a few Blues, helping Julia and Tanya up the ladder on board first then they radioed fire crews on shore, telling them that they were some kind of water police picking up civilians who had narrowly escaped the bloodshed.

The MDS boat was probably forty feet long, somehow managing not to run aground as it came into where the El Pato had been floating. Apparently it was a transfer vessel, usually used for taking thirty or so agents from one port to another. Cleo had climbed aboard last, greeted with the usual stares and whispers and then Julia and Tanya were hurried downstairs and checked for shock and injuries.

She'd had to sit there in an MDS tank top again—*practically under-wear*—while they sutured the cut in her wrecked shoulder because the chunk of wood had split her skin. The medical team was being mature but you didn't walk around in "sleep attire" unless you were headed to your dorm or you were fucked up and couldn't help yourself. She wasn't either of those things. It was only a flesh wound and she hoped it wasn't something she'd have to live down when she got home because the blue and purple bloody mess on her skin wasn't worth it.

Agent Starr had been in the room too, leaning up against the doorway answering all their medic-related questions in that calm and deep half-whisper voice of his when he'd secured the hard drive and made sure it was all going back to HQ. She'd kept her head down while a Green Tag Medic worked on her but she'd felt Agent Starr watching the whole time they were tending to the wound, probably pissed at her for the dock thing, exploding innocent civilians along with the *Truth for Life* assholes. She didn't know.

Now it was night and a familiar feeling kicked in her guts as she wandered the main deck in mostly dark. *It was almost time.* She was going to meet SpadeMan, the man Number One had a personal vendetta against. MDS even had his estranged family as collateral! She was the agent chosen above all the others to Delete him. Yeah, being fucking excited was an understatement. She couldn't wait to put bullets in him.

Cool air skimmed the black water and blew upwards when she walked the side of the boat, blood on her clothes now crunchy and dry. The guys downstairs had told her they had something else for her to wear instead, something she could rig up with a tonne of weapons for her run through the city. She was hoping her shoulder would hold up under it, it was throbbing like crazy in the strapping the medics wrapped it with.

Their ETA in Menas was set for almost three hours away. 21:00. SpadeMan's seminar was starting at 22:30. The MDS agents onboard had done her a favour and organised a limo to take Julia and Tanya to an MDS safehouse once they arrived. No one on The Outside gave a shit who was inside a limo, they didn't care about some rich civilian or forty seven kids on the way to a prom but they'd probably wave the thing through any blocks and get them to safety sooner. At least that was the idea.

The safehouse in Menas would be a medical facility or telecommunications building. MDS liked them because they were usually reinforced and bombproof, able to maintain phone lines and other ways of communicating if a disaster happened. Nearly every city in the country had one decked out and secure. Agent Starr would escort the civilians to the safehouse, Cleo would get Alan *SpadeMan* Pierce and put a couple of rounds in his ass then it was hometime. *Taco time.*

She walked to the bow and leaned on the guardrail to watch the boat power through the water. The metal was cold even through her uniform sleeves as she hung her top half over, just short of it getting dangerous. The water was blasting below, breaking white on the bow and being churned under. There was nothing but navy blue sky and black water ahead. The city was out there somewhere, she knew that, but for now it was like they were travelling through some dark corner of space and it felt good.

"Excuse me, Agent Darkrose?" Julia's voice came from nowhere but she'd known enough to announce her presence before approaching. Good for her, she wouldn't cop a RavenEye in the face.

Cleo glanced at her then back to the water. Julia hadn't spoken to her since before the detonation in San Freedom and it had suited Cleo just fine. She didn't need Julia to express her opinions, she knew them already, too evident in the disgusted looks being shot at her over the past hour or two.

"I need to talk to you," Julia leaned on the rail beside her and looked at the water like she was on some fancy-ass cruise, "I've never been on a boat before."

Cleo didn't say anything, small talk pissed her off. Julia caught on quick.

"I was angry at you for what happened in the motel, what you did to the owner and what you did in San Freedom," she said, "I thought Alan was right, these agencies twist people and make them into hollow machines just serving agendas."

Julia clasped her hands together over the rail then there was a lot of silence. Cleo started picking at the stitching on the Firing Glove. *Awkward.* The water splashed up the side of the boat and breeze carried scraps of the conversations happening downstairs but it wasn't enough to warrant a change of subject and Julia cleared her throat.

"I know you would say there's nothing to twist, that you've always been the way you are. I've been talking to Agent Starr about what being an MDS agent means. We spoke about the dock in San Freedom and how you're fine with what you did there, with the...explosions He told me to look at the magnitude, what it was to make that call, to put Tanya and I-*our lives*-above everyone else's at that dock," she said, "I could never make a decision like that. You're amazing, Agent Darkrose and maybe it *is* a great skill to be able to walk away from a decision like that without going to pieces."

Okay. The truth was Cleo hadn't thought about San Freedom much besides the way Agent Starr had taken it. He'd risked his life to come back and get her out of the car-*totally against the rules*-and then killed for her, after he'd told her he didn't want to do that anymore...and the look on his face after the Gold went up. As for the action itself, what she did, she'd left it somewhere in her mind to pick up later when she was doing the paperwork for Number One.

"Agent Starr told us that MDS has a whole floor in a hospital in the city. We're going to be picked up by other MDS agents once we get to Menas."

"That sounds correct," Cleo said.

"I'm grateful for you protecting us this far, what you've done for Tanya. You rescued us from people my husband sent to kill us. I've thanked Agent Starr already. They're saying there'll be no time when we get to the city, we'll have to hurry in case someone sees us. The other agents told us this is the part where it gets really dangerous for you."

"There will be many of his supporters in all areas of the city tonight," Cleo agreed. It was true, she didn't know what she was walking into and she was going to do it alone. Yeah, it was probably a little hazardous.

"You know, I think Agent Starr really cared about you," Julia said suddenly, "Maybe even more now that he's been stationed in the Middle East, been through what he has."

What. The. Hell. Cleo didn't look at her. She stared at the water and felt heat prickle her skin. She didn't know what to say to that, she didn't want to say anything. Maybe Agent Starr and Julia *hadn't* been running off in the woods to have sex, maybe they'd just been privately discussing her. She didn't know which was worse so she stayed quiet and waited for Julia to go away but she didn't.

"I don't think he agreed with what you did in San Freedom but he defends you. In that notebook Alan, *SpadeMan*, kept...he said the way Agent Starr looked at you was like nothing he'd seen before at MDS," she smiled, "He said if you'd do anything for each other, then you'd do anything for MDS and if you were ever *against* them, they'd be afraid."

She gave a small laugh and looked back to the water for a few seconds then she turned to leave. Cleo didn't stop her. She listened until Julia's steps faded and she was alone again. SpadeMan was really starting to piss her off. She couldn't wait to meet him.

30

MENAS LOOKED LIKE A PARTY. It came over the horizon like a star, lit up white against the night. That part reminded her of HQ; a city on the hill, the oasis in the middle of harsh desert where unlucky bastards died of dehydration. This place was similar, a panorama expanding out of never-ending black water to light up the night.

Cleo managed a quick costume change and now she was ready. The MDS catsuit was navy blue, an almost skin-tight unisex jumpsuit hugging every curve and leaving no extra material to be grabbed or snagged by an enemy. Probably left no imagination either. She had zipped it up, surprised she could still breathe when it was on properly.

The bridle on top was stiff black leather strapping, a pain in the ass to set up but functional, one big collection of holsters that didn't fit over her regular MDS uniform because they hadn't had her size bridle on the boat. It could hold knives, tactical mirrors, guns and ammunition leaving her hands free for combat. She'd almost forgotten how to put it on when the other agents gave it to her, she'd only worn one for training ops a few times in the early days.

The waistband on the bridle was tight up under her breasts to support the weight of the giant machete at her back. She'd put the M9 in the thin belted section around her hips and loaded the other pockets with a stungun, laser glasscutter, Pebble Scanner to find her way out of any complicated buildings and then good old fashioned OC spray.

Some Green tag had even donated a *CRONE* because hers had been missing since the truck outside HQ. The RavenEye was in the drop leg, spare magazine in the pocket hanging on her right thigh and she'd been given a flashbang to attach to her right arm.

There was *no way* she was going to pass for a civilian. She ran options through her head while the water licked up the side of the boat and they headed in towards the dock. She guessed she would have to stick to the backstreets and alleys when she made her way through the city. Simple enough. The less interaction with Menas civilians the better because she wasn't going to change back into her regular uniform, it couldn't hold as much firepower.

The POD was giving up the last of the instructions when she checked her route. The place SpadeMan was holding his seminar was called the *Stella Hotel*, in the main part of town, not far from the dock when the map flashed up. She'd jogged less on treadmills in the Red Tag gym. If they docked on time, it was probably going to work out because she could run the distance relatively easily.

The tall dark buildings on shore had a few lit windows but she couldn't see anyone working inside. The dock and piers looked empty too. She guessed the outskirts of Menas became dead once dark hit for favour of the inner city. She understood why as the boat began turning sideways to fit in a giant slip; the water smelled like shit. She spread her boots shoulder-width apart for balance and tried to hold her breath when the boat manoeuvred to line up with the dock.

A brief thought of Agent Starr sparked, particularly his ability to get the civilians to safety without her now. This was the part that could fuck everything up. She was leaving half the assignment to him, letting the collateral out of her sight and trusting he could get them to a safehouse. She still didn't know if he was operating at a hundred percent. The feeling nagged her as she sized up the cityscape taking over most of her field of vision.

Agent Starr came up on cue, standing next to her at the bow without a word. He was holding black nunchuks in his right hand. She knew he liked to fool around with them when he was bored but she hadn't seen him with any for a long time. Maybe someone on board had given them to him to pass the time. He looked like he was about to say something before he lost the words.

"You look like death," he said finally.

"Thank you."

"You can't wear that through the city, Cleo, there're civilians. They'll call the cops in five seconds flat."

She popped the button on the belt, took out the M9 and held it out to him. Maybe he'd quit his bitching.

"That just means you're going to use your RavenEye," he said.

"You're not getting my RavenEye."

Agent Starr smiled, one that came from somewhere a long way from the dark streets of Menas and the black water around them. Cleo put the M9 away and turned back to the cityscape to imagine all its restaurants and shops and back alleys, the paths she had to run. Agent Starr took a hesitant breath before he spoke.

"Stuff gets hardcore after this. With the bridle on, you've virtually no protection, no vest," he said, "That thing doesn't allow any space."

"That's correct."

Yeah, Captain Obvious, she couldn't fit body armour underneath. She couldn't get her regular uniform under it either. It was a fucking miracle she was even wearing underwear.

"I'm going to complete this alone," she said.

"I know, it's the only way this can be done. I just can't believe Number One made us come out here with a rifle, two M9s and a RavenEye between us. My phone died when yours did. It's like it's all harder than it has to be."

Cleo shrugged. It was standard Number One shit.

"Number One wants to push us. We haven't worked together for a long time," she said and instantly regretted it.

He looked at her then. No, she wasn't thinking about their past, being partners on assignment or other. But she'd noticed the succession of events too. Sending them out of HQ with minimal firepower, making them take the long way then killing Agent Starr's phone at the dock and not checking the progression of the assignment. Even pushing them together to complete the assignment in the first place had to be some sort of test. Or joke.

Number One's personality was at play again for sure but it didn't mean shit. She would prove herself anyway, keep that one hundred percent success rate and get another house in Australia with the credits after it was all over. She just had to battle the catsuit riding up her ass until then.

31

CLEO WAS FIRST OUT. She hadn't sighted visible threats from the MDS charter boat but she held her breath when she stepped on solid ground, trying to sense life-force from the shadows. The city began immediately, buildings across the tarred road stretching into the sky with random windows lit up.

Everything was silent motionlessness; a 2D picture tipped with moonlight. She stood on the main dock waiting for the others to disembark and catch up. The wooden boards on the ground stretched in both directions either side of her, lit only by various lamps along the slips and ambient glow from the moon and buildings. Seeing the city from out on the water had made it look bright but it was mostly dark where they were, only just enough light to see if anyone was approaching their direction and not much else.

Her group was exiting the charter at the top of a T-junction; if she walked straight ahead she would clear the dock, a footpath, the manicured strip of grass with park benches and eventually walk up a tarred road between rows of buildings. Left or right from her position meant she'd be walking on the road between buildings and the water.

She tried not to deep breathe the pungent seawater flavour in the air and scanned the windows in the buildings for lookouts. She bet Agent Starr was doing the same somewhere behind her while he helped Julia and Tanya onto the pier. It was impossible to spot a good sniper with a decent perch but SpadeMan didn't have access to many pros of the Sniper sort, the guy in the woods was dismal testimony. She hoped she was right as she stepped onto the grass.

Julia and Tanya shuffled with the oversized handbag after insisting they needed to bring it with them. Even the rifle and NovaRose hard drive had been packed up and left behind to save some trouble because Agent Starr didn't want to carry things around for nothing while he got the civvies to the safehouse.

Both Julia and Tanya were donning MDS jackets again and gazing longingly back at the boat. Agents on board were due in another port within hours and the crew had already started to head back out. Julia and Tanya's faces said they knew they were letting a safe place literally float away before they had to travel through an unfamiliar city with two agents they'd seen kill like it was a fucking sport only hours prior.

Agent Starr came up fast saying something about making good time despite the boat's ETA being incorrect in San Freedom but Cleo wasn't so excited about making time anymore. The last time they'd had a pickup, she'd had to blow up the joint. Standing there being told they were early and had to wait for the limo was like déjà vu, and being a sitting duck was the kind of thing that seemingly turned into a national incident.

"Arrival time for the transport vehicle, Agent Starr?" Cleo looked over her shoulder to check Julia and Tanya were behind them and not further back mourning the boat's departure.

"It's still set for twenty one hundred, fifteen minutes from now. We just gotta wait a few, that's all," he replied, "Apparently Number One requested I call HQ from the safehouse when we get there. Should be a fun conversation."

The guy had balls, she'd give him that. He wouldn't relay the details to her later but she could imagine what the conversation was going to be like. Number One and the other superiors were going to warn him there was hell to pay when he and Cleo got back to HQ, that they'd jeopardised everything by continuing with Julia and Tanya tagging along and now Number One was busy cleaning up their mess in San Freedom. She was glad she wasn't doing the honours.

"I'll get them to that hospital, Cleo," Agent Starr said, "Number One'll have them back at HQ in a few hours. We're doing good."

Hiding SpadeMan's family in the same city, probably only a short cab ride from where his seminar was happening...*wow*. Cleo may have found it amusing had her entire reputation not been staked on it. She couldn't tell if they were "doing good." Maybe she'd decide when the civilians were at the safehouse and she was kicking some Truth for Life ass or counting the credits uploaded to her chip.

Julia and Tanya's eyes were on the bridle when they made it to the grass and caught up, seeing her outfit in decent street-lighting for the first time. Cleo's weapons were right in their faces, exposed and leaving them to imagine what was going to happen when they separated from her and she carried on through the city, strapped up like she was in a warzone.

They were gauging how tight the outfit was too, both of them giving polite and quick glances over her body and trying not to let expressions show on their faces. Yeah, it wasn't the usual size, she'd had to hold her breath to pull the zip up over her chest and now she looked like something out of a comic book with gravity-defying breasts that seemed to be getting everyone's attention before her face did.

Fuck it. The civilians were Agent Starr's problem now. They would probably enjoy the next few hours cooped up in a room again with their favourite MDS agent, checking out his muscle tone and that grin that took over his face when he flashed it. The popularity contest had been well and truly lost to him over a day earlier, clearly.

Cleo took a few steps forward and bent to tighten the laces on her boots and check the RavenEye was secure for her run through the city. The only issue was having the POD accessible enough to check GPS and make sure she was on course to the hotel where SpadeMan was, she had to be able to grab it out with ease while running.

Agent Starr was staring when she stood and looked over her shoulder. The back end of her uniform was obviously as fitted as the front. It took a moment before he moved his line of sight from her ass back to her face. She pretended she didn't notice. He pretended to look elsewhere and the civilians started talking shit and pointing at the road across from them.

A black limousine was approaching their location, moving silently and gradually with the headlights dimmed. It slowed until it was barely moving, coming towards them front on. Cleo's left hand dropped for the RavenEye. Agent Starr went for his gun too.

"Get behind the benches." Cleo said. The benches on the grass weren't good cover but it was that or nothing.

Julia pulled Tanya back towards the one in the middle, jogging over and getting low behind the metal slats. Agent Starr joined them and squatted behind the left corner of the bench. Shots weren't going to be accurate if he opened fire, it was too dark and so was the tint on the limo windows. Cleo bet he was cursing Number One then for not letting him bring his RavenEye. A round from the RavenEye could take out the windscreen at their distance...unless it was bulletproof. Then they were probably fucked.

She pressed the release for her RavenEye and squatted down on the right side of the bench so they were flanking the civilians. The bench sucked. The only other option for cover was to make a run for the pier and dive into the filthy water if things got too crazy. She jammed the barrel through the slats in front of her instead.

The limo crawled to a stop in the middle of the T-junction, engine still running, positioned so it could turn in either direction. Agent Starr cocked his gun. She armed the RavenEye. They didn't look at each other. One of the limo's doors opened, flung hard so it almost bounced back. No one climbed out of the car. No shots fired. Cleo could feel her pulse in her throat, wanting her to make a move.

Tanya whispered, "Is that for us?" but Cleo didn't answer. Agent Starr was in her periphery, still looking ahead for an opportunity too, a shot lined up ready to send.

"Agent Starr?"

A male voice came from the limo and a hand appeared out of the door and waved them to come forward. Cleo's finger had the trigger halfway through the tension point before she saw the hand was empty and harmless. Unarming the RavenEye without taking a shot felt wrong. She did it anyway, carefully. She didn't want to blow the guy's hand off by accident, that sort of thing didn't go down too well with allies.

Agent Starr checked his watch and nodded in her direction. It was his car, just slightly earlier than expected. He stood up and unarmed his weapon then he reached a free hand down to help Julia and Tanya to their feet. He guided them towards the car fast, eyes darting around the dock and across to the buildings, scanning for threats. His firearm was still in his right hand, clearly visible, catching the streetlights and shining but tight by his side so it didn't come into contact with the civilians.

Cleo hung back, eyes on the surroundings too, slowly getting to her feet and bringing up the rear as the three of them crossed the grass in front of her. The back door in the limo opened as they approached. Good, because Julia and Tanya didn't need to spend any more time out in the open.

Agent Starr stood by the door and watched them push their bag onto the seat before they climbed in. He was spotting them in case they somehow fell out of the car or on the road. Julia probably thought he was a gentleman, helping them out like that.

Cleo felt something in her chest get heavy and spread to her guts watching them. Shit. It was instant dread and she was unable to catch her facial expression in time as she walked the last few steps to the limo. Her eyes went up to the buildings again, trying to sense if they were being watched. Agent Starr stepped around the door and came towards her.

"Are you all right?" He cleared the distance and put his gun away. They walked a few steps away from the limo, out of earshot.

"Yes. Do you have everything you need?"

"Civilians, check. My rifle and the junk from the car being sent back to HQ, check. A pissed off superior waiting for me to call them, yeah," he smiled, "It's all happening, eh."

"Make sure they're examined at the safehouse before Number One arranges a pick up. They have to be in good condition," she said.

"Understood," he took a glance back at the limo, "You do know one has a hole in them, right?"

Cleo thought about punching another hole in *him* but there wasn't enough time. She ignored the smirk on his face because the feeling in her guts was too strong to be light-hearted. Something was about to turn bad. Or maybe the build-up had been too much and now she was nervous to Delete SpadeMan? Surely not. Whatever it was, she hoped it wasn't showing on her face.

"Listen, maybe I can meet up with you after I sign them in at the safehouse," Agent Starr said, "I'm your second, Cleo. It's my job to make sure you have everything you need, that includes backup."

"No," she said.

"You're not even wearing a vest."

"You've said that to me already. A lot."

"Cleo, it's just that I just got back and–" He clipped his own words. Seconds ticked by. She kept her face neutral but she wanted to fucking leave.

The brick in her guts was getting heavier while she was standing there doing nothing, like things were falling to shit somewhere and she had to go and fix them before they came around to bite her in the ass. But she was holding the RavenEye and doing nothing. In the end she raised her eyebrows at him trying to hurry whatever he was attempting to say.

"I don't know if I can–" He was staring over her shoulder before he looked at her, "How can I let you walk away knowing what could happen to you?"

The question surprised them both. The look on his face told her the words had hit the air before he'd thought them through, despite the pause. She watched his throat move–apprehensive, maybe regretful–but he didn't retract the question. She didn't answer. It hung between them like a jack-in-the-box, oversprung and flailing. Not the sort of question an agent asks another, not the way he'd said it.

Another precious second flew by. Cleo put her free hand on his chest. She told him with just her eyes to back the fuck off, she appreciated his concern but it was not the time, however he'd meant it. Agent Starr breathed out and nodded once, soldier mode re-engaged. Time was up. She pulled her hand back.

"Good luck, Agent Darkrose," he said, "See you at home."

Cleo looked past the limo and down the street. When she started through the city she would have no idea who was a threat and who wasn't, civilians all looked the same. SpadeMan would probably have lookouts waiting around to slow her down or Delete her before she got to his hotel and gatecrashed his seminar if San Freedom was anything to go by. Yeah, shit just got real. Again. She gave Agent Starr one last look and started running, leaving him standing near the car watching her leave.

32

AGENT TRENT STARR WATCHED CLEO DISAPPEAR INTO THE DARK. She didn't look back. He wanted to go with her, leave the civvies to the agents in the limo and take off after her. He didn't know how he was going to wait out the action in a safehouse knowing she was out in the city trying to get to SpadeMan.

She was more than capable of finding the Stella Hotel and getting her man, he knew that. The feeling he had didn't come from worrying about her professionally...and he had literally confessed as much. Shit.

He got in the limo and pulled the door closed as it took off. The driver didn't waste any time backing up and changing direction. The vehicle was dark inside, navy blue carpet stuff for the interior and strips of small white lights lining the doors. It had standard tinted windows he could only just see through.

He shifted in his seat, got as comfortable as a man his height was going to in the oddly cramped limo before he looked up. Tanya was next to him on his left, Julia the other side of her. They were looking straight ahead at the two men sitting across from them with their backs to their driver. Trent didn't recognise them, they weren't wearing the uniform. *They weren't MDS.* One had a gun on him.

"Don't say a word, Agent," the gunman muttered and then the car changed gear and rocketed them further into the city.

Trent's eyes were everywhere, checking how many people were

186

in the car, their positions, potential exits—*ways to get out*—possible weaknesses in the windows, the doors, anything he could use as a weapon.

"They said we'd have trouble getting you in the car."

Trent met the guy's eyes and saw they were laughing but his thick lips were still. He was bulky and solid with dark olive skin and a short haircut. His dark blue suit was expensive and matching his tie over a white shirt, looked like he was going somewhere important. His gun was aimed at Trent's chest. The guy next to him was some skinny blonde kid, probably around Trent's age. No gun out yet, just a mean as shit look on his face.

Julia started crying. Trent didn't look at her, didn't need to. He could see her in his peripheral, taking tissues out of her bag and wiping her eyes. He could feel Tanya watching him intently now too, waiting for him to do something.

He had messed up. Big time.

"They told you you'd have trouble getting me in the car?" He frowned, "Who...do you think I am?"

"You're Agent Trent Starr, MDS," The large man said, Tongan accent mixed with American, "I'm Joe. Where's your gun?"

"It's in three pieces on a boat somewhere."

"Disassembled Sniper Rifle," the skinny guy said.

"What's in the bag?"

"Civilian shit." Trent shrugged.

"You got other weapons? I'm going to need them or your lady friends eat a round each."

"I have a side arm, that's all. Do you want it?" There was no point in dicking around.

"Yeah, hand it over." Joe kept his gun pointed at Trent and held out his other thick brown hand. Trent leaned back to take the gun out and pass it. The guy took it and flipped it over, only taking his eyes off Trent for a nanosecond. Not long enough.

"No modified handgun, *RavenEye*?"

"No," Trent said flatly, "I knew I was going to be around civilians, didn't want to hurt anybody."

"Oh, isn't that sweet." Skinny said.

"SpadeMan liked what he saw in your files, said he never saw an agent good at combat and own a scientist's mind. He thought your NovaRose was a bad idea, hated you for it. He told your boss it was unethical...then you finished it. He wanted to steal it and use it on MDS so you people knew what it felt like to be genuinely attacked rather than just simulate attacks on yourselves. He said he wanted you to work for us."

"He did?"

"Yes, But then he changed his mind."

"Oh."

"So now we're going to kill you."

"Right." Trent said.

Skinny laughed and cracked his knuckles. His t-shirt and jeans were old and worn, nothing special. Trent guessed he wasn't invited to wherever Joe was going. He looked typically civilian, the only thing worth noting was that he had the blondest hair Trent had ever seen. It was yellow, like a damn halo around the guy's head.

"How did you know I was on this assignment?" Trent asked Joe.

"We were tipped off when they told us Darkrose was coming for Alan. We knew you were due home, some of our guys are military too. SpadeMan knew you were coming back. He just thought it would've been earlier, you know, when you almost died," he laughed, hearty and loud, "We got the tape from the phone records there, the one with you calling Darkrose's message service, crying like a little girl."

"I'm sure I wasn't crying." Trent said.

"Close enough. Your superiors thought Alan would be worried when Darkrose was coming for him but he was *happy*. He wants to meet her."

Trent glanced out the window. He didn't recognise the streets but they were still passing restaurants and busy areas with people walking around and sitting down eating at sidewalk cafes. He had some time, the *Truth for Life* guys wouldn't stop the car to execute them in front of so many witnesses.

"You know how deep this runs, Agent *Starr*," Skinny said Trent's name like he was mocking it, "You know who Alan James Pierce is. SpadeMan served at MDS, his relationship with your *'Number One'* started before you or Darkrose were probably even born. Do you know how evil your syndicate is, what they've been doing to the people in this country and around the world for decades?"

"We just take out the trash, guys. That's all my job is, I wait around and take down threats to society *for* the people of this country." Trent shrugged, using the move to sneak a look at Julia and Tanya, check how they were doing.

The limo was a cheap piece of trash, no reinforcements, but if he kicked open the door next to him and jumped for it, there was no way he was getting Julia and Tanya out too. The seat they were sitting on was too long to pull them both across. Besides, he didn't want them injured and the car was travelling too fast to jump and not get badly hurt or worse. All right, next option...

"You're talking shit, Agent Starr. I could go on for days about what your syndicate's done," Skinny shook his head, "The geoengineering in the sky when you think we're not looking up, the poison in the drinking water, the experimental medicines for viruses *you* people made! You want us all sick so you can profit!"

"Do you think we're stupid?" Joe didn't miss a beat, "You dumb us down with drugs and media lies but we've still got questions. Why is it that all the towers and buildings that fell in New York went down demolition-style? Witnesses say they heard explosions go off before the main impact. Why was the rubble collected and recycled *before a thorough investigation?*"

His question ended in a yell and Julia jumped, Trent felt it through the seat. The guy was crazy. He was talking about something that happened a long time ago like it was fresh in his mind and still dictating policy.

"Explain how airplanes flew into restricted airspace over military and government buildings that day? Was there a Stand Down Order that day in September? You tell me, you Illuminati bastard! So many people died, and now we get our fucking balls squeezed and shot with radiation to get on a passenger plane. Tell me why! *Tell me the truth!*"

The gun in Joe's hands was shaking, not in line with Trent's chest anymore. His dark eyes were on fire and boring into Trent's, demanding answers Trent didn't have. He didn't know the "*truth.*" He was inclined to ask the same kinds of questions. The second an aircraft crossed into HQ airspace, Interceptor Jets took care of it, took it down–*no questions*–just procedure. He didn't even think there *was* an option of a Stand Down Order at HQ if anything like that happened.

He hadn't hung around on The Outside long enough to form his own opinion on anything Joe was saying. All he knew was some of it started a long-as-shit war he'd been dragged into and the friends he'd made overseas dropped like flies in a foreign desert miles from home. Regardless of the rumours and stories, the consequences weren't a lie, *the war was real* and good people were dying, fighting for what they thought was right. Sometimes both sides.

Images of the desert and the bloodbath overseas started forming in his mind. Memories joining together, melting and merging into scenes he couldn't afford to remember while trapped in a limo with a gun on him. The sound of his own voice shook him from the impending nightmare.

"I don't know the answers to your questions, you're asking the wrong person," he said, "I fought in the *War on Terror*, I served this country. Those soldiers are fighting a *real* battle, that part is not fiction or speculation. *People are dying.* They're defending this country for you to have the right to ask those kinds of questions."

They shook their heads like Trent didn't get it. He didn't give a shit, he had to make an escape and do it soon. The car was moving faster, taking them away from the city's populated areas through to dark streets and broken down buildings and warehouses. The dank unfriendliness around them matched the mood inside the car. It meant shit was going to go down and he was running out of time.

"You think you're on the right side but you're not," Joe caught the M9 before it fell off his lap as the car bounced over a pothole, "Don't talk to me about freedom when authorities are banning free speech and taking away liberties. We respect soldiers but they send you all over to fight and they lie about the reasons why you're there."

"Why didn't you try and get Agent Darkrose in the car too?" Trent tried.

Diffuse the anger. Waste time...cos he still had no idea how he was going to play it. He used the moment to check Julia and Tanya's positions again. He hoped they all got to the safehouse later. *If* they survived whatever was going to happen when the shit hit the fan.

"Darkrose was carrying more than we wanted to go up against, not going to lie," Skinny answered, "We called, asked to shoot her up on the pier. He said no, he's got plans for her. Your girl's walking into a trap and here you are with us, about to get shot in that pretty face of yours."

He turned to Joe and nudged him, "You see what she was wearing? I'd rip that shit off with my *teeth*."

They laughed and the gun dipped. Trent pushed his hands down either side of him. Both his legs came up fast, boots smashing the gun from Joe's hand, following through to his body, jerking him back against the seat, all the air gushing out of his lungs in a pained grunt. Trent knew the sound under it, he'd broken some ribs, maybe penetrated other organs if he was lucky. Joe was hunched over with Trent's gun when Skinny pushed himself from his seat, clumsily lunging for Trent in the small space.

Trent caught a body shot before Skinny lost balance, hit his head on the roof and fell into the window near a yelping Julia. Joe grabbed for Trent's shoulders and was rewarded with a palm heel up into his grill. The cartilage in his wide nose broke and twisted sideways, spitting blood as Trent's other fist came up and hammered Joe in the eye while he spluttered.

Skinny was somewhere behind, feeling around on the floor for one of the guns and yelling he was going to kill them all when he found it. The low roof kept everyone's leverage down but Joe launched himself at Trent again and they fought each other and gravity as the car fishtailed. Looked like the driver had noticed the scene in the backseat. He was driving insane, axels groaning and buckling while he executed wild J-turns and swerves to stop them fighting.

Trent kicked again, barely any power but enough to make Joe lose his footing and fall into Skinny the next time the car swerved. The two of them landed on their seat again before Skinny pushed himself up over Joe and pulled a knife.

Disarm. Put him down. Protect the civilians. Trent blocked the strike, forearm outward so Skinny couldn't get a shot at his veins, and caught it halfway down the limb. He felt the burning pinch. *The blade got through the stab-resistant material!* Trent grasped the guy's wrist and twisted it backwards. Skinny dropped the knife and Trent reached to his boot for his own, undeclared, blade.

He shoved it deep in Skinny's stomach and tore it upwards. *Death sentence.* Skinny's face transformed, finally realising the warning he'd been given about Agent Trent Starr was warranted. Trent kneed him off the blade and swooped down for the M9 while Skinny fell onto Julia and Tanya and they screamed, the type that shattered eardrums.

The car veered in another direction violently and Joe, the fucker, fell down to the floor. He was looking for a gun too. Trent's hand brushed over his and they both scrambled to find a weapon first but they found their guns at the same time.

Joe was bringing his weapon up, ready to fire. Then Trent could see flickers of some other place; he was behind a different gun out in a blistering desert, shimmering horizon while he was aiming at foreign fighters, already having taken incoming for days. He was ready to send the shot, arguing with himself whether *this* group was going to harm him and his squad or if they were just civilians caught up in shit. He didn't want to hurt civilians. *He wouldn't.*

Trent blinked and saw the inside of the limo. Joe was squeezing the trigger on his weapon. Another flash of the desert stopped his breath. He could see women in their Burquas or Niqab in his line of fire. He didn't know what they were wearing and the other guys didn't care enough to help him with correct terms. All they'd said was foreign soldiers dressed as civilian women to get close enough to kill western soldiers. Was he going to shoot? Wait, was he in the desert or the limo? He couldn't remember. He had less than half a second to decide.

Julia and Tanya screamed again.

Limo.

He fired. Double tap and muzzle flashes. Joe fell back into his seat, two smouldering holes to the chest. The driver lost control of the car. Trent felt the fishtail, sensed the car body strain and turn and seize up. A brick wall came up fast when he looked to the windscreen. They were mounting the curb and headed straight for the side of a building. He only had a second to put his arm across Julia and Tanya.

Metal screamed around them, bricks smashing the grill and busting the windscreen. Glass and screams filled the air. The car tipped up and sent everyone forward crashing into each other and the floor, bodies and blood and limbs entwining painfully. Then there was abrupt silence.

Pain drummed in the back of his head. He could hear glass start to fall and smash into smaller fragments on the road outside. His face felt like someone had tried to cave it in with their fist and he could tell without moving it was possible he had a couple of hairline fractures in his shins despite his conditioning. It was physics, tall guys didn't fare well in car crashes. *Too bad, Red Tag. Get up.* He forced his eyes open and pushed himself from the floor, ready for Joe and Skinny to somehow attack again.

Everything in the car was vaguely lit by streetlight coming through the broken windows. No one moved. He could see Tanya and Julia were alive as he got to his knees and felt pain shoot through his hip. They didn't look obviously injured but Julia was on the floor and both of them were shocked by the impact. He could tell by the way they didn't scream or cry now.

Joe's legs were half off his seat and he was lying on his side with his eyes open, facing Julia and Tanya. Blood was trickling from his thick nose onto the upholstery. The Perspex separating the driver from the passengers was broken where Skinny had gone halfway through and been spat back again. The skin on his face was shredded. One of his legs was bent the wrong way, a lump in his jeans where bone was trying to come through as he lay on the seat above Julia. Details were sketchy but Trent understood why the civilians were mute and the car smelled like an abattoir already.

He looked out the broken window nearest to him and saw they were flat against a wall at the front, wedged up against a fire hydrant or something else on Julia's side. They had to use his door to get out. Julia and Tanya had to cross over the dead guys and see the blood and gore up close as they squeezed around Joe's tree-trunk legs to escape.

Everyone was smeared with blood and he'd have to do a proper medical assessment on Julia and Tanya when they exited the car but there were no observable indications the two of them were in debilitating pain. He hoped it wasn't just hidden by shock while he located his gun again then made eye contact with Julia and nodded for them to follow him out of the car.

His boots crunched glass when he climbed out and smashed pieces caught the glow from the streetlight like glitter between his boots. Shit, his legs were aching, probably on their way to being nicely bruised up under his uniform. His thoughts were cut by Tanya emerging from the car wreck, reaching for his hands for help.

Her forehead was speckled with Skinny's blood but she was looking up at him, face neutral in the streetlight. She was able to stand on her own as soon as she was clear of the car and she didn't cry, didn't even say anything. Julia was slower, movements shaky and clumsy as she squeezed past Joe with her bag. She appeared with her eyes mostly shut to avoid the scenery, one hand out blindly so Trent could take it.

Dark smoke was creeping from under the car as he pulled her out but she didn't look back, crying softly and asking him to please make sure Tanya was okay. He made them step away from the wreck and then he checked them both over, asked them if anything hurt, if they felt sick, what their names were and did the usual procedure. When he stepped back, Julia rushed Tanya, hugging her, words gibberish as she held her and cried.

They weren't all right, didn't matter how it looked physically. He knew civilians, people not used to seeing death and extreme violence would carry the experience for the rest of their lives. It would affect everything they did, impose on all their thoughts after they finally had a chance to process what they'd been through. He was an agent, an assassin who thought he'd seen everything but even he was starting to realise how fighting in the *War on Terror* had done the same to him. He would carry what he'd seen there around with him for the rest of his life.

"I'm sorry," Trent said, "I should've checked the car before you got inside."

Julia and Tanya looked up at him like they'd just remembered he was standing there. Julia looked like Hell, face tear-stained and half crumpled but she swallowed and cleared her throat.

"No, Agent Starr. *Thank you.* I jarred my elbow on my window but I'm okay...Tanya is fine. We're okay."

Noise came from inside the car. *The driver.* Trent had forgotten about that fucker, figured he was dead too when he saw the state of the front of the car. Trent armed his gun. The guy was sliding over Joe's body to get out the same door they had just used.

He grunted as he pushed himself out, hesitating with his left leg. His white suit was bloody and torn across his shoulder. He froze when he saw them, standing just outside the car door, bleeding profusely from a cut on his forehead and blinking the blood away. The guy was Hispanic, good-looking, only a little younger than Trent, maybe early twenties. He didn't take his eyes off the gun in Trent's hand, raising his hands slowly but waiting for the kill shot.

Trent glanced at Julia and Tanya to make sure they weren't in his line of fire. Julia's eyes were shut, her hands clamped over her ears. Tanya was staring at him, calm and waiting in silence for the shot. The guy was unstable on his feet, shifting from one foot to the other like he was going to piss his pants. He was unarmed and panicking, on the edge of hyperventilating. Trent looked him in the eyes. Ah, shit.

He shoved his gun away before instinct and training took over and the decision wasn't his anymore. The driver blinked a few times, almost as shocked as Trent was then he ran away down the alley.

33

IT HAD BEEN COOL AT THE PIER but now Cleo was wading her way through the bowels of the city and things had heated up, figuratively and literally. She could feel sweat spring up on her temples as she jogged down another long-ass alley avoiding pieces of newspaper, crates and garbage bags strewn around.

The red brick walls flanking her were covered in graffiti; words and symbols she didn't understand. The next street was clearly visible up ahead, streetlight glow filtering into the alley, lighting up the end of it. She saw two large grey dumpsters on the left near the exit, half bathed in light and open, their contents spilling out over the side like someone had gone through them for scraps of food.

She was close. Another twenty minutes and she'd be gatecrashing SpadeMan's seminar and using the RavenEye to blow an extra hole in him. She could smell food now, the air laced with tomato and pasta and things civilians ate on dates when they were trying to impress the other person. It was going to be harder to stick to just the alleys as she neared the Stella Hotel. The POD said it was on a main street and there was going to be a tonne of SpadeMan's supporters outside.

She'd almost cleared the alley when she heard footsteps enter it back at the other end. *Someone running at full pelt headed her way.* She stepped into the shadows by the dumpsters and got low. Sweat was beading faster as soon as she stopped moving, body fighting discomfort as she tried to slow her breathing. She could hear the other runner panting, the type of breathing that told her he was male and he had been running for a while. His footsteps were messy with fear and fatigue, he was trying to get away from something.

The runner flashed by seconds later. He was wearing a white suit, pressed, pockets, a tailored jacket. It was all expensive. It was also covered in blood, a huge splash of it down the front of his shirt and his shoulder. Cleo got to her feet and took off after him, springing out of the alley into the next street, not totally sure why.

He wasn't far ahead when she left the corner. His white and bloodstained suit was a beacon flashing in the streetlights as he ran through the intermittent dark. She drew the RavenEye as she chased. It came up easily out of the bridle, everything flowing perfectly among the speed and adrenalin.

Cleo's boots pounded the sidewalk as she whizzed by streetlights and mailboxes and parked cars in a blur. Her eyes were on the man's back like there was a target on it. She was breaking the rules, running with the RavenEye clearly visible in her left hand but he was up to no good, no civilian walked the streets covered in that much blood.

Cleo jumped over dips and cracks in the pavement without slowing, boots slamming the path louder than she'd wanted but she gained on him easily. The guy started glancing over his shoulder still running hard, sweat and blood trickling down his tan cheek. One of his glances sent him off course, enough to clip a lightpole and spin around, fall and hit the sidewalk. Cleo almost skidded to a stop over him.

"*Get in the alley,*" she said, motioning to one on her right. The thing was dark, stinking of piss so strong she could smell it from where they were on the sidewalk.

The guy did what he was told, out of breath, shoulders slumped when he got up. He had some kind of look on his face like he thought he was going to get mugged. His dark eyes were on the gun in her hands as he walked into the alley, hands up, crossing into the dark. Then he spun around and tried to grab her.

She stepped sideways, smashed his arms down and ended up behind him. Then she clasped her hands around his face, RavenEye still in one hand when she jerked his head back against her shoulder and twisted him off balance to the ground. Planting a knee in his back with all her weight on top of him was the full stop. He was on the sticky asphalt, facedown, panting and breathing dirt and dried piss. She looked up at the walls of the alley for any lit windows. No witnesses. *Bonus.*

"Having a rough night?"

The guy was pseudo-fancy up close. The suit only looked expensive at a distance. She knew quality, Number One demanded it for events at HQ and the guy's suit was fake. He was paid for service, he was a doorman or something but if he was covered in blood, he probably wasn't a good guy and he obviously thought he could take her otherwise he wouldn't have tried to come at her.

"Policia?" He asked through gritted teeth.

"No. But that means I can harm you with no consequence if I don't get what I want."

"They do that anyway," he said breaking into English, "What do you want to know?"

"Where's all the blood from?"

"Nowhere."

"You roam the streets like this all the time."

"Yes," he nodded awkwardly against the ground, "It was an accident."

"What kind of accident, you kill someone?"

"Car crash."

"What kind of car was it?" Something in her chest scrunched.

The guy was good looking in the moonlight when she leaned down to get a side view, her knee still in his back. His black hair framed his tanned features and the suit made him look like an old school gangster. In another circumstance, she may have sized him up for a night in a hotel room. He was confused when their eyes met.

"I'm not inclined to repeat myself." Cleo said.

"People hire my limousine, it crashed."

"Were you alone?"

199

"No, there were the two men I was hired by and-"

"*Two females?*"

"Two females," he confirmed.

"What happened to them?"

"They were standing outside the car after it hit the wall."

"There was another man in the car, what happened to him?"

"I don't know about any other man," he said.

The RavenEye cocked itself, she didn't feel her finger move.

"You know who I mean. *Agent Starr.* Six two, black hair, green eyes...wearing black," She felt her finger stage the trigger, "What happened to him?"

"*Him?* He killed them, he killed the men who hired me. I think he stabbed them, slashed them. He-he *murdered* them. Then he let me go."

Cleo breathed out. She tried to keep her face expressionless as she realised she actually fucking cared. She wanted Agent Trent Starr alive and she was pretty sure it wasn't just because he was supposed to be getting her civilians to the safehouse. Dammit.

"He let you go?" She put the RavenEye away.

"He let me go."

Agent Starr liked civilians but when it was on, he was as dangerous as she was, trained to Delete. He did whatever he had to. He was told to protect the civilians and get them to the safehouse. If the driver had been in the way, it was a miracle he was still alive.

"You're a very lucky man," she told the driver before she took her knee out of his back and ran from the alley.

34

TRENT

TRENT SAT ON AN UNCOMFORTABLE-AS-SHIT GREEN CHAIR in the hallway of the local hospital, dull lights above already giving him a headache. Julia had lied to him. They'd been taken up to the MDS floor and he'd had his TC chip scanned and authorized before she asked for medical attention for a deep laceration to her hip, one he'd failed to notice earlier. She was going to be all right, it wasn't serious, but he hadn't done his job. He should never have let them get into the car without checking who was inside. Stupid. *Rookie mistake.* His mind hadn't been on his job.

His ass was going numb, padding on the seat was cheap and thin. He sat still anyway, nice and quiet, elbows on his knees and staring ahead. He was apprehensive, like a kid outside the principal's office while Julia and Tanya talked at the speed of light beside him.

Staff on-site hadn't been friendly but it didn't matter, the civilians were safe and now they all sat running down the clock until someone from HQ arranged transport back home. The conversation he'd had over the phone with superiors hadn't been good and they were angry but he hadn't had to speak to Number One directly when he jumped through all the ID hoops.

Julia hugged Tanya beside him. Between them they had a bullet wound, a cut that had required sutures and two slight concussions but, technically, they were still in one piece. He hoped it was good enough for Number One.

Shit, he was tired. His legs were aching, rivalling the pain in his wrist from firing a RavenEye with a bare hand and the slash from Skinny. His head still hurt too, even with the cold-pak they'd hastily shoved at him while they'd fixed up the civilians. He hadn't used it much, just flipped it over in his hands a few hundred times while he sat there feeling useless.

He was going to be home in the next few hours and it should have felt good but Cleo was without backup when she got to that fucker, SpadeMan. It was the plan, the way it was supposed to go, but it didn't sit right with him anymore. He leaned back against the wall and took a long blink.

He'd thought about her a lot in the Middle East, when he wasn't busy hiding scared, knee-deep in shit or shooting dead people the other guys called *"towelheads"* and worse. Things had ended badly between them before he left, he barely knew what happened but he'd lost her and she'd gone AWOL and he'd never worked it out with her because Number One sent him away before he'd had the chance to try.

MDS was Priority One. MDS was more important than anything else in their lives. Cleo had even said it to him that day before she disappeared, reminded him of the documents they signed pledging their understanding of that. Now he sat in a quiet wing of a hospital with two civvies, having completed his part of the assignment for Number One and MDS, feeling empty like he'd felt overseas without her.

"Are you worried about Cleo?" Julia's question was stark in the quiet.

She was leaning towards him, honing in on his thoughts with her intuition and degree in psychology. Tanya had conveniently left them for the drink fountain up the hall, out of earshot.

"I should be doing this with her," he said.

"Is it more than that?"

He didn't look at her.

"This is the first time you've seen her in a long time, you didn't expect to feel anything anymore."

"Somethin' like that," he admitted.

"She didn't think she'd feel that way either but she hides it better than you," Julia said. He couldn't help a glance at her while she spoke, "You've been out with the boys in our military, bonded with those guys, experienced extreme uncertainty. You've seen those boys missing their families, worry about getting home. You aren't different...but you were taught that being concerned for someone else or having a relationship is wrong. Other militaries *encourage* families to stay together, you know."

"MDS is priority. We signed agreements to leave each other behind if a mission called for it," he took a lengthy breath, "A long time ago I told her I'd never do that, I don't care what I signed."

"Is that why you went back, at the dock?"

"I gave my word," he said.

"She looked prepared to die back there. Do you think you'll be able to switch off again the way she does?"

"Cleo can kill and if she feels anything, you wouldn't know about it," he said, "I was like that but it changed after I'd had time to think. The idea that I could feel what I did for her, in the middle of everything MDS is...I didn't realise the importance at the time but then I saw it happen to some of the guys in my unit. It's like being over there woke them up to what they had, woke *me* up."

Trent watched Tanya turn on the drink fountain at the end of the hall by doorways to patient rooms. Julia's head moved into his line of vision.

"As I told you in the woods, I think you're *emotionally thawing*," Julia nodded and smiled, "It feels like hell now, but it's a good thing. This is normal. May I ask....what she's really like?"

"She's..." Trent started, rearranged his words, "From what I remember, Cleo is *strong*, smart. Very funny."

"*Funny?*"

"Yeah," he nodded, "People don't get to see it often."

"But you've seen it"

"Yeah."

"She's very guarded. No matter what I've said to her, she's never flinched. She must have regarded you highly if she was herself around you." Julia said.

"Words don't work on her. She is who she is and I appreciate that," Trent shrugged, "I loved that."

Julia's face turned guilt-ridden. She was awkward glances and fidgets in a matter of moments and Trent waited for her to crack. She looked over her shoulder to check Tanya was still preoccupied then she leaned closer until her cheek brushed against his and her lips almost touched his ear.

"Cleo's making a mistake," she whispered, "And I should have told you earlier."

35

CLEO WAS POISED ON A BLACK RUSTING FIRE ESCAPE four floors up in an alley beside the Stella Hotel. The thing was rickety as fuck and climbing it had meant straining muscles trying to keep it tight, not cause the stairs to rock or make any more noise than they had to. There was another floor between the top of the fire escape and the roof. She guessed there was a helipad up there if people needed to evacuate from level five. She had gone as far as she could without being inside the building.

The long window in front of her showed access to a lengthy beige-carpeted hallway, white hotel room doors lining the walls and small tulip-shaped wall lamps every two doorframes. She had the laser glass cutter ready in her left hand, extra work but fuck the front door, there was no way she was getting past security and the concierge dressed like a B-grade superhero.

A couple of people had stepped into the alley below to smoke cigarettes but they hadn't looked up. The street around the corner was alive, food smells and vendors yelling the prices of hotdogs and ice cream, cashing in on the influx of people rallying. It sounded like there was a carnival up ahead. She knew better, it was just the sideshow.

Truth for Life activists were crowded around the corner at the entrance to the Stella Hotel, all eagerly waiting for any sort of contact from SpadeMan. He was already inside, she knew by the time blinking on her watch. He had to be getting ready, dressing, preparing his speech, *some* shit. The people on the street outside of the building didn't know specifics either, they probably hadn't been able to get a ticket to his seminar inside.

Some of them walked past the entrance to the alley, moving ahead in the lights from the street in groups and alone, holding up banners and scribbled posters with catchphrases and one-liners. The sounds of their voices echoed back, general chatter and some sort of chanting and laughter.

She had approached quickly, not making eye contact with anyone on the street, and slipped through the crowd without taking the flyers they were handing out or stopping to talk. Their signs and t-shirts said *"No blood for oil,"* and *"You are not free, Big Brother is watching."* She'd seen stuff like it before, just never so much of it. Estimated, there were probably about a hundred and fifty civilians all standing around yelling about how their government was screwing them.

Some of them were wearing homemade costumes made from cardboard boxes with messages scrawled across them. A couple was dressed as a DNA double helix and talking about genetic engineering alongside some guy wearing a shirt that had said, *"The future is a micro-chipped population."*

That one had bothered her enough to be pausing on the fire escape ten minutes after she'd seen it, black laser cutter in her left hand and her right index finger at eye-level. She imagined the TouchCash chip under her skin, all the circuits beaming her business back to HQ.

The data appeared back in the depths of MDS every time she used it to make a purchase. It knew every time her vitals went up or down like she was a video game character and the damn thing kept records of every shot or Infirmary visit she'd ever had.

They'd made it sound so good when she was younger; she would never need to transfer medical records to other bases. By scanning her TC chip they would instantly know what type of blood she needed in a transfusion or who she was if she suffered amnesia after brain trauma in the field. But as she stood there, alone on a dark fire escape over an alley in Menas, she frowned at familiar thoughts; they would always know everything about her, nothing was private. Hell, it showed her vitals and heart rate so someone back at HQ could probably tell every time she had sex. She put her hand down.

She curved around the last part of a circle with the laser glass cutter in seconds. It was a thin purple line buzzing in front of her and slicing through the glass almost silently. The melting glass smelled like shit, changing from hard and still to bubbling and folding back on itself like ice melting. It reminded her of the signs she saw downstairs stating "Global Warming" was a lie. Yeah, she'd also heard some rumours about a whole lot of big players who got richer while the population became more naïve with stories of drowning polar bears. Number One and the others laughed at the slaves but the game was changing.

She understood now. She wasn't just there to Delete Alan Pierce, she was sending a message to his followers and dissidents who wanted to join them. *Truth for Life* had to suffer a serious blow because they actually had some power. They knew hints of the truth, maybe nothing complete, but it was enough. Number One, MDS and the rest of the government agencies obviously felt threatened, and it wasn't about the bomb *Truth for Life* was going to set off downstairs.

That bomb was going to backfire on those so-called activists. Number One was okay with the explosion maiming and killing because it would prove the movement was a real domestic terrorist threat. More force could be used against them in future, protests would be restricted, ruckus over policy for any reason would be stamped out before it began.

Civilians, slaves...idiots. *Most* of them.

It was beginning to look like Julia and Tanya Pierce were just two dopey women who were caught up in a mess they didn't understand. Admittedly, something about that didn't make her feel good now that she'd spent time with them. They were goddamm annoying and, no, they weren't part of any solution but they were not the problem.

36

NO SOUND CAME FROM THE OTHER SIDE when Cleo was standing in the hotel stairwell, pressed up against the door to the fifth floor. She'd come up from the fourth floor after approaching the elevator and seeing the big-ass mirror taking up the back wall of the thing. It had shown her the elevator was empty but there was a surveillance camera mounted inside, right above the door and ready to record anyone who entered.

It had been a feat to use the laser glass cutter while on the fire escape and make a neat circle big enough to fit through. She'd pushed the discarded chunk of glass through onto the carpet and prayed no one came out of the doors lining the hall to see what was going on. Then she had jumped through the cut out she made in the window, flexing her body, curling through the hole and flipping over. Rolling onto the carpet in that smooth perfect motion was ruined by the landing, half her ass had ended up on the glass circle she'd cut out and she was lucky it didn't break and skewer her, cushioned by the carpet underneath.

Things were quiet on the other side of the door because important, high-paying guests didn't like staying on floors where other civilian riff-raff could stroll past their rooms at all hours. She knew Spade-Man's type, deep down he was a rogue agent, and they all went a little crazy when they got on The Outside and found they could convert their TC cash to real funds. Yeah, he was probably spending up big in luxury on the fifth floor.

She would have put money on him having the whole floor hired out so only his people could disturb him and anyone sent to Delete him would have to come all the way up through the hotel. It was also why there was no point getting Agent Starr involved this far. Setting up a rifle to sit and wait halfway across town for a clear window wouldn't help, SpadeMan was too smart for that.

Cleo pushed the door open a crack, a sliver enough to see a guy in a navy blue suit, earpiece in his left ear and the wire spiralling down the back of his neck. The back of his suit had a tell-tale strap from a rig across his shoulders. He was armed and wearing the holster in full view. *Privately contracted security.* Spademan and his entourage *had* hired the whole floor and the guy was doing a shit job of guarding the hallway and stairwell.

She let the door close by itself, the click enough to call the guard over as she stood with her back against the wall, out of trajectory, feeling the air change as he approached from the other side. She heard him slide his weapon from the rig but he didn't cock it. His mistake.

The door handle dipped slowly then the door crept open an inch, the barrel of a small handgun appearing in the gap. She wouldn't be hit but it was close enough that she'd probably be sprayed with GPR, lucky if the shit didn't get her in the eyes.

The door opened wider and the guy stepped around it quickly. He was big, *six three, three hundred pounds, dark skin and wearing really nice cologne.* He needed the entire landing as he came into the stairwell, forcing the door back all the way so it pinned Cleo behind it.

She kneed the door away fast, strode out and grabbed the barrel of his gun with her right hand, bashing it out of his grip before he could fire. He was off-balance when she struck him with pointed fingertips, rigid and headed straight into his throat. He lost his footing and fell backwards down the dusk-blue metal stairs. She teetered on the edge of the landing as the door clipped shut next to her, security guard's gun in her hand and aiming as he tumbled, waiting in case he leapt back up but he didn't. He rolled the stairs, buckles and holsters clanging on the metal as he went down, then his giant body unravelled and his head hit the wall opposite. He was out cold instantly, and she was very lucky.

The door burst open again and Cleo snatched the CRONE from the bridle. The next guard took the shot in the chest, blue charges piercing his dark suit jacket and then his skin. His heart copped the blow point blank and he paled and dropped on the edge of the stairs.

She nudged him with her boot until he was writhing clear of the door and hanging off the first step. He was a shorter guy, stubby flailing arms and pale hands grasping at his chest as he started to slide down the stairs.

Cleo shoved the CRONE away and kept the first security guard's gun. Yeah, the guards in the stairwell would get found but by then the bomb would have gone off, Spademan would be dead and she would be on her way home. Maybe she'd even sort out some stuff with Agent Starr when they had more than three minutes alone to talk. She'd probably been too much of a hard-ass with him the last few days.

The hallway she entered was identical to the one downstairs but the white doors to fancy rooms were only lining the wall on her right this time. She guessed there weren't many people who could afford to stay on the fifth floor. It was expensive and exclusive. The wall opposite the hotel rooms was decorated with lame pictures of flowers, hung between more wall lamps.

A gaudy red and white *"Do not Disturb"* sign hung off a doorknob down the hall but she could hear talking coming from inside the room. Male voices, and she couldn't tell what they were saying. It was mostly low tones and quick exchanges as she made her way down. The gold numbers on the door were a little higher than her head, curves catching the light and shining the numbers 501. She snatched the sign from the doorknob and threw it over her shoulder.

Odds said it was probably SpadeMan in the room, talking to another one of his guys, telling them to check out the racket in the stairwell.

Yeah, she would catch them by surprise and the whole thing would be over in moments. Some big assignment...Hell, the only thing worth smiling about was that it meant her reputation was intact, besides the civilians stowing away thing, and she would be free to get that taco she'd been fantasizing about since the day in Number One's office.

Cleo pushed door 501 open and jumped back out of range. Everything was dead quiet. Seconds raced. She used a small SWAT mirror from the bridle to bend around the doorway and see into the room but it showed no one inside, just a big off-white velvet armchair that looked like it belonged to some royal. Whoever had been in there was gone already. Dammit. *How?* She pocketed the mirror and unstuck herself from the wall then stepped around the doorframe, security guard's gun nestled in her Firing Glove.

Her breath caught when she saw two men inside. She hadn't seen them a second ago because a large mirror had been strategically placed to reflect back at hers. It had only shown her the other side of the room. *Fuck.*

One of the men was standing with a tanned hand on the other one's shoulder while his paler friend sat close by in a cane chair. The first guy was good looking, dark eyes and caramel skin, Spanish, Italian? His features were set off by the heavy gold chain around his neck with a spades pendant hanging from it. *SpadeMan.* Okay, she'd found him and there was nothing exceptional about the sight, other than the man in the chair was *Agent Starr.*

Cleo exhaled and shot him.

37

AGENT STARR WAS ON THE GROUND holding his shoulder in mostly silence, save for a few small noises of discomfort. *Yeah, keep it dignified, you double-crossing bastard.* The security guard's weapon didn't have the velocity or caliber of the RavenEye but the force, maybe just the shock, had toppled the fancy white cane chair he was sitting on and taken him to the carpet.

Cleo only glanced at him once as she came into the room. She'd hit him in the shoulder or collarbone, she wasn't sure which but she hadn't punctured anything vital. She didn't want him dead yet, and he would know that too because if she *did*, he would have taken a round to the fucking forehead. When she was done with SpadeMan she was going to get some answers and then kill the treacherous bastard nice and slow.

"Welcome!" SpadeMan bellowed.

He was unarmed, just a glass of champagne bubbling in his hand like he'd been toasting something with Agent Starr before she'd interrupted. His dark grey suit and tie were tailored but buttons were still working hard around his gut. *Mid-fifties and out of shape but probably fitter than he looked.* He waited politely for her to sweep the room from the doorway, check for threats in all the corners like he knew she would.

The place was luxurious with white candles positioned all over, similar to a show home. A big-ass chandelier was dangling from the ceiling, complementing the short lamps on bedside tables to the right and the unlit fireplace looming behind Agent Starr. All the furniture in the room was white except for a wooden table, the stupid velvet pimp-throne and the blood-speckled fallen cane chair.

SpadeMan was standing between the bed and fireplace smiling and holding his glass towards her, did she want some? She pointed her weapon at his chest but he didn't drop his arrogant sneer. *Unease.* Maybe he had backup on the way. She had to work fast.

Cleo knocked the door closed with her hip and looked at Agent Starr. He was still on the floor holding his right shoulder and collarbone, frowning with the pain. She would kill him if he stood. The understanding passed between them without words and he stayed down proving he'd conceded. He wouldn't still be on the ground after a shot from a .22 otherwise, she'd seen him come back from worse.

"I saw what happened in San Freedom on all the news channels," SpadeMan nodded "They blamed a lone wolf *terrorist* again, said it was another attack, gave the fabricated group a new name for the papers to get into a flurry about."

He turned his back and put the glass down on one of the bedside tables as though she didn't have a gun pointed at him, taking his time and sliding a coaster under it carefully.

"Turn around," she ordered.

He turned back with a gun in his hand. She fired. Her gun jammed and she dropped it and ducked, snatching her throwing knife and flinging it hard. The blade tore the air, almost impossible to see as it flew towards SpadeMan. But he raised his right hand and *caught it,* blade inches from his throat, smiling like it was nothing.

What. The. Hell.

Cleo reached for the RavenEye and SpadeMan's face changed. Only a kill shot would do and she'd double tap, *at least.* Her first shot alone would nearly sever his head from his body.

"*Hold your fire, agent!*" he barked and, God help her, she did it. *Reflex,* "I'm Alan J Pierce, some people call me SpadeMan."

"*I don't care,*" the RavenEye was cocked, her finger inside the trigger guard.

"You should care. You should wonder why someone like me left MDS to spread the truth," he said.

"You spread lies and hysteria."

"Declaring national emergencies to be able to make Executive Orders is lies and hysteria for gain."

"MDS doesn't do those things, only presidents have that kind of power."

"Darkrose, you know as well as I do that presidents are friendly faces for the public to love or hate when attention needs to be diverted from the real issues."

"You have all the answers, huh?"

"No, just the *questions*," SpadeMan said, "And now so do thousands of people all over the world thanks to my websites and podcasts. They question *official* stories fabricated by the evil bastards you still work for."

"That's what this is about?"

"Are you actually surprised? No, no glorious plot to take over the country or blow up government property the way they pretend people like me desire. I only want ordinary people to have the truth and I'm helping them find it."

She took a step closer. Bullshit lies. He was going to blow something sky-high with his bomb any minute. She was about to tell him she knew all about his plan to pulverise nearby buildings but he pointed at Agent Starr and her focus shifted.

"I've had good fortune to read some of Agent Starr's files at MDS, courtesy of patriot agents, Stone and Hooper or Cooper–*somebody*–I forget. They were Green Tags I set up meetings with but they didn't show up the final time. You don't know anything about that, do you, why they would disappear suddenly like someone was ordered to *Delete* them?"

"I didn't Delete them, I don't know who did," Cleo said.

"I know a lot about both of you but I haven't told Agent Starr that I know what happened to him where he was deployed, for example,

I'll just point him in the right direction."

He gestured with his hand like some flamboyant professor in front of a lecture theatre, a little too dramatic to be standing in a hotel room talking shit. Cleo let him dribble it anyway, the RavenEye would allow it because they were his last words.

"Agent Starr either has run-off-the-mill acute Post Traumatic Stress Disorder, disallowing proper memory function or it could be more. The name for the latest variation of the project is classified but I would tell him to do as the civilians do and research *MK Ultra*, a *very* old program initiated by a sister agency, implantation of ideas into one's head–*brainwashing*–hypnosis and such."

Agent Starr was looking at him now, face tilted up watching and forgetting about the blood coming from his shoulder.

"I'd suggest looking at *Subproject Fifty Four*, the Navy's experimentation with what they called the '*perfect concussion.*' It involved a sub-aural frequency able to erase memory. Even Monarch projects could be a good place to start researching."

SpadeMan took a deep breath, looking at them both with a feigned pity he could only manage for a second before it faded. His mouth twisted into a smug smile when his eyes rested back on Cleo.

"Again, all this is old news but nevertheless possibly the starting point to finding out about whatever they used on him. *If* they did. They probably would've only wasted that kind of technology on him if he'd seen or done something over there that was beyond top levels of classification.

NovaRose.

Cleo didn't say it. She didn't even know why she'd thought it, the guy was full of it. He was paranoid and crazy, but Agent Starr was sitting up and leaning against the chair, full focus on SpadeMan like he wanted to let him keep talking. If she'd just fucking shot them both when she walked in...

But she hadn't. She actually *cared* about why Agent Starr had betrayed her. She wanted him alive so she could ask how he'd gotten to the hotel ahead of her, why he'd met with SpadeMan. He'd made her trust him alone with her civilians after his self-deprecating speech in the motel. Now she didn't know if Julia and Tanya were alive and SpadeMan was standing there in front of her still breathing and continuing his hysterics.

"Maybe Agent Starr didn't want to follow orders overseas so Number One took his memory for safe-keeping. I was about to tell him that when you arrived, Darkrose. We were going to exchange some interesting information."

"I'll bet." Cleo said.

The RavenEye was tired of all the conversation, heavy in the glove and trying to coax her into taking the shot. She glanced at Agent Starr again and this time he was looking in her direction. He wanted to say something to her, she could tell, but he stayed quiet.

"Agent Starr has an open mind, you could learn a lot from this man," SpadeMan said, "But you won't, you're MDS all the way. Deep in you, your blood knows their way is wrong though. I heard that you left MDS once. It's why you're coming with me."

Cleo jumped forward and rolled on her shoulder fast across the carpet. Her back was up against Agent Starr's chest and the RavenEye aimed at the door where she'd been standing.

Two armed bodyguards kicked it open, firing handguns, shooting at anything they thought was moving. Cleo fired the RavenEye, two shots for the first one through his dark suit, not fighting the harsh recoil so she could aim the second round.

SpadeMan dove over the bed and took cover near the window, laughing as his bodyguard dropped, still shooting as he fell, rounds going wild and hitting the walls and shattering one of the bedside lamps.

The other guard aimed straight at Cleo's face. *He'd get the shot without trying.* She raised the RavenEye again and squeezed the trigger the same time Agent Starr reached to her waistband for the CRONE.

The top of the security guard's head blew off, whizzing behind him and out into the hall like a bloody skullcap. The CRONE's charge scorched holes through his shirt and the body collapsed to its knees and then fell on what was left of the face while she caught her breath and swallowed.

She winced recognition at the sudden noise in her left ear right after. *Handgun*. Cocked then slammed cold and hard, flat up against her skull. SpadeMan had come back over the bed while she and Agent Starr were distracted and now she sat there, her RavenEye useless, Agent Starr's crotch at her ass and a gun at her head. Number One was going to be *pissed*.

38

SPADEMAN LAUGHED. He almost laughed his ass right off. He'd taken the RavenEye from Cleo and thrown it away like it was shit. It might have landed the other side of the bed near the window. She hadn't wanted to turn her head to confirm.

He'd taken the CRONE from Agent Starr first, then the flashbang from the bridle and the OC spray, the machete and anything else she could have used to Delete him and get the fuck out. He'd let her keep some Cyanoacrylate stuff she'd on her since leaving HQ, but only because she probably couldn't kill anyone with it. She'd used it in the past to seal wounds until she could get to an infirmary. She wished she could seal his fucking face with it.

He and his security team were talking and blocking the doorway out. One of the guards was in some kind of dark dirty green jumpsuit like a bug exterminator; *late thirties, six four,* heavyset with a shaved head sprouting tiny red hairs. He had acne on his face he picked at in between stroking the handgun in his belt. The other three men were suited up fancy, tailored dark grey triplets with lanyards around their necks displaying headshots and barcodes. They were all armed with one firearm on their belt and earpieces in their ears.

SpadeMan was glancing around his circle with a stupid wide grin, saying something about taking her somewhere soon and how much fun it was going to be. His staff didn't match his mood, grim and serious, glancing back at the two dead guards lying on the floor.

Cleo looked across the bed to the window. It was the only other exit. Fuck, she was actually starting to think of saving her own ass, bailing on the objectives and coming back for SpadeMan another time. There was a first time for everything. The only problem was escaping required her to get up, make it over the bed, jump on the sill and smash through the glass of a fifth storey window all before one of the four guards got a shot off. It was probably impossible.

"*Cleo,*" Agent Starr said quietly, "*It's not what it looks like. He's a liar, I'd never do that, I'd never tell him anything.*"

His breath was warm against her ear as she sat there, her back up against his chest like he was a human armchair. Her knees were almost touching her chin now, arms hugging them. She didn't want any limbs hanging out so she could be dragged away easily.

She was caught off-guard by the smell of Agent Starr's skin, recognition it was almost a comfort. She could detect it even under the metallic smell of his blood. She felt the urge to turn over her shoulder and look at him but she didn't want SpadeMan to notice their exchange. That and she was still pissed and didn't know if she could keep from punching his face in.

He was the reason they were in the shit. If she'd walked into the hotel room and seen SpadeMan alone, she would have handled it by now. The guy would be lying in a lake of blood with half a head and she'd be looking for a taco stand on her way back to HQ. She felt movement behind her and something clicked or snapped. Agent Starr's hands brushed her shoulders. SpadeMan and the bodyguards were too deep in conversation to notice.

"What are you doing?" Cleo hissed.

"Just look straight ahead," he mumbled.

He slipped something around her neck, some kind of garrotte, she expected. Maybe he was going to choke her to death and switch sides completely. The way he'd talked about the *Truth for Life* movement days ago...she didn't know what to think anymore.

She felt a small weight touch down on her chest. He'd tied something loosely around her neck, breathing sharply as the bullet hole in his flesh shifted. She looked down and slowly moved her hand up to grasp the necklace.

The glass pendant held its own temperature, almost freezing against her fingertips as she held it for a closer look. The vertical cylinder was an inch and a half long, silver caps on each end like a canister with a see-through compartment in the middle that must have looked like some precious stone from a distance. It was pale mint green inside, a mixture between liquid and air, swirling in and out of itself in a mist in constant motion, like it was alive. Cleo's pulse skipped when she realised what it was.

She looked at Agent Starr slowly over her shoulder. She had to remember to breathe. He'd just tied a vial of one of the deadliest bioweapons in the world to her body. His throat moved when their eyes met.

A flood of disjointed memories came back, piecing themselves together like a clichéd movie montage. She saw flashes of Agent Starr turning his back while he was changing his shirt in San Freedom but she'd seen the black cord around his neck near the ID chain. He'd seemed worried, even angry on the boat after he'd pulled her out of the SUV, clutching the neckline of his shirt, checking the vial hadn't exploded under it. He'd had NovaRose around his neck the whole time he'd been with her. He'd put them all at risk. *He'd endangered the civilians.*

"I don't know why I have it. I—I was going to kill people? I don't remember. I've had it since before I got back," he whispered, "Listen to me, Cleo, there're too many of them to fight, just go with them. If you're going to use it, throw it and run. It has to be away from you when it smashes or—"

"Okay," she said. She didn't want to hear the rest.

So this is what it felt like. Number One had originally issued Red Tags two Kill Pills each to carry with them at all times, some kind of Botulinum. She'd never wanted to know the specifics. She'd put them in a drawer in her dorm and forgotten about them because she didn't want them near her. Kill Pills were a stupid idea, she'd never think of suicide as an option...and why the hell would she need the *second* pill anyway?

"This vial won't open unless I destroy it?" She checked over her shoulder. He read between the lines. *How can I trust you that this won't open accidentally and kill me?* He'd even opened his mouth to answer but two security guys grabbed her and yanked her upwards before he spoke.

They had one of her arms each, twisting them painfully behind her back as they struggled with her to where they had been standing. Her boots barely touched the floor, like she was swept up in a wave. She hadn't even got a decent look at the guards either because she'd been looking at Agent Starr.

She could kick some serious ass, but shit, she was a lot smaller than many of her opponents. Their sheer size gave them the strength advantage if they got close enough sometimes. *Like now.* Their fingers were rough and dry, grating against the catsuit like Velcro as they hurled her towards SpadeMan. He'd already taken all her weapons but he looked up at the big security guard in the exterminator suit and asked, *"Do you want to search her, Roy?"*

Roy jumped like SpadeMan had interrupted his daydream, nodding quickly and sizing her up smiling. Cleo met his pale blue eyes and they changed from faraway to something predatory. He was a sex offender, she'd met plenty of them on The Outside to know. They were scum and it bubbled to the surface enough for her to see it in their faces, like the toxic shit in them was straining to push through their skin. He wasn't just a recruited security guard, he was some kind of paedophile or rapist.

Roy's mouth opened like a rabid dog and his saliva was breaking between his small yellow teeth. He went from dopey to animated instantly, lurching forward and grabbing her arm away from one of the guards, holding her like he was snatching a ragdoll back from his older brothers.

He wrenched her to one side, stumbling her with the force. Cleo went with it, no sense in fighting back and taking four or five rounds for her trouble, even after he shoved her in the back. She stopped herself from running into the table near the door and both hands were out on the table surface before reflex made her reach down for the RavenEye that wasn't there. SpadeMan smiled and left her watching his back as he exited the room and pulled the door shut behind him. There was no one in charge now.

Roy was holding her machete and raising it up and posing, prising chuckles from the other guards when he cooed high-pitched Hollywood Kung Fu sounds. She heard the blade slice the air a few times while he swung it around behind her. She hoped it didn't fly out of his hands by mistake and land in her fucking back.

He sliced the arm straps off the bridle slowly, skimming dangerously close to her skin. The bridle flopped dead, dangling from her waist like it had been hanged. Cleo held her breath to listen for another cue. She didn't know what was coming next but he put the machete down on the floor. *One less thing to worry about.*

"Bend forward, hands flat on the table," Roy instructed.

"My hands *are* on the table."

"Bend forward for me," he said.

Cleo only moved the top half of her body, feeling the pinch in her neck and strapped shoulder. She wasn't bending over for anyone, Roy could get fucked. Her fake effort seemed to be enough for him and he didn't tell her to lower herself any further but he took two more steps towards her and stopped, way too close.

He used both his thick hands to pull the bridle down her hips slowly like he was taking off more than just the rig, fingers passing over the straps and touching her body. She heard his breath accelerate as he pushed the bridle down to her ankles, taking his time on his descent, dragging his cheek down the catsuit and over her ass while he pulled the straps to the floor. He took a long time to stand straight again. She gave him a dirty look over her shoulder.

"Step out of the leg holes and spread 'em," he slurped.

Cleo ground her teeth. *Don't make a smartass comment, don't get shot.* She took small steps out of the bridle, no sudden movements in case Roy's friends still had their guns on her. She couldn't tell because they were mostly behind her, behind Roy, and piss-weak glances over her shoulder weren't going to let her see around his fat ass to be sure.

She could hear a cigarette lighter click out in the hall. Spademan was still there, waiting for Roy to search her for weapons he already knew she didn't have. *Bastard.* A stifled laugh from another guard brought her attention back to Roy and he began to frisk her. He was checking places where weapons could be concealed like it was a legit search, not that she had room for stashed weaponry in a damn catsuit.

Then he put his hands on her shoulders and squeezed like he was thinking of giving her a massage. Her bruised shoulder didn't want one; it wanted him to fuck off like the rest of her did. She kept her eyes forward, tried to ride it out but he moved his hands up slowly, kneading her neck and shoulders before he dropped them and leaned further over. His stomach was against her back. She didn't want to think about the rest.

He hung his head over her shoulder and moved his right hand past her thigh and waist and then over her breast and held it there. Cleo held her breath after he let out a perverted sigh. It smelled like pickles.

"Hope you're going to frisk *me* like that," Agent Starr growled from the floor, "*Can't wait.*"

Cleo didn't need to look at him. He didn't like the way things were going either. Sexual intimidation really bothered him—*an agent thing*—maybe more then. She couldn't tell and she guessed it didn't matter since they were both shit out of luck on options and neither of them could stop Roy molesting her.

She looked down at Roy's pale and freckled hand as he squeezed, wondering how far SpadeMan would let it go. She'd never been raped. She'd been *molested* a bunch of times over the years and she'd been *threatened* with rape but those threats were usually void about five seconds later when she killed the men uttering them. Another reason why she hated civilians; their men were one step up from living in caves with loincloths hastily tied over their genitals.

Roy's other hand moved across her left hip, trying to pull her back against him further, hand running along her curves slowly. Then it went down to the inside of her thigh and snuck across her crotch. She heard scuffling and someone cocked a gun. She guessed Agent Starr had gone to stand up.

Roy's words slithered, "Do you like that?"

"About as much as you're going to like me shoving my gun up your ass," she said.

Roy laughed before he whispered, "You can do that if you want...but only if you let me put my '*gun*' in yours."

Cleo kept her focus on the wall opposite. He was hard now. She wasn't completely sure, but she thought she could feel his small erection against her lower back. *Great.* Her patience was almost gone, bad news for them both since she was going to kill Roy in about three seconds and probably get her head blown off right after.

"You're so sexy...you look so good," Roy said, words breathy and halting.

The door flung open and SpadeMan appeared beside her like he was psychic. The fat and soggy cigar hanging from his lips smelled like shit. He looked over the scene and blew thick smoke in Roy's direction so he let go of Cleo, jumping back like she was a viper. She heard him swallow hard and back up to the rest of the security team, standing there like cardboard cut-outs just watching.

"Mr Pierce," Agent Starr said.

"What is it, my son?" SpadeMan smiled.

"Roy's a piece of shit."

"I'm more than aware of that, Agent Starr. Sometimes I let him have a little fun anyway...though this time, I admit, he displayed less decorum than I'd like."

"He'd better back off. If he touches her again, I'll kill you both."

"Ohhh! He doesn't like to share, Roy. Take her downstairs," SpadeMan waved his cigar like a conductor's baton, "I've got a few things to discuss alone with Agent Starr."

39

TRENT

THE SECURITY GUARDS RETURNED TO COLLECT THEIR DEAD, dragging them out of the hotel room and who knew where? He'd never been too clear on where someone would dispose of a body in a civilian hotel with countless witnesses outside, never stuck around to witness the clean up after he'd finished an urban hit. He'd watched the security guards in silence, overheard them saying Cleo was downstairs. It meant she wasn't dead yet. It was the only good thing about the situation.

Now it was just SpadeMan and one of his goons standing to the side, watching without interfering. He came up to the room when the others left and didnt look like a guard. Shorter than Trent, five ten, fit, maybe an amateur fighter, but probably not and his forehead was wide under blonde hair like he was some Neanderthal blessed with a time machine. He cracked his knuckles like a bad caricature when he looked over and made eye contact.

Trent was sitting on the carpet plotting some kind of escape plan. It wasn't going to be difficult, even with his injuries from the car crash and prior. SpadeMan was all of five foot nine *maybe*, overweight, probably not too good with hand to hand anymore, despite being ex-MDS and able to catch Cleo's knife like a superhero earlier.

It was just the gun advantage and if Trent could disarm him, he was a dead man. Shit, he could probably take the guy out in less than ten seconds if he wanted, the bullet in his flesh didn't matter. Pain was normality, always had been and he'd go through SpadeMan to find Cleo. That only left the goon standing there all smug and Trent was sure he could deal with that fucker too.

"Either of you going to talk or just keep trying to taser me with your stare?"

"I see what you're thinking, Agent Starr," SpadeMan smiled, "Right behind those bright eyes of yours, behind that pretty face," he blew out a cloud of thick smoke, "You're more than a pretty face though, aren't you?"

"Not *even* a pretty face."

"You think modesty will get you out of this?"

"I think killing you will," Trent said.

SpadeMan took another inhale and smiled, "That's unlike you."

"Is it? You have no idea what I am."

"I know you have an affinity for civilians...like my estranged wife and daughter. I've heard what you've risked to get Julia to safety, Agent Starr. Is there something you need to tell me?"

"Yeah, we talked. I'm disgusted at the way you've treated Julia and the way you've treated your daughters," Trent said, "*Both of them.*"

SpadeMan put the cigar in his mouth and started a slow clap.

"Ohh, what a revelation! It doesn't take a genius to realise Cleo is my biological daughter, Starr but you sure took your time, even had to get Julia's stamp of authentication, huh?"

Trent jumped up, bullethole in his shoulder screaming fiery protest, but the kick came hard anyway. He closed the distance and threw it high, shin smashing through Spademan's hands and futile block and sending his firearm across the room and crashing through the window. The follow-through saw SpadeMan take the kick to the side of the head. He fell but he wasn't knocked out.

The goon leapt forward police-attack-dog-style but SpadeMan yelled for him to stay where he was, coughing from the ground with one hand held up, cigar burning next to him. Trent knew what his kicks could do, SpadeMan was lucky as shit that something wasn't fractured. He could have been out cold if his arm hadn't taken half the impact but the guy still didn't want his friend's protection.

Compulsion pulsed Trent's veins goddamn hard, *commanded* him to go forward and deliver fatal blows and finish it. *That piece of shit.* He didn't dare move. If adrenalin hit for real and he killed the guy, he wouldn't know where to find Cleo.

"You've got some power, boy, but this isn't how it goes," SpadeMan stood up clumsily and brushed his hands over his suit. He was in pain, Trent could see it on his face, but he wasn't going to make a big deal of it, "I've watched you do that before from Number One's office, seen holograms of you sparring. You want to fight an old man? I've seen what you can do, with the right combo you'd have me dead in seconds," he said, "That won't make you a respected agent, you may as well be beating up a Yellow Tag. Sam?"

Ah, so the goon had a name. Wasn't going to matter in a few seconds.

"Agent Starr probably wants to fight someone worthy of his skill before he kills me. He likes people but you see it in his eyes, don't you? He's trying to hide it but you see it? That hunger, the way just challenging him alone has made him want the kill. *Like an animal.*"

"I see it." Sam murmured.

Trent watched SpadeMan scoot backwards and Sam came to stand in front of him. All right. The Sam guy was a joke, already red-faced with anticipation, eager to impress his boss.

"Starr, show my friend here what you can do with those," SpadeMan said.

"With what?"

"The weapon I didn't take from you, the one in your back pocket."

Trent kept his eyes on the goon as he reached for the chuks in his back pocket, pushed half out already from sitting on the floor. He'd forgotten them. The agents on the MDS charter had been cool enough to loan him some to mess around with when he was bored as shit on the way to Menas.

SpadeMan's other goons hadn't bothered to confiscate them, probably thought they were useless to him with a bullet stuck in his flesh. Or they thought he was carrying them just to look cool. They were half right about that, who actually fought with them? He thought it was for overpaid actors in action movies. But if they wanted to see what he could do with them he would show them.

Sam shot him a mocking smile when he slid them out. He had a handgun drawn, gripping it proudly like it was his dick.

"Sam, do you not have the stomach for a fight without your gun?" SpadeMan chuckled.

Spade Man was playing them both, seemed to want entertainment, and that was cool with Trent. He wanted to take it down a notch anyway, make sure he wasn't going to catch another bullet before he'd worked out a game-plan to get out of there. He wanted Sam to come out with a blade or something close-range then he'd shatter the bones in his hands with a strike. Sam shrugged and tossed his gun on the bed as if he didn't care about losing his weapon advantage but his baby blues said otherwise.

Trent could feel his body prepare itself to execute technique. The Nunchucks began to move on their own as his eyes locked onto Sam's, vaguely noticing the black blurs spinning around him as he manoeuvred the weapon.

He could move Nunchucks wherever he wanted; overhead, low strikes, over-handed twists and spins. He could swap hands, wrap the chain half around his waist. Oh yeah, a regular circus act, incorporating all the grips and anything else SpadeMan wanted to see. The look on Sam's face was worth it. He guessed Sam would figure he wasn't just playing soon enough and he didn't really want to kill the guy but he'd make him hurt real bad. It was what SpadeMan wanted to see and if it bought him some time to scrape together a better plan, hell, he'd do it.

"Why are you looking at me like that?" Sam growled.

"Because...you're pretty much fucked."

SpadeMan laughed at their exchange and kept rubbing his forearm where Trent's shin had struck.

"Careful now, Sam, this man will break your bones in one move. I've seen him do it. He wields that weapon professionally, his tricks aren't empty threats. He can strike in excess of ninety miles an hour."

"Well, why'd you make me drop my weapon?" Tension rode Sam's voice.

"He gets off on manipulating people, the way he's done with his daughter," Trent said, Nunchucks still spinning pointless paths around his body.

"MDS has manipulated Cleo more than I ever could," SpadeMan held his hand up. Trent let his eyes slide to the side, no big deal, the Nunchucks were still flailing, carrying on the inane sideshow and intimidating Sam.

"For someone who's just discovered one of the best-kept secrets in MDS history, you didn't ask many questions." SpadeMan said.

"Cleo is who she is, nothing you say changes that. I don't need to ask anything."

"You should've asked though. How did Darkrose wind up serving MDS? Why was her lineage hidden from her? Why did Number One keep this secret? If I let her go, would you let her Delete me without knowing we're related? A myriad of questions! But you should have asked one question in particular."

"Oh yeah?"

SpadeMan's grin was sly before he spoke.

"With all the scuffling in here earlier, Starr, where, oh, where did the RavenEye go?"

Trent felt his face change. He was fast—*ridiculously fast*—but even he couldn't do the impossible. SpadeMan laughed. He had the RavenEye in his left hand before he pulled the trigger. The gun was aimed straight at Trent.

40

SPADEMAN HAD GIVEN HER A RED TAG UNIFORM to throw on over the top of the catsuit. It was like he'd correctly assumed Cleo was uncomfortable as fuck in the unisex-but-overly-revealing costume. The MDS uniform even looked like an old one of hers, like he'd stolen it from home somehow but she hadn't complained or asked questions when she pulled it on and discovered it fit.

Dammit. She'd let Trent Starr fuck with her head again. So...had he betrayed her? She still didn't know. She'd been trying to figure it out for the last ten minutes. He'd trusted her so much he had given her the sample of NovaRose but did it matter now that she was sitting on a chair in the middle of an empty stage with two guns on her?

The dark red curtains in front of her were long, reaching from the high ceiling to the floor of the stage, fluttering at the bottom as people entered the room on the other side. She'd been able to hear a few whispers and dull sounds before but the room was filling with people now. She sensed nearly a hundred talking and shifting in the seats.

There was no way she could fight off all of them if she managed to get out of the chair and disarm the two monsters standing either side of her. Both of them were over six foot tall and built like tanks, off the same assembly line as every other guard she'd seen around the hotel. She didn't know where Roy and the other security team had gone after they'd handed her over but the new guys hadn't tried to molest her yet so she guessed things were looking up.

"Welcome," SpadeMan was a silhouette bathed in a spotlight the other side of the curtain, "I'm Alan Pierce, some of you call me

SpadeMan. You sit here before me as loyal Spadians–the *Truthers*–who will change the fate of the world."

The crowd cheered and the curtains flapped open. Cleo saw a flash of the audience jumping out of their seats with hands in the air. Yeah, they were excited. The guys either side of her were trying not to smile too when she glanced up. Then the curtains began to part and they left the stage in opposite directions, out of sight of the crowd but guns still on her when they stood in the wings.

"We talk about governments and agencies and all the factors which control our lives. The woman onstage with me has changed the course of the seminar tonight, this is *Agent Cleo Darkrose,* a highly-ranked agent with *MDS.* As some of you know, the *Majestic Defence Syndicate* is one of the main agencies taking away your freedom. They control everything."

The crowd fell impossibly silent. She could feel eyes all over her, analysing her uniform and red arm bands. Then they started booing, crescendo ending up in ear-splitting growls and cursing. Cleo's eyes went everywhere, looking for weapons, searching the crowd for immediate threats as they started getting out of their seats to scream things at her.

The guards either side of the stage were watching with their guns *up.* The even better news was she wasn't tied to the chair but things were going to turn bad anyway, she could tell by how angry the crowd was and how fast they'd gotten that way.

"This woman has seen things you can't imagine. She's one of the people who created society's grasp of what terrorism is and all the Psy-Ops and Big Brother technology around you. They sit around all day and decide what you should believe!" SpadeMan's microphone distorted and screamed. Some of the audience flinched.

"What are you doing?" Cleo asked the back of his head.

"No, we're not a violent movement but have you asked yourselves where we're headed? Questioning the agenda is good but these bastards still exist. They are still getting away with everything, telling sheeple that this is all *conspiracy theory* and that *we* are the dangerous ones!"

SpadeMan finished and turned to look at her. He was smiling.

"You *know* what I'm doing, my dear. We're not violent but I can bet my life there are a few members of the audience who won't be able to stop themselves when I do this."

Cleo jumped. Freezing liquid splashed her shoulders and rained through her hair over her face, down her back and her sleeves, cold and thick and halting her breath until she gasped for air. When she did, the odour shot through her nostrils and stole her oxygen. It was razor-sharp and acidic. It burned her throat and the membranes inside her nose. Her eyes streamed tears immediately.

The crowd was roaring approval and clapping like trained seals. She pushed her hair back to stop the liquid falling into her eyes but the fumes burned them anyway. *Kerosene, Gasoline, something so damn toxic and flammable it was choking her.* They were going to kill her. The security guards had come up and emptied buckets of it on her and stepped back. One spark, and she was going to turn into a fireball.

She tried to stand but her ass hit the chair again and she fell half off the side, screeching the chair legs—eyes still clamped shut—disorientated as fuck. She couldn't make her eyelids come open, they didn't want to be roasted by vapour. The chemical smell induced hot bile reflux while laughter and shouts hollered from the audience and she tried to brush off as much of the flammable shit as she could. But it didn't work, she was spreading it.

"The floor is open, ask her your questions." SpadeMan purred into the mic. The bastard brushed past her as he stepped back, far enough that if someone threw a match he wouldn't be set alight too.

The audience went *crazy* and her vision came in tear-filled blurry flashes. Fumes rose off her hair and the sides of her face, snaking into her eyes while the chaos boomed around her and she barely caught questions over the din.

"What happened in New York? How did the towers really come down?"

"Are you inducing economic crisis to force a one world currency?"

One of the guards kicked the back of her seat. She coughed on impact, midway through a painful breath stripping and scorching the back of her throat.

Someone yelled, *"Why are they trying to make civilian armies commanded by presidents?"* And there was another hard kick to the back of her chair. Oh, they wanted her to answer the mob.

"I–I don't know," she spluttered. The corners of her mouth stung like they were already on fire.

"Do you orchestrate natural disasters with Tetonic plate weapons so the military can occupy different countries, take their oil?"

"I don't even know what that means!" *Frustration.* Cleo opened her eyes and they stung hard, only permitting a glimpse of the scene before she had to slam them shut. *Fuck.* Her face was feeling it too now, patches of burning, irritating her skin all over.

The audience was out of their seats, waving hands and pointing. She didn't know what to say to them. Her answers weren't going to be good enough unless she started making up shit. She didn't want to, they were irrational. Another flash through sore eyes told her the guard on her right was wiping his hands with a towel, furiously scrubbing away the substance and standing by an empty gas can near his shoes. She was definitely covered in something dangerous. But she was fucking dangerous too.

She shot up and thrust her fingers into his throat–*supersternal notch*–feeling the V in his neck give as she struck. He dropped the towel and gasped, electrifying pain shooting through his arms and she ducked. Flammable liquid splashed from her hair, some into her mouth, tasting like shit as the chair she'd been sitting on zoomed close overhead. Another painful blink and the other security guard was on her, both hands around her neck.

She moved side on, *record speed*, out of the trajectory of his body and slammed her arm over his. Then she smashed her elbow into his face. He let go. It took less than a second to turn further and throw a knee so his groin was fucked and he had to drop.

SpadeMan was watching from a few feet away, face aghast. He glanced at the audience like he wanted them to stop her but they were already shoving their chairs back and making for the stage as she forced another stinging glimpse at her surroundings. Yeah, Cleo would Delete if she had to. *Fuck the body count.* Number One could sort it out later, tell the media one of them had a psychotic break and slaughtered everyone, paranoid tinfoil fantasies taking over.

She blinked again and SpadeMan was behind her, one arm tight across her neck so she was trapped, his other in front of her face. He held an orange plastic cigarette lighter in his hand, thumb about to roll the ignition. Yells and banter from the audience faded out like someone turned down the volume. Time slowed and everything moved like a dream. Her eyes fixed on the lighter, so close, her heartbeat thumping in her ears.

She kicked backwards, boot into SpadeMan's groin the same time the cigarette lighter burst and sprayed shit everywhere; orange pieces and liquid ejecting themselves through the air. SpadeMan made a choked sound and pulled back, blood running from his hand.

His audience was rushing the stage, stepping over fallen chairs and each other to get to her. Some were scrambling up the edge of the suede platform already. She looked down at SpadeMan all hunched over, saw the butt of her M9 sticking out of his jacket and swooped it up to start running. Agent Starr was emerging from the crowd in her periphery, darting out from the unfamiliar faces and up onto the stage in one neat, preternatural leap that defied gravity and all the fast motion around him.

He swapped his gun to his left hand and grabbed her wrist, pulling her to the left of the stage and shoving past other security guards coming out of nowhere drawing their weapons. She got it, he'd blasted the lighter and clipped SpadeMan's hand when she'd kicked him in the crotch. *Yay, team work.*

Cleo pointed her gun at raging audience members as she crossed the stage attached to Agent Starr. He had pace, pulling them away so fast she only had time to take two messy shots into the crowd before they cleared the area. The audience cowered and screamed but they surged forward again when the shock wore away.

Agent Starr turned them around the corner to a narrow white bricked corridor only wide enough for them to run single file to a door at the end. He wrenched it open with a hand she noticed was red with blood blisters and scraped up from firing the RavenEye the day before. Then he pushed her bruised shoulder for her to go through first.

She couldn't see shit when he closed the door behind them. Everything was black. *Literally* black. No matter how wide she strained her eyes open, there was nothing to see.

"*Stop,*" Agent Starr ordered; harsh, true MDS commander-style, "There are stairs."

She waited for him to move past her and grasp a handrail to take a step down, hissing air through his teeth as he moved. He was in some kind of pain and their descent down the stairs was probably going to take longer than usual if he was injured and she couldn't see anything. Regardless, the raring *Truth For Life* audience wasn't far behind...

Cleo ripped the necklace from her throat and felt the sharp pinch against her skin as the cord snapped. Agent Starr said something, perhaps asking what she was doing, but she didn't answer. The crowd's voices thundered down the corridor as she opened the door and threw the NovaRose vial.

41

CLEO'S EYES HAD ADJUSTED. Finally. It wasn't much of an improvement but she wouldn't complain, the stinging had waned and she had vague lighting from smoke detectors and signs lighting her way. It was only when she moved her head too fast that the fumes from her clothes and hair hit and left her breathless and a little disorientated. She and Agent Starr were in a new section of the hotel after descending the stairs and she hadn't heard the door open again behind them, like the audience members had stopped trying to follow after she tossed the vial.

Agent Starr was ahead of her. She could see him limping in the bad lighting as he moved forward trying to keep their pace fast despite half-tripping over his own boots. She felt along the walls as she followed. The bricks were cold and damp, almost wet, and the air tasted like mould on her tongue. They were in the basement. Her eyes were on Agent Starr's back when he turned right, sharp around a corner she hadn't even seen, like he knew which direction to head.

"You know where to go?"

"Yes, sir. Located a map in an upper hall, memorized it." Agent Starr said, monotone.

"We have to get out but we're headed further *into* the building. I won't let failure turn this into a suicide mission, Agent Starr."

"Can't exit at street level, sir. Hostiles outnumber us approximately a hundred to one up there, possibly more now, every direction. I assume NovaRose was deployed. We have to take the goods lift to the roof and wait it out, wait until the gas is gone and the enemy is neutralised."

"*Stop.*"

Agent Starr stopped, instantly and completely still. Seconds went by. Cleo could hear banging and chairs screeching on the floor above them. People screamed as NovaRose devoured their skin and disintegrated organs. Agent Starr's body seemed to stiffen as he stared up at the ceiling, almost like he could see through it.

"SpadeMan," Cleo couldn't help cocking the gun in her hand, "I didn't Delete him, now we're running from him. I have to go back."

Agent Starr grabbed her free hand before she could turn.

"*No,*" he said.

"He isn't dead, Number One requires him Deleted. There isn't going to be another opportunity," she hissed. *Fuck the NovaRose gas*, "I'll wet something and breathe through it."

"No, that doesn't work. You *know* that, Cleo," Agent Starr dropped formalities, "We'll Delete that fucker–*you will get him*–just not tonight. The assignment doesn't matter anymore, it's time to bail. We've got to retreat."

"Look at yourself, Agent Starr. We're *MDS*...and we're *running*."

"Sometimes you have to," he said, "We don't know this place well enough. I know what it's like to have no other option, the reality you might die somewhere totally foreign and no one will care that you were ever there."

Something burned behind his eyes, unsaid ache and something raw. She watched his throat move in the lowlight, then his gaze changed and he was back, looking at her calmly.

"Cleo, if you go upstairs, you'll die. What's worth more than your life?"

"I don't...understand the question," she confessed, "MDS is worth more than our lives, why are you saying this?"

"I care about you. Let your reputation take the hit, just once."

"Not an option, he has to be Deleted. You're talking like them–*like the civilians*–the slaves!" She snatched her hand back and left him off-balance.

"The shooter in the woods told you Alan Pierce is your father," he snapped. His words echoed, vibrating back from all directions so she couldn't pretend she'd never heard, *"Julia told me and so did SpadeMan."*

Fuck. Cleo looked at the floor. She'd refused to consider it when the shooter whispered it in the woods, putting a round in his head had ended the shit. She'd thought he was full of it at the time, that it had just been an odd, pain-induced taunt. But she'd put a bullet in him anyway to make sure it wouldn't get out if it were true, not before she'd had a chance to investigate.

She'd avoided even thinking it was a possibility; that Number One had sent her on some fucked up vendetta assignment that didn't make sense and that there was a backstory, a *real* conspiracy. But it was right in her face now, standing in front of another elite MDS agent in some civilian dank. *Everyone had known except her.* She was a fucking joke. Agent Starr hesitated before he started talking again, eyes low.

"Julia told me, back at the hospital. She's not your mother but he *is* your biological father. She's known all along that you're SpadeMan's...daughter."

"The signs outside," her voice came out quieter than she'd planned as she unarmed the gun, "One of them was like the yellow flag in my room, the one we never figured out who put there. I folded it up, didn't look at it for years, thought it was a bedsheet but I remember what it said now, *'don't tread on me.'*"

Agent Starr had the grace not to say anything else. Screams from the *Truth for Life* people filled the silence between them. Audience members were coming, despite the gas. People were still going to come through the door back where the two of them had entered the basement.

Logic was screaming for her to run, reminding her they had to move out, get up to the roof before they were surrounded by *Truth for Life* or lethal gas but she was glued to the floor. *SpadeMan was her father.* They were related. *Blood.* Closer than she and Number One, she and MDS. Her head went racing off in a thousand directions and none of them let her move her boots.

"What...does that mean? *All of it.* What does it mean?"

She turned to look at Agent Starr when he didn't answer right away. She didn't know what the fuck she was supposed to do. She was dirt, lower than dirt. *She was a part of the problem.* Her breaths were coming faster like she was going to break. The thought horrified her.

"Cleo, it doesn't mean anything," he shrugged finally.

His face wasn't hiding anything. It was what it was. He didn't even look like he felt sorry for her. He gave her a few seconds to realise that even if it did mean something, standing in the basement with noxious gas loose above their heads wasn't where she should work it out. She was the agent in charge, tainted bloodline or not.

She patted Agent Starr's hip twice–*teammate-style*–and turned away to start jogging again. She got about four steps before she stopped sharp and he ran into her. She was straining to see her fingers through the dark. They weren't just smeared, they were *covered* with blood. She turned and held her hand out to Agent Starr for the explanation.

"It's nothin," he said. She could just make out his shirt, sodden wet and clinging to his right hip. She reached out to touch it again but he took a clumsy step backwards out of her reach and said, "Doesn't matter, sir. We have to keep moving."

42

SIX STORIES UP AND THE SKY WAS SAPPHIRE, speckled with white stars and smeared with grey brown smoke from surrounding buildings. The air had bite and hints of food smells from below. Cleo could see the rooms in the building next door and light steam billowing up from other places in the city and lower roofs belonging to restaurants. She was standing, back up against the door, keeping it closed in case they were being followed. Agent Starr was disappeared around the small structure they had come out from, trying to find something to wedge against the door. She could hear him breathing, straining on the inhale.

The roof looked empty, a rough rectangle with red-brown bricks lining the edge, tall enough to come up near her shins. The rest of the roof was halved, right side covered in large wooden crates and pallets stacked high, some weird kind of maze. The other side was clear apart from metal ventilation pipes and ducts on the far end and a large round water tank about her height.

"What now?"

"The gas will disperse in approximately an hour," Agent Starr appeared with a large wooden pallet, dragging it to the door. It looked like it was hard work, "I'm pretty much black on ammo. I have a security guard's weapon, no magazines."

"I've got a full magazine in the M9 minus one or two rounds. SpadeMan had the gun," she said. It was dismal.

"It'll have to do until we get an extraction, *if* we get one."

They needed cover. It was either waiting for an Evac once the situation made the news and Number One deciphered the carnage enough to figure they needed assistance…or they were waiting out the gas and walking down through the hotel to step over mangled bodies of dead *Truth for Life* people. Cleo didn't want to see that shit. Watching the test animals burst and bleed out after NovaRose exposure had been disgusting enough.

Both options were probably redundant if infected people broke through the door. Agent Starr was barricading it but they both knew it wasn't going to hold anyone desperate back. Expelled air was enough to spread the airborne NovaRose particles so if anyone tried to come through on her watch, she'd Delete on sight but she only had so many rounds left.

Her eyes settled on the water tank ahead the same time Agent Starr's did. He was standing close to her then, she knew without looking. She could taste his blood on the air and hear him breathe, almost like long gasps.

"You get in it and I'll take a look around, make sure there's no one else up here," he said.

"Say again?"

"You're flammable."

Oh yeah. She'd forgotten, despite the smell and the stinging in the corners of her eyes. Her gaze was fixed on the tank while she weighed up her options and wondered if he remembered she hated being submerged in water. Her pulse quickened already just thinking about the icy discomfort. She could feel his eyes on her like he was reading her thoughts before he looked back to the water tank.

"Just in and out," he said, "You'll be thirty seconds, sweetheart, but do it now, we got no time."

Cleo watched him break into a painful jog towards the stacked crates with the security guard's weapon in-hand. *"Sweetheart."* There wasn't time to be annoyed or feel awkward. She doubted he even realised he'd said it. His mind was racing, he was in pain severe enough to be half-hunched over, strain on his face to keep back audible grunts when he passed her. If they got the extraction, she'd call him on his slip up when they got in the bird. She'd even punch him in that pretty jaw of his if he got smart about it.

The water was fucking *cold.* Making the decision to get in the tank was a memory shoved violently to the back of her mind as she fought tension in her chest. Her ribcage was locked up and shocked, trying to force her to let go of the precious breath she held. She was totally submerged underwater, forcing her eyes open and flushing the shit out of them. She wanted the Gasoline or Ether off everything, including her eyelashes and she had to be fast. Her weapon and the magazine were balanced up on the ledge.

She sucked in mould-flavoured liquid and spat it back out, somersaulting underwater and tasting the chlorine in buoyant dirt. Bonus, at least the water was treated at one stage. She just hoped the chlorine wasn't strong enough to make her flammable again. Irony was a familiar bitch.

Her hands were slipping off the metal rungs before she broke the surface and pulled herself from the water. She hung for a moment to listen for movement or voices before she raised her head over the lip of the tank and grabbed the gun and magazine.

The door she and Agent Starr had come through was rocking ajar when she rounded the side of the tank and saw their crude barricade scattered on the ground. They weren't alone anymore. Water off her pants slapped the ground and left wet pools around her bootprints and dark stains on the concrete so whoever else came through the door was going to know which direction she was headed but the thought disappeared when her attention moved to a trail of blood shining in the moonlight in her periphery.

The blood source had been moving fast, drops throwing up tell-tale info and leading steadily to the maze of stacked up crates and pallets on the right side of the roof. She aimed her gun, eyes darting for a target warily when she followed the dotted red path into the first aisle.

The low-lit passage was an *electric blue glow from the moon and shadows* combo. She was a soaked rat in the dark labyrinth looking for a bloody piece of cheese, unable to fucking Silent Step because the run-off from her clothes was so heavy. The gun was out and ready to engage anyway, despite residual stinging in her eyeballs and the soundtrack of cars and off-putting random shouts from the street below.

The smears of blood on the ground were thick. Someone was bleeding heavily, probably on their way out, some big-ass injury that worsened as they moved. It led down the aisle away from her and around the corner at the end, disappearing into another section of the maze like a trail of sticky red breadcrumbs.

Her pants were clinging to her legs, slimy and uncomfortable like wearing a cold leaky diaper. *Disgusting.* But not worth the risk adjusting when stacked crates and pallets either side were sneaking moonlight through and playing with her scratchy vision. Silver light cast striped shadows over half the aisle, then all the way down to the other end, forcing her to blink hard and refocus every few steps.

Her eyes were flicking back and forth between the gaps in the walls for anyone waiting in a parallel aisle for the perfect shot before she hooked a left into a small walkway halfway down. The moon was barred from the new path instantly but the dark blood on the ground was still visible and led to another aisle on the right.

Cleo ears picked up someone breathing the second she stepped around the next corner; laboured creepy rasping. *Dying breaths.* He was lying face down on the ground halfway up the aisle when she saw him. The blood was a shiny dark halo around his body like some kind of sick deity but he was still alive. Barely. The volume of blood meant he didn't have much time.

Cleo didn't recognise him from her distance. There was no uniform, no distinguishing clothing as she approached. The short sleeves on his shirt showed her the length of his mashed forearms with parts of his flesh missing. She could see down to bone when she was closer.

His right arm was stretched out in front of him, fingers wriggling as the skin shrunk back and peeled away. His flesh was thick melting sludge, dripping something between a liquid and solid. *Decaying.* Cleo held her breath, right hand tightly over her nose and mouth, squeezing so hard it hurt.

He sensed her and tried to look over his shoulder. She choked. *Half his face was gone.* His jawbone and teeth were visible on the left side through congealing blood and oozing drool. It was like a fucking Halloween mask. She could see his flesh shrink back across his cheek up to his ear as she watched invisible fingers recoiling and ripping skin until bone showed.

The guy was in his forties maybe, crazy-eyed, looking all around like he didn't know where he was anymore. He mumbled quickened gibberish, all run together then he started calling her 'mommy,' and crying that he wanted to stay home from school.

She swallowed hard. He was a fucking hallucinating monster. She wanted to put him out of his misery, fire a round right into his head but she didn't want anyone else on the roof to know she was armed. There had to be others up there, more injured *Truth for Life* people who had made it to the roof to die of NovaRose inhalation. Seeing one meant there were probably a lot more nearby. Like roaches.

Agent Starr's voice came through the wooden crates from the next aisle and woke her up. He called her name quietly like ventriloquism, voice low with no echo. She turned away from the infected man and dashed to the end of the row. *If Agent Starr was in the same condition...*Thoughts scorched a track through her mind, all jumbled and speeding as she turned the corner. *What if? What if he was just as fucked?*

Agent Starr was sitting up, leaning against the left wall of crates and pallets when she saw him. His chin was almost touching his chest. She put the gun up and jogged over, stopping a few feet from where he was, weary he was rotting too. She didn't need to see that shit up close again—*not on him*—not on that model jaw.

She was waiting to see signs that he was as far gone as the guy in the other aisle when he raised his head and looked in her direction. She held her breath, expecting to see half his face disintegrated and peeling away but his jaw and lips were intact, perfectly formed and normal, no melting sludge. He even looked more boyish and fresh in the blue light from the stars. Her boots moved without instruction and cleared the last few feet up the aisle so she could squat down in front of him, face to face.

The lighting was eerie where they were, half-obscured and striping him and the pallets he was leaning up on but it was enough to see his uniform was heavy with blood down his entire right side. She shook her head, she shouldn't have shot him in the hotel room when she saw him with SpadeMan. It wasn't a kill shot—*and it could have been*—but she shouldn't have shot him at all.

"I'd never've sold you out," he said quietly like he could read her mind.

"I know," her lips ended up on the side, short for admitting her mistake, "Why did you tell me about SpadeMan?"

"I didn't want you to find out after you'd Deleted him, didn't want you to regret it."

"What made you think I would have?"

"I didn't think that," he said, "But I thought you should have the choice, all the information. For once."

His eyes were clear in the dark light, glowing their supernatural chatoyancy. They didn't suit the scene. Cleo frowned and looked down at his chest and hip and then back. The darkness didn't help her diagnosis but he looked pale as fuck. Bloodloss and pain. His shirt was *so* wet, too much blood to have come from just one small caliber hit to the shoulder, and the blood she'd noticed on her hand earlier in the basement wasn't from some scratch.

"What happened to you?" She put her gun on his thigh and reached for his shirt. The uniform clung to his skin, defiant until she pulled it up with both hands. He flinched when it stubbornly tore away from his body.

She couldn't see past the blood first. His skin was wet and dark and glinting in the lowlight. More blood started flowing like she'd ripped out a plug. She kept her face blank, teeth gritted inside her mouth trying to prevent an expression appearing on her face. She sighted the wound after a few seconds trying to make sense of the bloody anarchy on his body. The hole was between his right hip and stomach and she could see *into* it, see his shiny insides move with every breath. She pushed his shirt back down and pressed it tight.

"You're hit,"

"Yeah," he said, "RavenEye."

It felt like someone slapped her across the face when she met his eyes. She had to fight her mouth dropping open. He was going to bleed out. His body was going to go into shock, fit and healthy as it was. She looked down at the blood all over his shirt again. The wound was too big, the velocity the RavenEye fired at had left him with a hole in his side she could probably shove her fist into. *Fuck.*

She was sure the round had perforated his intestines. It smelled bad and he was sweating but his skin felt cold. Trans-abdominal and visceral injuries needed medical attention immediately. She was surprised he wasn't already dead. When she looked at him again he was still watching her, amused at her determination to appear calm for him.

"What's on your mind, agent?" He smiled weakly.

"It's bad. I don't know how you've survived this far, even *your* body can't handle this."

"Even *my* body? Do I detect some...*appreciation* for this physique?"

"Not anymore, it's ruined," she said. She didn't dare laugh. He did. Her mind was racing as she picked up the gun and felt her shoulder twinge. *A RavenEye round to the abdomen.* Her gun. *Fuck.* She'd never had to treat a RavenEye wound for real.

"Cleo...I can see it on your face, it's not your fault. Shit happens."

"I have Medi-Glue. I'll glue you," she said. He smiled.

247

They both jumped. Shotgun pellets blasted through crates back toward the door they had come from. Their eyes locked into each other's. There was nothing else like a shotgun blast.

Pellets began exploding through row after row of crates, one blast after another headed their way. Someone was systematically blowing holes in every stack to flush them out. The sound of metal and wood bursting and splintering repeated, growing louder like an impending thunderstorm rolling across the roof.

Cleo could hear a helicopter in the background between each blast but she couldn't see it. Even if she stood, they were blocked on both sides with no view of the sky apart from the strip above their aisle. She wanted to hear someone yell that it was a medevac and they were okay but there was no indication it was their ride and it didn't matter if it was friend or foe anyway, they needed to move now or they were going to end up red swill dripping down the crates and pallets.

She was about to ask Agent Starr if he could stand but he was staring through her, eyes glazed, hands moving to cover his ears. The next two shotgun blasts didn't register for him. His face was blank, asleep with his eyes open. Then something *big* exploded down the street.

Cleo's eyes zigzagged, checking the aisle, scanning for threats again. The building vibrated under her boots. There was screaming from below. A bomb had gone off. *The* bomb. Had to be. She didn't know how big it was but it was enough to shake the building's foundations. That meant people were dead and others were missing limbs. Chaos was coming.

It was only a few seconds before she could hear sirens in the distance. When she glanced at Agent Starr he was still motionless. She thought she'd seen him jump when the bomb went off but he was back to being a zombie.

"Agent? Can you hear me?" She tried. She saw a flicker of recognition behind his eyes. *Not enough.*

"Agent Starr? Agent Starr. *Trent.*" Cleo shook his good shoulder and leaned closer to his face, "Trent, look at me. You're on the roof of the Stella Hotel in Menas. *We need to move, now."*

"Cleo," he murmured. It was a start. He took his hands away from his ears and another shotgun blast shattered crates before he looked at her again.

"The bird—I remember the unit—my squad. I was breathing moon dust and they were all dead, and it kept circling, trying to extract for too long," he said, "I didn't want to be a Meateater in the first place, I didn't know I was over there to kill, I didn't—"

"*Look at me,*" Cleo hissed, "It won't be long this time. We're going to get off this roof. Trust me."

"I trust you, with *everything.* You know that," he said.

Cleo got to her knees and armed the M9. He was watching her, ignoring nearby crates shattering with another shot. They were in danger, seconds to get out of the aisle before they were next. She was about to push up to stand when he spoke again.

"You didn't ask me why I said I'd never hurt you, back at that motel," he said, "It's like you're afraid of the answer. I told you before, I don't care about the circumstance, I'd never hurt you or leave you behind."

"Are you sure you know where we are, the time period we're in?" She asked, double-checking her gun was ready to go, "What *time* is this, Agent Starr?"

"Cleo, I know this isn't before. I'm at the Stella Hotel, I just got back. We're on SpadeMan's Deletion," he breathed in sharply, "They've got me on strong meds I haven't been taking, they make everything hazy but I remember the important stuff. The plans I made still have you in them when I think about them, took me this long to realise how important that is."

"Are you turning this into a goodbye speech? You're going to feel *stupid* about this tomorrow,"she whispered. It didn't matter that he probably wouldn't see the next day, they both had to believe he would, "We have to get out of here, *now.* Can you walk?"

His eyes changed, attention on something over her shoulder. When she turned she saw SpadeMan, Roy and another giant bodyguard blocking their way out of the aisle. Roy was laughing. The other guard was holding a pump-action shotgun and SpadeMan had her fucking RavenEye.

43

SPADEMAN'S TWO OVERSIZED FRIENDS CARRIED AGENT STARR toward the other side of the roof where the ventilation pipes were. Roy the pervert was smiling. Cleo didn't know who the other guy was but he was big too, good looking with caramel skin and muscles bigger than her head, wearing an expensive suit like all the other security she'd seen throughout the night. They had two of Agent Starr's limbs each, shakily swaying him between them.

The sirens and yelling were still happening below, more people arriving at the scene to help the injured on the street. No paramedics had managed to make it into the hotel and up to the roof yet. Good for them. But it wouldn't be long before someone entered the building to help and got hit in the face and lungs with NovaRose.

Cleo was walking beside SpadeMan, close on his left with her eyes on the cracks and dried bird shit under her boots. His lackeys struggled with Agent Starr's long limbs and weight distribution, stumbling a few feet behind them. SpadeMan's gaze was on her though, unwavering despite their commotion.

When she glanced back at him, she saw blood seeping through the white bandage he'd wound around his hand and she noticed, again, he had been good looking once. Still was. And he could have made a decent life for himself. It was a shame he was a bastard. He wasn't even watching where he was going, dark eyes on her the whole time, sparkling and analysing her like she was some oddity in a freakshow.

"You're beautiful," he said finally, "You've probably heard that from a lot of men over the years."

What the hell was that supposed to mean? She wasn't going to say it, but for his information, there was only one man who had ever called her *"beautiful"* and they were carrying him behind her like a dead Trophy Buck after a hunt.

"Don't pretend to be interested in who I am. You know all you need to, your wife even has a book about me."

"Julia is no longer my wife, Darkrose, just as you are no longer my daughter. *Stop here,*" he instructed everyone.

Roy and his partner dropped Agent Starr where they stood and waited for him to push himself off the concrete awkwardly and stand on his own. He coughed and tried to get his breath back from impact while they chuckled either side of him. Cleo heard him let out half a groan before he caught it and went silent.

They were all standing in the far corner of the roof now, on the left side behind some of the clinking ventilation pipes. Cleo could hear the same helicopter in the background nearly covering the noise of the sirens from underneath, closer than before, circling and weaving between buildings nearby but still out of view.

Agent Starr looked like shit when they made eye contact. He was vertical but only *just*, swaying where he stood with his teeth gritted and straining to take a full breath. SpadeMan hadn't taken any chances, even with Agent Starr's life-threatening wounds. Roy and his partner had disarmed them both and Cleo didn't want to fight hand to hand. They were all bigger than her and she also had the handicap; wet clothes and an injured agent to factor in.

"Are you worried about what Number One will do to you if you don't die here? For two of the highest ranked agents at MDS, you haven't executed my Deletion very efficiently." SpadeMan smiled.

"There's still time." Cleo said.

"I see. Pass me a weapon, please, Roy." SpadeMan pocketed the RavenEye as Roy threw him Cleo's confiscated M9. He caught it, flicked it around, clicked the safety off and shot her in the right shin.

The exit wound erupted, blood and searing heat blown out the side of her calf as she dropped. An involuntary yelp fell out and she slammed her eyes shut until she could see flashes under her eyelids. *Fuck!* She didn't want to give them satisfaction by grabbing at her skin vainly to stop the burning but it was *bad* and someone else was screaming on her behalf in the echo.

Julia and Tanya were running across the roof towards her when she raised her head, two security guards gaining on them like racing greyhounds. *Julia and Tanya? What the hell?!* She shot Agent Starr a dirty look. He was trying to explain while Roy and his partner held him back. They didn't have to try hard, he was on the verge of dropping to the floor if they let him go.

SpadeMan was laughing, enjoying the looks between them all while her leg pissed blood. It hurt like *fire*. She'd been shot before, first time as a Green Tag wanting to prove herself. She'd caught that one in the left shoulder blade and thought she was dying but she couldn't remember it being so painful.

SpadeMan pointed Cleo's gun in Julia's direction next. She put her hands in front of her, pushing something invisible and backing up into one of the security guards coming after her. He snatched her hands and pulled them behind her back while his partner grabbed a fistful of Tanya's hair, gripping the clump tight in his hand so she couldn't move away.

"Darkrose represents everything I stand against. They've used her against me, she has to be made an example of." SpadeMan said.

"But she's your daughter." Agent Starr severed the look between Julia and SpadeMan and he stopped pointing the gun at her. Cleo heard the effort it took for Agent Starr to speak, he wasn't going to be standing much longer. SpadeMan looked him up and down a few times and narrowed his eyes.

"Do you know what it's like to have a child and watch her grow up from a distance? You can't have a child at MDS. I wasn't allowed to touch her or talk to her, then I wasn't allowed to be *near* her. All I could do was leave the flag in her dorm, get the hell out of there and hope she figured it out one day," his voice brimmed with something heavier than his words, "I had to view her as a separate agent while Number One decided what was best for her. You and I are alike, Starr."

"How?"

"Before you were stationed at MDS HQ, Number One showed me your work, told me why we needed you. They knew what you were before *you* did. I read about your exploits at an MDS compound in Canada where you were developing a new Bioweapon. I saw holographic replays of your fights played right in front of me," SpadeMan said, "I listened to recordings of you pitching dangerous ideas but you still kept your humanity, chivalry, respect. I wanted you to work with Darkrose before I left. Do you remember the curriculum for male Yellow Tags at your home base? You were taught how to treat the opposite sex if you went undercover on The Outside before they scrapped it and said it was a sexist program but you excelled because you wanted to be skilled at anything and everything. I knew you were different."

"Full of secrets tonight." Agent Starr said.

"Better than full of lies," SpadeMan cleared his throat, "How is the 'War on Terror,' Iraq, Afghanistan? I heard you were critically injured in Kandahar but you spent time in many areas."

"That's none of your business."

"No, really. How is it, soldier? How does the world look now? You must be a hell of a lot smarter than all of us. They must have trained you well, Starr."

"Who I was there is not who I am here. I'm just a guy who wore a multi-cam uniform and got told to do shit," he said, "I'm just some guy."

"I did worry that you wouldn't return. I respected your humane qualities."

"What I did over there was not humane." Agent Starr murmured.

"No, I imagine it wasn't but certain qualities remain in you. Darkrose has given herself over to MDS completely. Haven't you noticed she thinks of civilians as nothing?"

"You killed a lot of people with that bomb downstairs, I wouldn't act so righteous." Cleo grunted.

"That explosion wasn't me," SpadeMan looked hesitant like she'd actually knocked him down a peg or two, "Where would I get anything I needed to make something like that?

"You tell me, you're the terrorist." Cleo said.

"They use that term a lot but they're usually behind it somehow. This is text-book. This was *Number One*, they're trying to frame me. They have the means to do this. You really don't know who you work for, do you?"

"You tried to have your family killed! You sent gang members to Delete us in San Freedom, you got a *truck* through perimeter security back home."

"What?" he shouted, "I don't know what you're talking about. How could I manage those things? You *know* that's impossible."

Cleo wanted to tell him to eat shit but she could feel blood running down the inside of her pant leg into her boots. She couldn't risk another round in her flesh or Julia's and Tanya's. They were standing close by crying, eyes zipping all over the scene and watching her struggle to a lunge position to support her injured leg.

Cleo stole a look over her shoulder, trying to sight the helicopter she could still hear. It was closer and it didn't sound military. If it was MDS, they were taking their sweet-ass time finding a landing site...but it didn't sound like one from home either. She just hoped it wasn't a civilian news crew because they were fucking useless and she didn't need to be on national TV, she needed an Evac. *Now.*

SpadeMan slammed his elbow between her shoulder blades and she hit the ground, sprawling with her hands out in front and tasting leftover Gasoline. She heard Julia call SpadeMan by his real name, pleading with him to stop and let them all go home but her words were muted by the sounds of a struggle.

Agent Starr disarmed Roy like magic; a too-fast flick of hands in the lowlight, snatching the gun from him then smashing a fist into his face. Roy was out cold before he hit the ground, jaw so obviously fractured. Cleo may have paused to appreciate the gore factor but her body was already forcing her towards SpadeMan.

He was ready for her as she closed the distance and threw a kick with her good leg. He checked it with his own, his shin smashing into hers—*bone on bone*—then he rushed forward and punched her and she fell, the sway of an almost-knock out thickening her spit and fogging her head to mush before she rolled. The concrete was sharp on her face, scraping her cheek and grating off her skin. She was inhaling dust and sand when she came to a stop, pushing up weakly, ready to get out of the way of any gunfire but no one fired while she scrambled low and dizzy. SpadeMan was just laughing.

Agent Starr's disarm had ended up a waste of time. He was kneeling in front of Roy's unconscious body, hands on the back of his head and Roy's partner behind him, weapon pointed at the back of his skull.

The mysterious helicopter was real close now, behind the pallets on the other side of the roof. It *wasn't* MDS and it wasn't military. The noise coming from the main rotor blades was loud and uneven. Old tech.

The blades chopped the air and blew Julia's and Tanya's hair around their faces as it came up over the side of the building into their view, hovering like a giant steel spider. The metal body was blue grey and clunky, matte and rusting in parts. It was SpadeMan's. It even had a big-ass tacky Spades suit symbol painted on the side.

Agent Starr was trying to get her attention but SpadeMan stepped in front and blocked their line of vision to each other. He was shouting over the blades of the helicopter, gun on Cleo, ordering her to stand.

If the other guards knew who she was, they'd want her to fuck up and draw their fire so they could get the kill for status. It meant her ascent was careful and so painfully slow. Her muscles were protesting and compensating instantly, begging her not to put pressure on her injured leg. The side of her face was raw and sparking the same as her calf, hot spines scratching under her skin like she was blushing from having all their sights on her.

SpadeMan was holding the M9 pointed square at her chest when she was upright. Julia and Tanya were struggling against the men holding them back behind him and Agent Starr was nearby, still on his knees fighting to stay mostly vertical. They all had the same look on their faces.

"Things would've been different between us if it wasn't for MDS, you know that right?" SpadeMan shrugged, "They want a *New World Order*, using the people as slaves and batteries to build it. They want this planet to be a prison with their Police States and surveillance. So many liberties are being taken away in the name of National Security! They want people *scared*, willing to hand over their rights to authorities who say they offer protection but what they want is ultimate control."

SpadeMan's face showed sincere concern. He really thought he'd done the right thing by quitting MDS and not going into hiding like the other rogues, instead going public and creating a movement that actually made Number One apprehensive. A *New World Order*? Hell, it was part of the oath, what Cleo pledged to create at *Call* every single time she was home...It wasn't just a muster call, it was prayer dedicating her soul.

She felt regret flicker, one second where it felt like there was no one else on the roof but the two of them. Time slowed all the way down so she could hear her breaths ringing deep and deliberate in her ears. Shit, there was so much she wanted to ask him. The look between her and SpadeMan stunned her into stillness and said things that didn't come in words she knew how to say with her mouth. She saw something similar dancing behind his eyes too.

He had a lot to tell her—*she could see it pushing to break out*—but the moment passed before either of them grasped it and timeflow normalised. He wouldn't say those things in front of his people or Julia and Tanya. It couldn't happen, not there with all the guns and blood and time running out.

Sounds of chaos rode the air they were breathing, muffled screams and groans and more emergency vehicles approaching below. She was bleeding and Agent Starr didn't have long. She could smell his guts and taste his blood when the breeze changed. He wasn't going to make it off the roof alive unless they got reinforcements immediately and even then, if Julia and Tanya were on the roof, that meant the hospital safehouse was compromised and they couldn't take him there.

Shit had gone too far.

SpadeMan's face said he'd reached the same conclusion under the spinning blades of the helicopter behind him.

"You're my biological daughter. I loved you once, Cleo, *I did*. You could never understand something like that," he said, "You're just one of them, an Illuminati-loving bastard who wants control of the world."

"I told you I don't know what you're talking about!" Cleo yelled over the helicopter blades.

"That's even worse! You're just an enforcer, a pathetic Foot Soldier. They don't even trust you enough to let you in on the big picture. You're everything I hate," SpadeMan armed the M9, "*Pawn!* They sent you to test *both* of us. Neither of us can back down. *This was always going to be a fight to the death.*"

Roy's partner hauled Agent Starr to his feet and shoved him in her direction. He came at her, full force like a cannonball, weak from blood loss and unable to change course. Then he ran into her. *Hard.*

The two of them tripped clumsily and off-balance. They had fucked up. The assignment was over and they'd failed Number One. They'd lost...and they were both going to die.

Agent Starr stumbled sideways. Cleo had enough room to see around his bicep, see SpadeMan raising the gun, aiming at the back of Agent Starr's head. A nanosecond whooshed.

No. He'd saved her ass so many times the last couple of days...and then there was all the stuff he'd told her and the permission slip he still had. He genuinely cared about Julia and Tanya, *maybe he could still get them out of there.* He was a good guy regardless of what he'd done overseas, or what Number One thought of him.

She blinked, a short as shit glance up at him then she flattened her hand, fingers rigid up against each other, and plunged it into his bleeding wound, violently embedding it in slimy things; warm, moving flesh and intestines and blood. She threw a knee to his groin before he had a chance to jump back and dropped him.

SpadeMan's rounds were already on their way. His face was wrinkled in concentration, thick valleys above his dark eyebrows. Time decelerated again. The muzzle flash from the gun blinked like a slow-mo strobe light, one spark after the other, recoil jerking the gun back before time skipped to the present.

Rounds hit.

Impact was hot, scorching holes through her uniform and forcing her backwards. She struck the safety wall with the backs of her knees and teetered.

Julia and Tanya were screaming again. She heard Agent Starr yell something she couldn't understand. SpadeMan was running towards her, still firing his weapon, one hand out ready to push her off the roof.

She'd lost count of the shots. Rounds devoured her strength and her body went into shock instantly.

She didn't know where she was hit. She could feel blood pressure draining, the sucking falling feeling squeezing from all over, so fast she was lightheaded. *Fuck.* Her civilians were still in danger. Agent Starr was still in danger. She had to get them off the roof but her eyesight blurred.

SpadeMan's gun jammed or his ammo ran out so he snarled and threw it away then he was up in her face instantly—like he had teleported—grabbing her by the shoulders while she tried to make sense of it. His sweaty face was so close. She could see the look in his eyes, *so angry* when their foreheads touched and she breathed his air. There was only one option left. She hooked her arms over his and dropped backwards, eyes on the sky and feeling him come with her over the edge.

Read an excerpt from RED COWBOYS

TRENT WAS DRUNK AS SHIT. He had left the Blue Tag building knowing he was down for the count. The rest of the night was going to be spent leaning over the toilet in his washroom and sleeping on the tiles. He'd managed to excuse himself, said he was coming back but he knew he wasn't. He'd gone through almost two bottles at dinner before Number One had given a Yeti a look and signalled him to collect the other bottles nearby and distribute them elsewhere.

He was staying up on the fifth floor of the Red Tag Building. He'd thought getting the whole floor was a pretty good deal for weeks before realising it was probably because Number One didn't want him infecting other agents with his sudden weakness, his failure to come back from what happened to him overseas and at the Stella Hotel. The thought nagged at him, trying to squeeze through the drunken brain fog.

He didn't want to be on Level 4 anymore anyway, right around the corner from Number One's office and Cleo's old room. He had lived in a massive tent with about forty other guys in the Middle East and before that, mostly slept in assigned cars, dorms and his place on The Outside but his condo was out of the question. He was smart enough to know he didn't want to be alone there so Level Five it was.

Everything was blurring in and out of his vision as he coasted down the hallways towards his room, trailing his hand along the wall to remind himself to keep upright while his steps dragged and tempted him to drop. Something about the flicker rate in the mutant-fluorescent lights above was playing tricks on his mind enough to make his guts churn. He knew his room was a few doors up from the far end, well away from the elevator where he had got out but heading that way was proving hard work.

He wanted a rest stop when he hit the halfway point, a few seconds to make the feeling in his stomach go away but a wall came up out of nowhere and blocked his path so he shoved it back with his left hand. The coolness on his palm didn't budge and he didn't want any trouble so he stepped back instead and just gave it a dirty look.

He continued the stumbling journey down the hall and repeated the action over and over. Whenever he pushed one wall back it was like it propelled him across towards the other until he was tripping down the hall from side to side like a human pinball. *It was great.* Drunken haze was so perfect, he was void of everything and he didn't care. All he wanted was to go to bed, after he'd thrown up a few times maybe.

He laughed and the sound bounced around him, boyish and kind of pussy while his head spun and threatened to dunk him on his ass. He took a long blink and Cleo was there when his eyes shut, her finger on his lips, dark hazel eyes resting on his. He knew what that look meant. Shit, he wanted to kiss her, start something that wasn't going to finish until dawn. His eyes sprung open when he crashed into something hard enough to jar his scraped up elbow.

It was solid and rectangular and taller than him, covered in a thick grey plastic tarp. He was pretty sure it hadn't been there earlier when he flashed past to change his clothes and race to dinner but he didn't know. It was almost at the end of the hall, maybe far back enough for him to have overlooked it, it was possible. He swayed as he pulled the corners and yanked the tarp. It stuck a few times, throwing him off balance and making him bow his back. He overcompensated and fell forward when it suddenly came away, slamming his hands out on the glass in front of him.

It was an expensive display case for trophies or fine china; thick glass up front and wooden frames, sturdy enough to take his weight if he'd wanted to climb it for some reason. It hadn't even shuddered when he'd fallen into it. His hands were pressed up on the surface while everything spun around him, his full weight on it waiting for his balance to return.

He forced his eyes to focus on his dirty square fingernails, move down his fingers past minor cuts and scrapes across his knuckles and then back up again. He pulled away from the case and left white prints slowly waning with the air. Trent saw the contents of the display case behind them and choked, halfway between a gasp and a yelp.

His back hit the opposite wall hard, driving all the air from his lungs, leaving him coughing and unable to get a breath. He couldn't take his eyes off the case but he was caught, bent over trying to clear his throat and get some oxygen. His eyes were watering with the strain. He hadn't realised he had shoved himself backwards so violently until impact.

He could see a grimy female Red Tag uniform with grass stains and dirt on the knees and blood spatter on the arms and chest. Two bullet holes graced the torso area and then one near the shoulder. The words *"Agent Cleo Darkrose—Deceased"* were printed on a small gold plaque below the glass on the wooden cabinet area of the display case, engraved in thick stamped-out italic font. It looked authentic, it matched his memories.

It was the uniform Cleo had been wearing when she fell from the Stella Hotel and died.

Thank you

I invite you to share your thoughts or give your support for the series by visiting

EverEdenAuthor on Facebook

Pinterest and

EverEdenAuthor.com